The Brisbane Line

First published in 2020 by Brio Pty Ltd
PO Box Q324, QVB Post Office, Sydney NSW 1230
www.briobooks.com.au

Text copyright © Judy Powell 2020

ISBN 978-1-922267-09-2 (print)

ISBN 978-1-922267-10-8 (digital)

A catalogue record for this book is available from the
National Library of Australia.

Cover design, internal design and typesetting © Brio Books Pty Ltd

The Brisbane Line

J.P. Powell

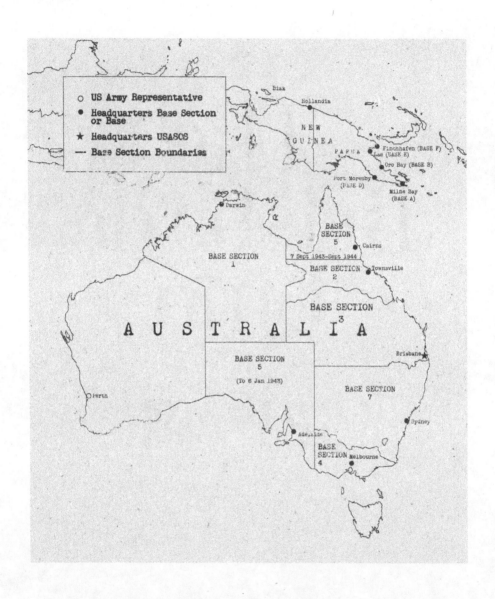

'One had only to pass through the city streets at night to be
convinced that decency had largely vanished.'
Archbishop Sir James Duhig
The Courier-Mail, 8 March 1943

For Libby,
who remembered the Americans 'making a line'.

FRIDAY 8 OCTOBER 1943

Chapter One

Sergeant Joe Washington watched from the southern end of the Victoria Bridge as arm in arm they came, a ribbon of colour braided between the metal arches of the bridge that spanned the oily river. Loose-limbed girls with bobbed hair or tight curls pasted to their foreheads, giggling and nudging each other, arms linked. Bobby-soxers and dames, broads and beauties. Blondes, brunettes, redheads. Long evening dresses shimmered under the weak lights of the evening brownout, short skirts twirled. Every now and then a slim figure was in uniform, the drab green and khaki of the AWAS relieved by a sprig of mimosa or a pink-throated orchid pinned to the collar. A colourful flock, Joe thought. Like the gaggle of birds that swept the sky in the early evenings, a flash of emerald and crimson, a swirl of silver.

'Thank heavens for the Rubber Control Board. The army needs all that rubber, eh?'

Joe smiled at the expression — true in both meanings.

The skinny man in the rough serge of an Australian private slapped Joe on the shoulder. 'Whadya reckon, you bastard?'

He turned, brows raised in anticipation of a response, but drew back when he saw the insignia on Joe's shoulder. 'Not here to cause a blue, are ya?'

'Hell no,' said Joe, as he cleared the fog from his glasses. Sweat pooled in his eyebrows and he wiped his upper lip.

Joe returned his attention to the women. Too many fights began like that and anyway, the man had a point. Since vulcanised rubber became a protected commodity, corsets had gone out of fashion. Not that corsets would appeal to jitter-bugging dancers whose short skirts were designed, it seemed to Joe, to show off soft parachute silk knickers.

Funny how it'd taken a war and thousands of miles packed in a cramped destroyer for him to become a regular at the Trocadero.

A crash, followed by the sound of breaking glass.

'Get your hands off me! Fuck off, you bastard!'

The men around him turned to watch.

A group of Aussie soldiers was gearing up for a brawl. Only a matter of time until Monroe and his gang would descend as if from nowhere, batons at the ready, rifles unslung. Let them deal with it, Joe thought, relieved to be off-duty, if only for a couple of hours.

In the eighteen months since he'd landed, he'd seen Brisbane change, and the Trocadero along with it. Long gone were the young women in wide fairy floss skirts and bouffant sleeves curtseying to the Governor as they made their debut at the Masonic Ball — he'd seen the sepia-tinted prints in the foyer. Now the dance floor heaved with soldiers and sailors — sunburned faces and crew cuts, nervous rookies and middle-aged daddies boasting rows of ribbons — gyrating young women shimmering in slinky material. All of it sliding seductively over non-girdled flesh.

Across the road Joe glimpsed someone among the milling

crowd. Jostled, but aloof, she released the rope of beads that hung from her neck, lifting a gloved hand to secure the tortoiseshell comb in her raven hair. A familiar gesture, and for a fleeting moment Joe smelled the lavender water in his grandmother's bedroom, saw again the string of yellowing pearls on the dressing table, her hair combs laid out neatly beside the hand mirror. He had them still, packed in tissue paper in a metal trunk in his mother's bedroom, fragile threads of silvery hair still clinging to the tines.

If only he'd brought his camera. The evening light could work, he thought. In a studio he'd set the lights to highlight the tortoiseshell comb, leave her face in shade, and catch the poignancy of the moment the second before the hair fell loose. But here — on the street — she would be the point of focus among the milling crowds, the stillness among the noise. Time held in check, the way photography should be.

A tall, thin man with receding hair and a thin moustache draped his arm across her shoulders, the monochrome dress uniform worn by off-duty Americans now crumpled, his tie askew. She half-turned as the soldier shepherded her past the ticket office.

The crowd surged forward and Joe lost sight of the woman as the partygoers funnelled through the entrance.

*

Two hours later, he clattered up the metal steps that hung from the back of the South Brisbane Town Hall and tapped a soft shoe shuffle, surprised that his footwork remained agile although he'd long ago moved from bantam to welter to middle weight. The fight at the Troc had petered out with few casualties and Joe hadn't seen the woman again. But he'd kept to himself; he went for music not company.

From the cells at the back of the yard came the gentle rattle of Private Archibald Teague's ragged breathing, the sound amplified against brick and bare cement. Joe should have interviewed him earlier in the day but had decided to wait till he'd sobered up. He marvelled at how peacefully the man slept; only the dishevelled clothing and blood on his boots gave any indication of what had happened. From the adjoining cell, Corporal Dwight Duke's deep snore formed a weaving bass with Private LeRoy Bryson's grunting percussion. The final cell in the row held a Japanese storekeeper from West End who slept silently, hands resting at his side; the only prisoner Joe had seen fit onto the narrow bench.

No new arrests since the last shift, then.

He glanced into the mess where two MPs, rifles propped against the wall, slumped around a table messy with dirty cups and Mrs Lakursky's grey sandwiches. Glasses in the sink retained a yellow residue and there was the familiar smell of whiskey.

'Quiet night?' Joe asked.

'Nothing much. A punch-up near the PX. A knife fight at the submarine base. No one hurt.'

Private Wilbur Bland was a lonely man from Illinois who spent his evenings writing maudlin letters to his wife. He often asked Joe to check his spelling.

'Monroe around?' Joe asked. Corporal Butt Monroe took a flexible approach to working hours, as he did to most matters military.

'He went out,' Bland said.

'Did he say where?'

'Nope. Never does.' Bland flattened the curling edges of a sandwich and took a bite. 'He took the Willys jeep, though.'

A corridor led past a series of offices, now empty. Joe entered the large room at the end and walked to his desk.

During daylight hours he would sit and gaze over the spindly trees in Memorial Park, the concrete air raid shelter, and down the slope to the dry dock and the khaki river ribboned with rainbow slicks of oil, the morning light picking out the red and green swirls. Usually a submarine — low, dark, sleek — lay wounded at the dock, its conning tower looming over what passed for a suburb in this part of town.

Now, Joe glared at the tower of folders that confronted him. Ochre files tilted sideways in a bizarre stratigraphy of paperwork. Carbon copies of typed statements, drawings of crime scenes, his case notes. All typed in the colourless language of officialdom, with photos bleached of life. He lifted one folder after the other, reordering to see what he could leave a bit longer. The knifing outside Nick's café, another drunken brawl at the PX, two soldiers charged with the rape of a ten-year-old girl, twenty more men AWL, the theft of a jeep by a sailor who made it as far as Ballina. Lucky man. Larceny, misuse of a weapon, knifings and assault, impersonating a captain — at least that showed a sense of humour. He pushed the files away, reached for the paperback novel he'd been reading earlier in the day and slammed it on top. For whom the bell tolls indeed.

He stood and moved to the window at the end of the room. Hot air hovered like fog beneath the ceiling. The neatly pressed shirt he'd donned this morning clung to the sweat under his arms and around his waist. He pushed past the blackout curtains. With luck some of the humid air might escape, though he held little hope of a breeze.

Joe removed his glasses and flicked sweat from his eyebrows, watching the drops fall to the mosaic floor. Had he imagined the brief flare of white from a welder's torch? He looked toward the dock but couldn't see any more flashes. Midnight and dark as pitch. He closed the blackout curtains, muffling any sound from the outside world.

Life in the army hadn't turned out as he'd expected when he'd queued with those thousands of others at the recruiting office in Lower Manhattan. Unlike the futile battles his father and comrades fought, Joe knew this was a war he must fight. But his eyesight was poor and when a military doctor found a heart murmur from a childhood bout of rheumatic fever, Joe's fighting future died before his myopic eyes. It had been too bad. And too late to pull out. So here he was, stuck in a backwater in the South Pacific investigating petty crimes no one cared about, writing reports no one would read.

He remembered that first year in Brisbane, the anticipation as the convoy tied up. When they disembarked it'd been his first time ashore since leaving the States. He'd walked from Brett's Wharf into a small country town, almost a hick town if truth be told, a tinpot town straddling the khaki river, the streets mostly unpaved, children playing ball in the middle of the road. A few brick and stone buildings playing at being a grown-up city, most of the place just wood and tin. It all looked temporary, as if everything could be picked up and moved to another location. But what a place! Palm trees and purple jacarandas, the rich perfume of frangipani. They'd been billeted in private homes or boarding houses perched on the ridges along the river, bivouacked in tent cities on the racecourses at Ascot and Doomben. And the reception. Impossible to ignore the invitations, the generosity of families who would share their Sunday roast with these exotic visitors, hosted singalongs around the piano. A welcoming place.

No one understood their accents, of course, and Americans in their turn struggled to translate the Aussies' oddball sayings. But slowly they adjusted, rubbing along as allies, if not friends.

And then MacArthur landed, corncob pipe and all.

Thousands claimed to have seen him arrive at the South

Brisbane Railway Station with his wife, young son and Arthur's *amah* in tow. Lennon's Hotel became known as 'Bataan'. Every day he drove, complete with armed escort, the few hundred yards to his headquarters in the AMP building on Edward Street.

Such a showman. Almost a clown, Joe thought. But we all longed to join the circus.

All that was over a year ago. The novelty had worn off. When Joe walked into a room now there were always people who turned away. Sure, the invitations still happened from time to time, but the small-town ways had mostly gone. These days men roamed the streets at all hours, sailors and soldiers moving in packs. Dockyards and munitions factories worked around the clock. It wasn't unusual to see men and women heading home from work at midnight. Mothers worried if their daughters were late back from the pictures, fathers wondered how their sons paid for the American cigarettes they'd taken to.

Mostly the problem was booze and women, Joe thought, mentally riffling through the files on his desk, listing the cases. Fights and knifings. His job was to deal with the aftermath. Sweeping up, hosing down.

On a raised platform at the end of the room Major Mitchell's desk was, as usual, spotless. No night shifts for the major.

Where was Monroe? Who knew what his helmeted MPs got up to. Circling the city boundaries day and night on patrol, dragging soldiers out of nightclub brawls, pulling sailors out of brothels. If at times they strayed into the nightclubs or stayed longer than absolutely necessary in the cat houses — well, he could hear Monroe saying, what did it matter? So long as the MPs kept the troops in order.

Trouble was, sometimes they stirred up more than they quelled.

Joe dealt with the aftershocks — the fights, the stabbings, the arrests. As a provost with the Criminal Investigation Command his job was to investigate crimes and prepare the cases for military court. But there was little enough support, even from Major Mitchell. Sure, some crimes like rape and murder couldn't be ignored, but all too often Joe knew the top brass dismissed the work of Criminal Investigation as a distraction from the main game, of fighting the war.

The distinction made no sense to Joe. Wasn't justice the game? What was war if not crime on a grander scale?

He sat down at his desk, leaning backward to inspect the intricate designs in the plastered ceiling.

Where was Monroe?

Jeeps. Ah yes. The gasoline mystery. Barrels of the stuff had been disappearing for months now. There was little enough to go on but *something* was going on. The 'why' was simple. The trick here was to work out the 'how'. How it was happening and how to catch who was doing it. Until he knew more he'd keep it to himself.

Rationing had begun early in the war. Some locals abandoned gasoline altogether and learned to live with the stench of fish oil from the gas converters attached to their car hoods or trunks. But most people had to apply to the Fuel Control Board for coupons and these quickly became collateral to be traded, hoarded and swapped. The slips of paper passed from hand to hand like cards in a game.

Opportunities for black market deals proliferated. Every army unit had a requisitions officer or quartermaster. Not difficult to imagine that some of them had found an easy way to boost their army pay. Even here at Base Headquarters no one had been able to tell Joe how much gas they went through, although Bates, the quartermaster, had used longwinded words that explained nothing.

Joe opened the top right-hand drawer of his desk to retrieve his notes.

A photo slipped out from the papers: a woman in New York's Central Park, leaning back with her arms resting along the top of a park bench, eyes closed. Behind her the trees were bare, their naked branches reaching for the sky. Nancy hated having her photo taken. She said black-and-white photos sucked all the colour and movement out of life, and it was those things that mattered. He'd sneaked this shot on their last day together, a spy watching from a distance. Now everything seemed so distant. The elastic band around the bundle of letters in his apartment was stretched thin, close to breaking. Their easy banter was long gone. Jokes weren't funny without an audience, punchlines lost their velvet fist when delayed by the postal service. Joe found it hard to remember the days they'd spent together. Nancy wrote about the world she knew, the office intrigue, cocktails at the Cinderella Club every Friday. He'd left that world behind and couldn't describe this new one. 'Somewhere in the South Pacific' told her nothing of the life he lived now — of the fights and knifings, the whores and pimps, the parties in the streets of West End, the all-night boozing at the sly grog shop in Spring Hill, the birds screeching in the trees outside his room, the evening skies darkened with bats each night. The sweat. Always the heat. Sometimes he struggled to breathe. What was it — October? Nancy would be waiting for snow to fall in Central Park while Joe was here praying for rain or a gentle breeze.

In the corridor a phone trilled until answered. Moments later Private Bland poked his head around the door and flicked crumbs from his shirt. 'Woolloongabba's got a body, Sarge. Looks like one of ours.'

SATURDAY 9 OCTOBER 1943

Chapter Two

Joe cut the motor and propped the motorbike onto its centre-stand beside a police Harley and sidecar. Steam rose from the exhaust. From close by came the asthmatic cough of a train — the last one to Beenleigh. He checked the luminous hands on his wristwatch. Half past twelve. A brawl? In the South Brisbane cemetery? Unlikely, but nothing's a surprise in this town.

He slung his helmet across the handlebars, retrieved a flashlight from his camera bag and followed its yellow strip of light through the wrought iron gates. Something squished beneath his feet and he steadied himself against a tree trunk. Down the slope he picked out a large figure leaning against a stone column. Closer up he recognised the dome of a bobby's helmet, the baggy blue serge of the Queensland Police uniform straining against the metal buttons.

He introduced himself with a handshake and vague salute. 'Sergeant Joe Washington. Criminal Investigation Command.'

'Constable Guymer, sir.'

'Woolloongabba said you've got one of ours.'

'Yes, indeed.'

'Odd place for a fight,' Joe said. 'Pity they didn't pick a more respectable hour. Did you get the others?'

'Respectable? Dutton Park?' The constable looked at his boots and sniffed his displeasure. 'Used to be a fancy place, but things change, I guess. More's the pity. And no. There's only one soldier.'

'Where is he?'

'Down here, sir, near the burial vault over to the right.' The constable pointed to a mausoleum of sorts. 'Good place to hide crates of whiskey.'

'Have you checked it out?'

'Nothing there.'

'But there has been?'

'Looks possible. There's a couple of crates broken open, empty now. But they don't look like anything you'd have at a funeral.'

Joe followed the constable down the slope to where he stopped in front of a lumpy shape on the ground. Joe's flashlight traced the angular lines of a tall, thin man lying face up, legs and arms akimbo, eyes open. An army private. Something about him looked familiar but then soldiers in uniform all looked pretty much the same.

'Who found him?' Joe said. 'You can't see the body from the roadway.'

'We got a call to the station. Man said he heard a car stop, thought something was being dumped. We've had lots of complaints about goings-on here. Black-market deals, women meeting soldiers, all-night drinking. That sort of thing. We thought it might be sly groggers. The CIB are on their way and they'll want to talk to the caller, no doubt; he lives across the road.'

Joe's flashlight moved along the body, pausing to take in

the details: polished boots, drill trousers, leather belt, undone. The shirt was unbuttoned too, the tails pulled out from the waistband. Had he wandered into the darkened cemetery to piss? The soldier's right arm lay outstretched on the ground, his shirtsleeves rolled casually above strong forearms, fingers curved around an open palm. One of his shirt pockets — the left, above the heart — was ripped and ragged. A single incision, from the look of it. But why was there so little blood? Close up Joe could make out smears of red along the man's forehead that looked like scratch marks. The pencil moustache above the open mouth was blurred at the edges, merging with a five o'clock shadow. Had someone once told him that hair and fingernails kept growing after death? He shone the flashlight around the body, finding leaves and twigs but very little blood. Had the body been moved?

'Any sign of a weapon?' Joe said and looked up. 'Got to be a knife.'

'Nothing,' Guymer said. 'We may find more in the morning but the river's no distance, easy to dispose of a knife. I've no idea what type, of course. You'd know more about that.'

Joe was used to knives. Most American servicemen carried them and he knew the locals were shocked at how often they used them. Aussies preferred fists; thought it more manly.

He kneeled beside the body and felt around in the trouser pockets. It was moments like these when he thought of Nancy and his life on the other side of the world. Would he ever tell her he went through a dead man's pockets looking for ID?

'Here's his wallet,' a different voice said. Joe turned to discover a second man emerging from the shadow of a tree. The sallow-faced sergeant handed over a leather billfold and Joe flipped it open. A few stained notes, a couple of local coins: a few bucks.

So he wasn't robbed.

Tucked inside one end of the wallet was a photo. He drew it out, held it under the flashlight. A fair-haired woman in a patterned frock, head tilted to the right as she smiled for the camera, her arm draped around a boy with combed hair and short pants who held a teddy bear awkwardly under his arm. The background was too blurred to give any context, but Joe felt sure the woman knew the photographer. A family snap on a day out? He remembered a similar photo in his childhood home, his mother dark not blonde, but the bear he'd held was almost identical, its black button eyes and smug stitched smile. He couldn't remember where they'd been when his father took it, although he could still see the box brownie, his father peering down into it before lifting his head to smile at his mother. It remained — that single photo on the mantlepiece — the only reminder of a younger man, one who could make his mother smile. All his life he'd wanted to smash it.

The commander would be writing to this woman soon, but the death he'd report was not a soldier's. There were always more victims in war than you realised, and now she'd become one.

Joe checked for the man's dog tag. 'Hold this, can you?' He handed his flashlight to the constable, who held it steady as Joe pulled a notepad from his pocket and copied the details. Robert A Foster. 24683595. Next of kin Doreen — was it her in the photo? An address in Sandy Springs, Georgia. Protestant. No point in recording his tetanus shots or blood type.

Joe looked into Robert A Foster's eyes, reading the lines on the face, the hair of the thin moustache. Why were you here? He smelled blood and booze — you'd expect that — but also something else. Lilacs? Perfume? His eyes worked their way down from the head. Ah. A smear on the left shoulder, easily mistaken for blood. He leaned in and looked more closely. Lipstick.

*

'So young man, what do we bloody well have here?'

Joe swivelled as a square hand clapped him on the shoulder like a slab of beef landing on a butcher's block. He took in the big man in front of him, the three-piece suit, red cheeks and fleshy lips topped by black hair and an unnecessary hat. He was an imposing figure — over six feet tall, Joe guessed, and around fourteen stone. Joe had seen men like this at the police youth club when he was a kid — soft and flabby, but with a sharp right. The man might look like a clown but he'd caught Joe unawares.

Senior Sergeant Frank Bischof wasn't based at Woolloongabba Station but it didn't surprise Joe to see him here. Local police spoke of the Big Fella's uncanny knack for always being in the right place at the right time, even if no one knew precisely how he did it. Rumours circulated of a vast web of contacts — other detectives, police on the street, barmaids and touts, hustlers selling cigarettes in the alleys around North Quay, the man selling meat pies on Petrie Terrace.

This town is a mystery, Joe thought.

He noticed how both uniformed police stood at attention, their chests puffed up, heads raised. But neither made eye contact with the detective. Odd.

'Sergeant Joseph Washington,' he introduced himself with an unnecessary salute. 'An American soldier's been knifed. Here.'

'Let's have a look,' Frank said as he sank to the ground in an uncomfortable crouch. He kneeled for only as long as it took to take in the single knife wound, the blood smears on the hairline, the grazed knuckles. He stopped when he saw the red smears.

'Lots of lipstick,' he said, standing to neaten his cuffs. 'A whiff of perfume — something tarty by the smell. A knife's usually a woman's weapon. We'll check around the brothels and boarding houses. No shortage within a close radius. Should be pretty straightforward.'

'We don't know what he was doing here,' Joe said. 'There was a report of something being dumped and there's a stone crypt over there. Should we check it at least?'

'Found a weapon?' Frank turned to the sergeant, dismissing Joe with the wave of a hand. 'It'll be a kitchen knife or something similar, is my bet.'

'Nothing so far from what I hear.' Joe stepped forward. 'But it looks like a single blow to the chest did for him. He's got a few other scratches, grazed knuckles from maybe a fight. No other cuts. Whoever did this must have got lucky — or not, depending on your point of view, of course. My guess is he would have been dead pretty quick. There's no shortage of knife fights among soldiers, I wouldn't dismiss a fight gone wrong. Right this moment we've got a private in the—'

Frank ignored him and strode toward Constable Guymer. 'How did you come to be in the vicinity tonight?'

'Road patrol.' Joe watched the constable straighten his back, to the extent that his belly would allow. Reporting to the boss, giving a full account. Yes, sir. 'We've had to increase road patrols in recent months. Lots of complaints from the public. Assignations with soldiers. Loose women. Sexual impropriety. We were nearby when the phone call came through to Woolloongabba.'

'Good man,' Frank said.

'I found this,' Guymer added. He handed over a slip of paper. 'And here's his hospital day pass.'

Why hadn't they shown those to me? Joe thought.

'Who called the station?' Frank said. 'When?'

'One Jim Fletcher. Lives down the road in Princess Street. Said he heard a car park, something being dumped.'

'We'll need to talk to him,' Frank said. 'One of you go and check if there are any signs of a car having stopped on the roadway.'

They turned at the crash of metal being dragged and bumping against stone. A shaft of light pierced the dark and an angry voice whined, 'For fuck's sake.'

Two men emerged from the darkness, a balding middle-aged man in a yellow shirt hauling a ladder and a young, red-haired youth staggering behind, bandoliered with camera bags and flash equipment.

The older of the two bent to rub his ankle. 'Bugger. This place gives me the willies,' he said. He growled at Frank and nodded to Joe. 'Where do you want us, then? Talk about the middle of the night.'

Man and boy followed Frank's pointed finger. The two uniformed police stood guard. With scarcely a glance at the body on the ground, the cameramen began unpacking his gear, arranging lights. The tripod stood askew, one leg propped on a tilted slab of marble. Once set up, the older man moved to the body, now the centrepiece of an elaborate show. Lights, action. The man crouched, inspecting the body from each side. He stood and reached for a camera bag.

'Make sure you get him from all angles,' he said to his younger partner. 'You know how pernickety Baty is. Long shots of the placement. Close-ups of the chest, lipstick, knuckles.'

The boy held the lights, struggling with the apparatus while he shielded his eyes from the glare each time it flashed.

'Nothing moves till we're done here,' the man said, raising his camera. He lined up shots through the eyepiece, without needing to look at the body. Joe knew how the lens worked to bring you closer to your subject, but at the same time kept you detached. Removed somehow. Each burst of light illuminated a part of the body — the pale arms and face, the smears of red, the open mouth. Everything reduced to black and white.

Joe watched Frank check the linen handkerchief peeping from his coat pocket was straight.

'You two,' Frank spoke to the uniformed police, a general leading his men. 'Sergeant, you'd best call the van. There'll be a public phone up on the road and while you're there, check for tyre marks. Footprints. Let these clowns know so they can photograph it all, for what it's worth.'

The men turned at the sound of a shoe slipping on gravel and a low growl. Another flashlight shone into the night and Joe began wondering what the point was of all the blackout regulations.

'Is that police? What's happening?'

Behind the narrow beam Joe made out a wizened face above a grey checked shirt. White hair, sun-weathered face, rheumy eyes and a gentle smile. Beside him, a tan dog twirled in delight.

Frank raised a foot as the kelpie edged toward him. 'What's your business here?'

Joe held his hand out to the dog, feeling its warm tongue inspect the space between his fingers. He patted a nose surprisingly cool and the dog shuffled.

Ignoring Frank, the old man glanced at Joe's peaked cap and uniform then bent to pat the dog. 'Sit, Bobby. There's a good boy. What do you think the Yanks are doing here, then?'

'Are you the one who made the call to Woolloongabba Station? We'll need you to make a statement.' Frank moved toward the man but retreated as the dog snarled.

'I'm Sergeant Joseph Washington, sir.' Joe proffered a hand, anticipating a strong handshake. An outdoorsman by the looks of him, not a city dweller. 'Perhaps you'd like to tell me what you saw earlier tonight? We could sit over here.' He led both man and dog to a low brick wall wide enough to make a seat.

Frank stood apart.

'I understand you reported something to the police?' Joe said. 'Mr —?'

'Fletcher. Jim Fletcher. From number sixteen. Most nights Bobby and I go for a walk, you know. After we've listened to the late news on the radio and finished our tea. We had a chop tonight, didn't we, Bobby? Bit of a rarity these days but my brother was down from the farm and Bobby needs a bit of gristle on the bone. Keeps his teeth strong.'

'And you saw something?'

Jim spoke to Joe, his voice even, his face turned away from Frank. 'Yes, it was all a bit strange, we thought. Not easy to see details, of course, not now there's no streetlights. And not much moon. But I've spent a lot of time in the bush and your eyes adjust. We were getting ready for our walk when a vehicle stopped. Out on the road there. And I heard voices arguing, but in whispers. Then I heard something being dragged along the ground, bumping along, then dumped. Doors slammed. Whoever it was drove off fast, over the bridge and up the hill past the railway station. It didn't look right, that's all I can say. Have you found something?'

'What seemed unusual? Was it a car? A truck?'

'Not a truck, the engine wasn't that big. I think a car of some kind. Maybe a jeep.'

'Arguing, you said? Did you hear what were they arguing about?'

He shook his head. 'Too far away to hear any words. But the tone of voice, you know, that's what made me think they were arguing.'

'Do you see people here often?'

'On weekends people come, to visit graves. But not at night.'

'Was there a fight? Could you tell if they were American?'

'Sorry. I can't be sure.'

'Do you think you could show us the spot? Where the car stopped?'

'Course I can.'

Behind him Joe heard Frank clear his throat and spit.

Chapter Three

At five o'clock, on what was now Saturday morning, Joe parked the unit's old jeep beside a neat row of white stones that marked the entrance to the 42nd hospital at Holland Park. They'd paced the streets with Jim and his dog, searching for signs of a parked car, trying to identify tyre marks. Frank was sure the lipstick was the key but Joe was more interested that the body had been found so close to the tomb. He'd checked it out himself while they waited for the morgue van and had little doubt it'd been used as a store — apart from the empty boxes and scraps of hessian, there were marks along the floor where something heavy had been dragged. It wasn't possible to be sure when the goods had been there, nor when they'd been moved, but it was another angle.

Frank eased himself out of the front seat and Joe took grim pleasure in noting the handkerchief hanging from the top pocket, the crumpled coat, the grey smear on the back of the shirt collar.

Joe had rung ahead and an MP with a profile as bulbous

as the bottle trees in Anzac Park waited for them at the hospital entrance. He led them to the administrative head-quarters where Chief Medical Registrar Major Boole sat behind a wooden desk.

Joe saluted.

'You've found one of our men,' the major began.

'Yes. Robert Foster.' Joe handed over the patient's day pass and waited. 'Murdered. We can get you photos.'

'He was recovering from malaria and nearly ready for release. Had done good work at the PX from what I hear. Any further details?'

Joe told him what they knew. It wasn't much. Knife wounds but no weapon found. Cuts to the head and hands. Lipstick on the collar.

'He won't be the first patient to get drunk and find a prostitute. Won't be the last, either.'

Joe noted Frank's nod and they turned to leave. They followed the MP in single file along raised walkways toward the rear of the building complex. A group of men in white singlets and striped pyjama bottoms performed callisthenics on a small parade ground. Arms up, arms down, twist and turn. Like a slow dance to barked instructions from a muscular sergeant who sweated with the effort of keeping the men in time. The smell of bread from the hospital bakery reminded Joe that he'd missed breakfast. They skirted warehouses stocked with medical supplies, a hut marked 'narcotics' and a building that obviously housed the motor pool. Carpentry workshop, a steam plant, what looked like a chapel — everything that could be made, regulated, dispensed or policed happened within the grounds of the hospital and Joe wondered what contact the staff and patients had with the surrounding town; apart from prostitutes, barmaids and fellow drinkers, that is.

They passed a garden with the letters P and X marked out in purple and pink petunias in front of a long wooden building. Up a ramp to the reception area where a group of men, some in dark blue dressing-gowns, a few in the white uniform of hospital orderlies, drank bottles of Coca-Cola. A pair of crutches was propped against the counter. Rooms ran off the main corridor and Joe heard the whirr of a hair dryer, the metallic clip of scissors. Joe saw Frank raise his eyebrows at the shelves groaning with tins of jam, packets of biscuits, boxes of ice cream cones and bars of chocolate. Joe knew the hospital's PX was a quarter-million dollar business from listening as Lieutenant Bates waxed lyrical.

The MP led them to a small office where a short, tough man sat behind a desk chewing a cigar stub in the side of his mouth. The man reluctantly stood, removed the damp cigar to balance at the edge of the desk, looked toward Joe then smiled at Frank.

So this was Staff Sergeant Moses Ackerman. Joe had heard Bates speak in hushed tones about Mo, the man who knew how to find what he wanted, who always had a ready supply of greenbacks to ensure he got it.

'At your service, gentlemen.' Mo's voice, sharp and rough at the same time, could have grated blocks of granite.

Joe returned the smile. 'Joe Washington, Base Station Criminal Investigation Command. This is Detective Senior Sergeant Frank Bischof, Queensland CIB. Mind if we sit?' Joe waved away the MP, who moved toward the ice cream counter like a cow toward a field of clover.

Frank slid a piece of paper across the desk. 'Know this man?'

Mo glanced at the writing. 'Sure. Slim. He hasn't come in this morning. Should have been here by now.'

'When did you see him last?'

'Two days ago.' The answer was quick and definite. 'He was on day leave yesterday, wasn't rostered. Why? A detective, did you say?' Mo chewed on his cigar.

'I gather you're in charge of this PX,' Joe continued. 'Can you explain to Detective Bischof how it all works?'

Mo cracked his knuckles and retrieved the wet cigar. A businessman pausing to discuss his favourite child.

'I like to think of the Postal Exchange as the heart of the hospital,' he said. 'The doctors might get you well, patch you up and stitch you back together, but we're the ones who make life worth living. Food and drink, a place to get a suit made, have your hair trimmed. We can find pretty much anything you want, and we make sure you get it at a decent price.'

None of which answered the question directly. Surely this man's future was going to be in the new world of advertising, Joe thought. Assuming any of us have a future.

American Postal Exchanges had become something much more than a simple postal service. Goods in a PX were tax free, and that price difference was the source of much resentment toward the American soldiers. In November the year before, thousands of drunken Australian and American soldiers had rioted outside the PX on Adelaide Street, drawn like moths to a flame — lit by the price of Lucky Strike cigarettes. A soldier had died and hundreds had been injured. The authorities had tried to hose things down but the town was still feeling the consequences, and Joe knew it.

'So what does Foster do here? "Slim", you called him?' Joe said.

'He helps behind the counter. Sells things, mostly. Part of his rehab. Doesn't do a bad job, either.'

'Tell me about him.'

'Bit of a sad sack if you ask me. Always hanging around the beauty parlour, mooching over the nurses. He's not any trouble, just a bit pathetic. Keeps showing you photos of his wife back home in Georgia or some dump.'

'What was he here for? What's wrong with him?'

'They never tell me. I never ask.'

'Any friends?'

'Corporal Jones. He's a bit dim. They went on day leave together, I think.'

'Did he tell you what he planned?'

Mo smiled, a Groucho Marx smile. 'Dames. Always dames.'

Joe remained seated as Frank stood. He paced the room, inspecting the shelves on all four walls, the tins and bottles, the cellophane packets, a stack of cardboard boxes. He pulled one down, lifted the lid, fingered the flimsy patterned silk. Negligees.

He pirouetted on large feet, surprisingly agile.

'Lot of stuff you've got here,' he said. 'Not exactly hospital gowns and nurses' uniforms. I bet a lot of people would like a piece of this, get their hands on some of these goods. Perhaps some of the businesses specialising in tarts? Had dealings with some of them, have you? Make a bit of profit then plough it back into the business?'

There was no reaction from Mo, who knew when to hold his cards to his chest.

'Well, you won't have to bother about Foster's rehabilitation anymore,' Frank said. 'He was murdered. Last night. Knifed and left for dead.' He made for the door, waving for Joe to follow.

*

The neuro-psychiatric ward housed dozens of patients, eyes glazed, bodies gaunt from repeated bouts of malaria, and more were arriving as war advanced through New Guinea and the Pacific. When Joe had arrived the previous year, the troops were fresh-faced and eager. Few had seen action of any sort but all that had changed. Sure, Aussies could boast of successes in the Middle East but Joe assumed many of the patients in this ward had seen action in Buna or Sanananda. Markham Valley. All battle weary now.

Joe spoke to the nurse who approached them, a thickset woman with just the hint of a moustache. He explained their business indirectly. She led them between the rows of bed-steads, men lying or sitting, reading or simply looking at the ceiling.

'Only the most severe cases are in locked wards,' she said.

Corporal Jones sat beside a bed at the end of a long ward, one hand clutching his head, the other cupped awkwardly over a cigarette stub.

'When did he get back?' Joe asked.

'Sometime around midnight,' she said. 'We're used to them coming back drunk. It's what happens. No matter how many times we tell the ones with malaria that alcohol simply lengthens recovery time, they don't listen. Heaven knows where he's been — although I can guess. Came back dirty and shaken and hasn't stopped shivering since. Almost suits his nickname, poor lad. "Snow" they call him, although he's not so lily-white now.'

She tucked wiry hair into her nurse's cap, lifted her watch from a chain that lay across her ample bosom, held Jones's wrist and counted. Her lips moved silently.

'We'll need to interview him,' Joe said.

'You're free to talk to him but I don't know how much sense he'll make until he sobers up.'

Frank and Joe stood in front of Jones, who barely regis-tered their presence.

'What's the matter, lad?' Frank was unusually gentle. 'Had a fright? Seen something ugly? Done something maybe? Which is it?'

Jones looked up blankly but turned away.

'Know someone called Slim, do we?' Frank's gentle voice seemed more sinister than his normal tone. 'Seen him lately? Want to see him again?'

A jerk of the head as Jones's eyes quizzed Frank and Joe in turn.

'Come on, lad. Let's go for a ride. Get a bit of fresh air, maybe sober you up a bit.'

Frank leaned down to haul Jones upright.

Joe nodded at the nurse, who simply shrugged. She had too many serious patients to be worried about this one. 'You'd better sign him out at the front office. He's all yours.'

Joe led the two men back to the jeep and watched as the big man pushed the smaller into the jeep.

'Let's take him to see your mate, eh?' said Frank. 'Just for the formalities.'

Joe looked in the rear-vision mirror at the figure slumped in the back seat. The sweat on Jones's face made his skin oily, like wet pastry. Once a week Joe's mother made pasta. She'd leave the dough on the landing to rest, flipping it over once in a bowl slicked with olive oil. Pale, yellow and spongy. Was that what made Jones seem familiar?

*

At eight o'clock Joe pulled into the circular driveway off Fairfield Road in Yeerongpilly and parked in front of a low brick building. The flag on its pole hung languidly in the morning heat, the bare earth bleached white. This was American territory, the victim was American, the autopsy would be conducted by an American doctor, so it was Joe who led the two men into the building that housed the 5th Medical Laboratory and the Army Quartermaster's Morgue. He strode through the entrance, Frank and Jones trailing in his wake. It was his show for a brief time. Not Frank's.

He led them through a maze of corridors, glimpsing metal benches and test tubes in rooms to either side, the pungent and pervasive smell of chemicals. At last they reached a room at the rear of the complex, out of sight of the main laboratories. He'd been here often and every time, as he pushed open the door, he was reminded of the smell from his grandmother's kitchen, scrupulously scrubbed clean with soapy water and Brillo but overlaid with a whiff of the chicken liver she chopped to make paté on Sundays. He really did need breakfast.

Joe saluted the American major who stood at the dissecting table, a cigarette holder in his left hand, a scalpel in his right, looking for all the world like a diner ready to sit down to eat. On the mortuary slab a white sheet covered a long, low mound. A shape with few lumps and a gentle slope toward the exposed feet. Long toes, Joe noted, with the ingrown toenails common to those who wore heavy boots.

Frank padded around the room's periphery, indifferent to the nameless blobs of pink flesh that floated in bottles of formaldehyde.

Jones slunk into the corner. Joe watched as the doctor flicked back the sheet.

A naked man lay on his back, a stab wound now clearly visible on his upper left chest, a further three cuts to the top of his head. The same pencil moustache. Receding hair, strong forearms, circumcised. Six foot three, or thereabouts, Joe guessed, but not heavy, with more muscle than fat. Last night Joe had thought the man familiar. Now he couldn't be certain. This body held nothing. Just a lump of muscle and bone, all movement stilled, emotion frozen. All the lines of a life flattened out somehow. Still life, he thought. Like a black-and-white photo. Briefly he remembered the photo he'd found last night, of the boy and the woman.

Frank hauled Jones from the corner and spun him round to face the table.

Jones whimpered, unable to look away.

'Recognise him?'

The corporal, skin flaccid and face already drained of colour, looked like he wanted to lie on the slab beside Foster and give up any pretence of being alive. His hands shook as he covered his bloodshot eyes.

He nodded. 'Yes. It's Slim. God.'

Frank let him go and he slumped against the wall, concentrating on his feet and swallowing so as not to vomit. His mouth opened and closed, each breath bringing in the smell of disinfectant and bodily fluids.

The detective towered over the pale man, stepping on the toes of his boots. He stabbed a finger in Jones's chest. 'Feeling a bit crook, are we? A blue gone wrong?'

Joe added 'crook' and 'blue' to his growing list of incomprehensible Australian words.

Jones gagged, covering his mouth, looking around for a sink. He dry retched and flecks of spittle fell at Frank's feet.

'Watch the shoes, mate. First rule of interrogation: Never chunder on the detective's shoes.'

Joe filed away another word.

'Spit it out,' Frank added with no hint of irony.

'I didn't hardly know him.' For a moment Jones forgot his headache and shook his head. He groaned. 'Only met him a few weeks ago. Went drinking last night. That's all. Jesus Mary.'

'Enough of the Hail Marys. I want information. Details. That's what's called for now. What time were you drinking?'

'From about ten o'clock, I reckon. We had day passes.'

'From the hospital?'

'Yeah.'

'What then?'

'Well, we had a few beers, maybe three or four. Slim wanted to head into the city so we got a taxi.'

'Type?'

'I don't know cars real well, cream coloured, was it? I can't remember.'

'What then?'

'The driver took us to a hotel. Somewhere in the city. And to a dance hall. We ended up in someone's house. Where there was a girl. You know. Not a cat house. Just someone's house.'

'San Toy used to be a house, pretty flash in its day,' Frank said for Joe's benefit.

Jones looked past Frank toward the body on the table. He looked sick from booze, sicker still from the smell in the room.

'We'll need a statement,' Frank said. 'But first, let's go for a bit of a drive to see if it jogs your memory.'

*

Joe engaged reverse, turning to look at the sickly corporal hunched in the back seat. Not contagious, he hoped. 'You went on pass together?' he prompted, releasing the clutch as he turned into Logan Road. 'Where did you go first exactly? And when? How about we go back over it.'

'We had a snack at a café,' said Jones. 'Around 10 am. It's up the road from the hospital, on the right.'

Logan Road provided the southern exit from Brisbane, down the east coast all the way into New South Wales. A small but steady trickle of cars headed south in the opposite direction, their tyres thumping rhythmically as they crossed the tram tracks that ran like a seam down the middle of the road.

Southport was a coastal settlement of fishing shacks and fibro boarding houses where families rented rooms during the school holidays. Joe had taken the train there once or twice, had wandered up and over the Jubilee Bridge to the beach. One weekend he'd stayed in a boarding house and went to the picture theatre that hung precariously over the water on the ubiquitous wooden stilts. That would forever remain his most vivid memory of this part of the world.

'Here,' Jones said from the back seat. 'Opposite the hotel. We went there afterwards for a drink.'

Joe slowed as they drove up the hill, stopping at the large hotel on the corner, its fake Tudor panelling out of place in this Southern Hemisphere summer. Opposite was the tram terminus. Inside the dark interiors of waiting carriages, buxom matrons in broad hats fanned themselves with magazines held in gloved hands, the damp on their upper lips shining with disapproval as they eyed the Mountain View Hotel.

Joe pulled into the kerb, ignoring the 'no parking' sign.

'This where you mean?' Frank took over. 'Foster with you all the time?'

'Yes. Here. We met a taxi driver here. He took us into town.'

'To the San Toy, I'll be bound.'

'A Chinese restaurant? No, we went to a pub.'

Frank threw back his head and laughed. 'That's a good one. Must tell Betty that one.' He looked sharply at Jones. 'You'd better tell the truth, lad. No harm in wanting a bit of slap and tickle now and then.'

'I don't know what you mean. Here.' Jones reached into his top pocket and withdrew a notebook, its cardboard cover creased and bent. He offered it to Frank. 'The taxi driver wrote his name down. In case we needed him again.'

Joe watched Frank read the address slowly, close the notebook and slip it into his fob pocket, dismissing it with the wave of a hand. 'No point wasting our time here then,' he said to Joe. 'Let's keep going. Jones can make a statement back at headquarters.' Frank seemed animated in a way he hadn't been earlier. 'Just drop us at the Town Hall, Sergeant. I'll collect the car, Jones can come with me. We can have a little talk on the way. Discreet like. Suit you?'

It didn't, but Joe had no authority. Yet.

'Okay. Up to you,' he said.

Joe followed the tram tracks, a navigational trick he'd learned when he'd first arrived. He drove down Logan Road to Woollongabba, turned left into Stanley Street and parked at the back of the Town Hall. Frank eased himself out of the low jeep and led Jones to where he'd parked the police V8. Joe was uneasy with the arrangement but couldn't be sure why.

'I'll follow soon as I can,' he said.

The body in the cemetery was Frank's for now; Joe had no official role until they charged Jones. And perhaps they would, though he seemed an unlikely perp. Maybe this investigation would end up straightforward, after all, just another fight between soldiers. In the meantime Joe had other things to deal with.

Chapter Four

B ack at his desk, Joe made a space for his forearms and held his head in his hand as he confronted the tower of folders before him. Other cases. Already this month he'd investigated LeRoy Bryson's attack on two women in South Brisbane, Corporal Duke charged with carnal knowledge of a minor and now Private Teague arrested for the murder of one sailor and the knifings of two others in a brawl at the Army Motor Pool.

And barely a week into October.

Not that you'd call them real investigations. Just reports for officers to flick through while waiting for the court martial to reach its predetermined conclusion. Fines, slaps on the wrist, transfers.

He found Bryson's folder near the top of the pile. A dozen sheets of paper — his own sketch of the scene of the attack, the streetscape neatly ruled, participants marked in red crosses. A black-and-white photo he'd taken of the fence with the paling prised out — a gap in a row of white teeth. A story in loose sheets of paper but with so much missing. Most of all the 'why'.

Duke's story was simpler. A corporal with the Darra Ordnance Ammunition, he'd done what so many soldiers had done: gone and got a girl pregnant. He'd sent her money, written to her from New Guinea, all seemed on the level, but it turned out she was only fifteen.

'You're late,' Major Mitchell said. Uniform immaculate, buzzcut the regulation millimetres, boots glistening with polish. The major never walked into a room, he arrived like a galleon entering harbour. Flags hoisted and brasswork gleaming. He laid a thin briefcase on the raised desk at the end of the room, adjusted the angle of the photo of his wife, two neatly dressed children and a well-brushed dog and reached for the in-tray. 'Where's the report on Private Teague?'

Joe lifted his head, aware that he needed some breakfast and a shave.

Bryson had been charged yesterday but Duke would have to wait. He'd put off interviewing Private Teague. The MPs had hauled him in on Friday so he'd had a day to cool his heels. Joe had questioned the others involved — well, those still in hospital. Teague wouldn't be going anywhere soon.

'Have you interviewed him? His court martial's only a day away. It's a simple enough case. I'll need the files on my desk by this afternoon.'

'Just on my way there now, as it happens. After that I thought I'd double-check some details on the Duke case.' Joe took a notebook from the top drawer and slung his bag over one shoulder. He'd keep the gasoline story to himself for now. Taking the initiative wasn't high on the major's list of virtues. 'And I'll check in with the CIB. There was another knifing last night.'

'Anyone charged?'

'Not yet, the police are investigating.'

'Don't spend too much time on Duke. He's been charged, he'll get what he deserves.'

'Yes, sir.' Joe saluted.

Prick.

'And Washington, don't interfere with the local police, they don't appreciate it and I don't want to hear about them not appreciating it. You've no business getting involved in a knifing at this stage. You know the rules.'

He did. No one liked them.

The Criminal Investigation Command, to which Joe had found himself reluctantly attached, was established to investigate crimes committed by their soldiers — one thing there was no shortage of — because even in a foreign country, American soldiers were only answerable to American military courts.

Local police weren't happy with the arrangement and it had become another complaint among many. Joe had heard them all. Now the threat of direct attack from the Japs had faded, locals were getting cheesed off with the Yanks. More money meant they got the best of everything. Quicker service, more beer and the best looking girls. It all came to a head last year during Thanksgiving. The Queensland Police Commissioner blamed the American Military Police, and if the gossip Joe heard around the base was anything to go by, he may well have been right. Grant, the American MP charged during the riot, had been transferred to Syria even before his court martial — and of course he'd been found not guilty of murder.

Joe had heard police complain about the weeks spent on investigations that led nowhere. As soon as they nabbed an American perpetrator they had to hand them over. No satisfaction of preparing a case for the courts and no chance of seeing a conviction. It stank.

Even so, the police maintained — strenuously — their

right to investigate all crimes committed on their patch. It was their town, and until an American was charged the local police held sway.

Joe had a dead American soldier on his hands, but no American had yet been implicated in his death. He didn't doubt they would be. Most fights were between soldiers and most Americans carried knives. He'd give Frank Bischof a day or so to find someone. Only then would he know what official role he could play in this investigation.

*

At the bottom of the stairs Joe collected a set of keys from the rack in the guardroom. The three MPs studying their cards at a table scarcely looked up. Poker was serious business.

He slid a key into the door of the cell nearest the road and withdrew a notebook from his top pocket. He took a chair and sat at right angles to the bed.

Private Archibald Teague lifted his body to a seated position to look at Joe directly, eye to eye. Teague must be six feet tall, Joe calculated, and thin. God, he reeked. Stale booze, sweat, the metallic tang of blood. An Adam's apple worked in his scrawny neck as he raked fingers across his forehead. Blood from a cut under his eye had dried, forming a brown crust.

'Had time to think? Sleep it off?'

'What happened?' Teague asked.

'You tell me. Remember Thursday night?'

'Not a lot of it. I've been trying to remember. Me and some pals took a streetcar into town, wandered around a bit until the bars closed. Up Spring Hill way we found a joint selling wine and moonshine. Must have been there a while, drank a couple of bottles, did our dough. I wanted to head back to camp but on the way we met a bunch of sailors. Down the hill near the wharves, must have been. They were all shouting and throwing bottles, looking for a fight. Christ, got a fag?'

Joe kept a pack in his fob pocket, always three cigarettes to use as collateral. He'd never got the hang of it himself. He nodded for Teague to go on.

'We were all pretty mad. I got cut.' Teague lifted his hand and picked at a scab on his chin.

'Where was this?'

'Must have been near the Motor Pool on Edward Street. That's where we saw the sailors. Then the Shore Patrol arrived, a bunch of them jumped down from the cage, took to the sailors with clubs and batons. One of them had a knife.'

'Who?'

'A big man, with white hair. He was going gangbusters, beating heads.'

'You had a knife yourself,' Joe said. 'When the MPs searched you they found a pocket knife in your trousers. The tip broken and covered with blood. Do you remember using it? Or how it broke?'

'No,' Teague said. 'But that don't mean I didn't. Everything's mixed up, fuzzy. I know everyone was throwing things, bottles, maybe a knife. There were a lot of us by the end.'

'Did you know any of the other men? Not the men you went drinking with, the others? What were they doing near the Motor Pool?'

Although Joe toyed with the idea often enough, he struggled to understand how you could kill someone so casually, someone you'd never known, who'd done you no wrong. But that was war, he guessed. No difference really.

'What were *you* doing near the Motor Pool? Why did you stop?' Joe said.

'Just passing, on our way to the streetcar. I do remember

there were sailors loading drums onto a truck and then some sort of argument. Fists thrown. We just thought we'd have some fun, help out. But we'd been drinking most of the day, they were too good for us.'

'What was in the drums?'

'No idea. Maybe gasoline.'

'This Shore Patrolman, the big man with the knife. What do you remember about him?'

'Nothing much,' Teague said. 'Just that he seemed off his nut.'

'Describe him for me.'

'Massive. A bull neck and white hair. He spoke funny, not that he said much. Just yelled like a Nazi in the movies.'

'Did you see him use the knife?' Joe said.

'No. We were all in a heap together, punching and kicking. He just stood out somehow. Don't know why.'

'I'll have Private Bland type up your statement,' Joe said. 'But I have to say it doesn't look good.' As he stood and turned to leave, Joe pointed to the floor. 'You may not have noticed, but there's blood on your boots.'

*

The Willys was gone and so was the motorbike. He might have to jump on a tram, he reminded himself — but at that minute the army jeep veered into the courtyard, screamed to a halt and disgorged a large man in the white puttees and helmet of a uniformed MP. As Corporal Butt Monroe unfolded himself from the driver's seat, an imprint of the steering wheel deep into his belly, Joe wondered how he managed to drive. Monroe slurped from a squat bottle of Coke and munched on a handful of peanuts. He licked salt from his hands before flattening ginger strands of hair across the purple birthmark that slipped over his forehead and down over his left eye, a pirate's eye patch.

'Finished with the jeep?' Joe asked.

'Yeah. I was out at Darra checking on the little girlie that nigger knocked up.'

Joe hadn't asked.

'Gotta go get ammo from the Q store later, though.'

Joe held out his hand for the keys and slipped into the driver's seat as Major Mitchell appeared at the top of the steps.

'The report?' he called, but the sound was lost in the rev of the engine as Joe backed out and into the side street.

Chapter Five

Joe parked in front of CIB headquarters between another Willys and a delivery truck laden with wooden pallets. Morecombe House was a small building on the corner of Queens Gardens with stained-glass windows, carved arches and peaked roof; Joe thought how unlikely the former church was as a setting for what happened within. On second thoughts, perhaps the architecture served to instil in detectives the authority they needed. He remembered sitting beside his mother on the hard wooden pews in St Patrick's, waiting his turn to pass through the velvet curtain. Inside the darkened space with only a grille on one wall, the smell of tobacco overwhelming, the whistle of Father O'Flagherty's breathing terrifying for a small boy. He'd learned an important lesson there as Father waited. The power of silence, how the silence made you want to fill the space, to talk, to seek absolution.

He'd heard locals call this building the Confessional.

Joe raced up the stairs, hoping he hadn't missed too much. It was half past ten and at least an hour had gone by since he'd left Jones with Frank.

A constable with buck teeth and dandruff led him down a narrow corridor through heavy double doors. A rough pine table and four metal chairs sat in the middle of a room, the bare walls painted ochre, the only light from clerestory windows. Frank Bischof sat on one side, arms on the table, all smiles.

If Joe had briefly thought the man sitting opposite Frank familiar, now he hardly recognised him. In the short time since Joe had left him in Frank's care, Jones had sobered up. He'd also acquired a swollen left eye and scraped the knuckles on his right hand almost to the bone.

'What happened?' Joe wasn't sure to whom he addressed the question nor who would reply.

'Nothing,' Jones said.

'What have you done? I left this soldier in your care.'

'Custody, you mean,' Frank said. 'Fell climbing the stairs. Put out his hand to stop himself, hit his head. That's the trouble with drink. Makes you unsteady.' He motioned Joe to an empty chair. 'Now Jones, tell the sergeant your story. There's a good man.'

Joe sat beside the private. He could feel the vibration from his jiggling left leg. 'I'm here to keep an eye on you,' he said.

Jones stared at the floor. 'I've only known Foster — Slim — for a week, met him at the hospital. We both had day passes yesterday and went out.'

'What time was this?' Frank leaned back and crossed his legs.

'Around ten o'clock. Like I told you. We had a meal at the café and a few beers at the hotel. Then we got a taxi into town, to another hotel.'

'Did you and Foster stay together the whole time?'

'Mostly. We had a few more beers, went over a bridge. Slim wanted to go to a dance hall but I don't like crowds so I waited outside, at a bar.'

'Where?'

'No idea. I've only been out on leave twice before, don't know my way around town. Not far.'

Joe leaned forward. This may be a Queensland police investigation but the man was American, after all. Surely even the major couldn't argue with that.

'Did the taxi driver who dropped you hang around?'

'Yeah. He said he'd take us someplace after. Not a cat house, just somewhere private he knew.' Jones kept his eyes on Joe.

Frank uncrossed his arms and planted them on the table. 'Where did you end up?'

'I don't know. Not far from the dance hall. A wooden house on a steep hill.'

Joe remembered the streets they'd driven through on the way from the mortuary, the streets around the Town Hall. Rows of houses propped on wooden posts, their tin roofs sloping over open porches. Well, that certainly narrows it.

'I was pretty far gone by then. There was a bit of a party,' Jones said.

'Who was there?' Frank said.

'The taxi drivers — both of them — a girl, an old woman. Slim wanted more hooch so they went off to buy gin.'

'What did you do while you waited?'

'Well, you know.' Jones blushed. 'There was this girl so, you know, we had her.'

'Did you pay for this service?' Frank said. 'Are you sure you weren't at the San Toy?'

'Never heard that name till now. But yes.'

'And then?'

'There was a fight. I was skunk drunk by then. Can't remember a lot. I just know I ran, I don't like fights. I ran away. I always do. I'm not proud of that, but it's the truth.'

'Where did you go?'

'I kept running till I found a road, followed the tracks till I saw a streetcar. Not sure how I managed to get back to the hospital but I made it.'

'Doesn't anyone have a name?' Joe said. He saw a notebook lying on the table, remembered Jones handing it over to Frank. He flicked it open till he found a name on the final page. 'Eddie? Is this who took you there?'

'Yes. Leonard was the other one.'

'And the girl? The one who got into the fight?' Frank said. 'Her name?'

Jones shook his head.

'Could you find this place again? We could backtrack down the tramlines?' Joe said. Frank frowned at the idea. 'We can use Uncle Sam's gas. Don't want to needlessly waste the resources of the Queensland Police.'

'Right,' Frank said, hauling Jones to his feet. 'Let's go.'

The three men left together. As Frank passed the front counter he stopped for a word with one of the detectives. 'Check around the taxis, will you. And the brothels. You know the most likely ones.'

*

Joe drove across the Victoria Bridge and past the Trocadero, sleepy in the mid-morning. Queues had formed outside the Blue Moon skating rink and it looked like Artie Shaw was coming to the Cremorne. He'd remember the dates.

He edged the jeep along, following the tramlines until he came to a place Jones thought familiar. From there they made their way through a maze of alleys and side streets that climbed Highgate Hill. On the side of the hill the wooden houses slumped sideways like soldier amputees, their left-hand stumps longer than the right by a good three feet. Huddled so close together their unpainted side walls were only a few inches apart.

'Down here a bit. No, maybe that street — to the left.' In the rear-vision mirror Joe watched Jones concentrate, retracing in reverse the steps he'd taken when he'd fled the fight last night. Or so he said.

'You sure? Not Gladstone Road? To the right? That'll take you back to Montague Road.' Frank seemed to hold firm views on where they were headed.

'No, I'm pretty sure this is it,' Jones said. 'I remember the cane chair. The girl was sitting there when we arrived, reading under a light on the porch. See?'

Joe took in the tin awnings drooping over sash windows, the ripped lace curtains hanging limp. He hauled on the handbrake. Frank opened the rear door to pull Jones out. Together they walked up the wooden steps. Frank knocked, his face blank.

The door was opened by a fat man with rough-cut features, greasy wisps of hair over a burnished skull and an afternoon stubble. Baggy trousers and a blue suit coat as shiny as his head. The hand that gripped the door was red, the skin on the palms flaky, and the smile he gave Frank died when he saw the others.

'What do you want?' the man spat as he flung a cigarette onto a pile of stubs in what passed for a front garden. 'What's this all about?'

Frank stepped over the gob of spit. 'Hello, Leonard. A word.' He pushed his way into the front room. Joe followed with Jones in tow.

The living room scarcely fit them all and Frank's head grazed the sloping ceiling. A settee and two sagging armchairs, their patterned brown velvet worn thin, formed a circle around a low table covered with stains and grubby glasses. Beside a chipped plate with a half-eaten slice of toast smeared with black paste, the Brisbane *Truth* praised the Allied bombing of Bremen and gave odds for the mid-week races.

Frank lowered himself into one of the armchairs, the stuffing moulding to his huge shape. The fat man sat opposite, with Joe completing the circle. Jones stood in the corner of the room, beside a chair on which sat a brown cardboard case of the type he'd seen kids carry to school. Inside, neatly folded and packed, were threadbare towels and bottles of yellow liquid. Medicine?

'Is this the place?' Joe broke the silence, looking to Jones for confirmation.

'Yes. This is it.'

'Tell us what happened.'

Jones looked to the window, past the lace curtains onto the street. Never once did he look at the man he called Leonard, nor did Leonard register his presence. The only real communication, Joe sensed, was between Frank and Leonard, but he couldn't read what was being said.

'The taxi driver — Eddie — brought us here. We drank beer. Eddie and Leonard went to get some gin. I didn't see them again. There was a girl.'

'You had sexual intercourse,' Frank said, rousing himself.

'Yes. While he was away.' Even then Jones didn't look at the man opposite Frank.

'Did you pay? Prostitution is illegal in this state, you know.' Frank looked sternly in Leonard's direction.

'Yes. Slim paid. I don't have any money.'

'How much?'

'Twenty pounds. Five a time. While we waited for the gin.'

'Not bad money.' Frank whistled softly and Joe guessed Frank's weekly wage was much less.

'What time was this? How long were Leonard and Eddie away?'

'An hour? Maybe more. I went to sleep for a while.'

'When was the last time you saw Foster?'

'Here, last night. Like I told you, there was a fight. Him and the girl, the old woman. They were yelling and screaming, throwing fists. I ran.'

Leonard had still not spoken.

'What about you, Leonard? When was the last time you saw this man? And the other soldier, Foster?' Frank turned to face Leonard. The two men assessed each other as in a game of chess or poker. Each one deciding how much to tell, when to raise the odds. This would make for a great shot, Joe thought, mentally checking exposure levels under the single bulb.

Leonard nodded. 'I went for the gin and when I came back they'd both gone. You still owe me,' he said to Jones.

'Looks like you're out of luck,' Frank said. 'This bloke has no money and the other one's dead. You don't seem surprised.'

'Nothing surprises me about the Yanks. They fight all the time. Knives, pistols, batons. It's nothing to me. They came here, that's true. But they'd gone by the time I got back.'

'You live here alone?' Joe said, looking around the room. Few enough creature comforts.

'With the wife. She's in the kitchen.' Through a doorway Joe saw a table and chairs, an ice chest.

'Where was she last night?'

'Here. In bed,' Leonard said. 'She's not right in the head.'

'And a girl?' Joe looked to Jones, who nodded.

'She comes to look after the wife. Comes most days and does the cooking and things. Can't help if she does a few jobs on the side.' Leonard tittered.

'Where's she now?' Joe asked.

'No idea. She disappeared with the soldiers last night and hasn't come this morning. She should be here by now.'

All three men turned at a click as the doorknob turned.

On the doorstep stood a woman, her businesslike navy skirt pinched at the waist, the cotton blouse buttoned to the neck. No rings or other jewellery, no tortoiseshell hair clip to hold back her blonde hair, just a simple bobby pin. Something about her reminded Joe of the woman he'd seen at the Trocadero last night. It couldn't be, of course. This woman was blonde not dark, the exposure levels would be quite different, the effect more Jean Harlow than Greta Garbo. She was, in many ways, a moth to last night's butterfly. But even so. Something suggested the possibility of a metamorphosis.

She paused, looked at the men waiting with open mouths, and turned to leave.

'Not so fast,' Frank said. 'Well, well. Fancy seeing you here, Rose.'

*

Joe watched the woman — Rose — step into the living room, indifferent, it seemed, to the overflowing ashtray and dirty plates, the unshaven man slumped in the threadbare couch. He wasn't sure she'd noticed him. It was Frank Bischof, moulded to the brown velvet, who held her attention.

'Is this the girl?' Frank said.

'I was pretty drunk,' Jones said. 'Could be . . . I dunno.'

Rose surveyed the group. 'What's going on? Who are these people?'

'Are you sure this isn't her?' Frank looked directly at Jones who avoided his gaze, eyes downcast.

'Didn't look at her face,' he said. His face seemed flushed, his breathing shallow. He wouldn't look at Rose.

'What are you all talking about?' Rose said.

'Where were you last night?' Frank leaned toward her, a bulldog straining at the leash. 'Anyone with you?'

'What's it to you where I was?' Rose stood resolute, her foot on the step.

'Just answer the question.'

'I was at a meeting at Dutton Park if it's any of your business, which it's not.' She and Frank faced off, players on either side of a chessboard. Not that Frank looked like much of a chess player.

'Can anyone confirm that?'

'Of course. I was at Clem Christesen's. He arrived later, after work.'

'The communist? With the Ruskie wife? What time did you leave?'

'Around ten thirty, why? And you know Clem's no more a communist than I am.'

'Anyone with you? No one walked you to the tram stop? Bit risky at that hour of night. Or did you take a little side trip? Pop over here for a bit of fun.'

'Laurie Collinson was with me,' Rose said. 'We caught the tram together.'

'Ah, the poofter poet. Sure you didn't meet anyone after? Just a quick root on the side? Make a bit of money to pay the bills and fill the house with more books and dolls? The cemetery's not a bad place, wouldn't get disturbed there. Dead quiet.'

Joe saw Leonard's smirk, a snigger at the shared joke. Poofter? He hadn't heard that one but could figure it out.

Rose turned to leave.

'Not so fast,' Frank said. 'We found something in the cemetery last night. You were in the vicinity. We'll need a statement.'

'I didn't see anything,' Rose said. 'If that's what you mean.'

Joe watched the two of them, characters on centre stage. He and Jones — even Leonard — took only bit parts.

Frank stood. 'I'll have questions for you later,' he said to Rose, his interest suddenly elsewhere. 'You can go for now, I know where you live. You, too,' he said to Jones. 'I'll check things here, bring Leonard to the station, get forensics to look at his vehicle for what it's worth.'

They were all dismissed, it seemed. But why?

'In fact,' Frank said, looking back at Rose, 'why don't you let the sarge here take you home. He's going to take Corporal Jones back to the hospital, I'm sure he'll give you a lift.'

Joe caught Frank's glance. Was he still part of the investigation? he wondered as he ushered Rose and Jones toward the door.

Chapter Six

'Sober now?' Joe said, opening the passenger door for Rose but directing the question to the corporal slumped in the back seat.

Jones nodded.

'Want to tell me anything?'

'No. I've said it all.'

'What happened at the police station?' Joe asked.

'Like he said. I fell.'

'Sure,' Joe said. 'And I'm Fred Astaire.' He saw Rose smile. 'So what really happened last night? You're better off telling me the truth.'

Joe reached into his top pocket for the pack of stale cigarettes. He offered it across to the back seat. In the rear-vision mirror he watched Jones slide one from the pack awkwardly with his left hand. He gave his lighter to Rose, who swivelled to light Jones's cigarette before taking the pack. She lit one herself before returning the empty pack to Joe's pocket, her fingers patting soft against his chest.

'I ran,' Jones said. 'I always run. Like at Buna.'

Buna. Only a few weeks ago Joe had seen it on the front of *Life* magazine, three dead soldiers half-buried in the sand, the sea lapping at their feet. The photo had caused a stir, although Joe thought it a beautiful shot. Dreadful and brutal, but honest.

'We all run away from something,' he said, wondering if soldiers like Jones would ever return to normal life.

At the hospital gate Jones got out, but Joe didn't wait to see him inside. One thing you could say about the army, they made it easy to track down soldiers. There'd be plenty of time to question him again, double-check the details. Not so Rose and he needed to talk with her while he had the chance. Other than giving him brief directions she said nothing on the drive back across the river and through town.

Near the Roma Street goods yards an enormous tree with multiple trunks and fleshy dark leaves stood lookout on the corner opposite a warehouse emblazoned with the logo of the South Queensland Egg Board. Rose indicated for Joe to park outside a wooden building, the front verandah enclosed in fibro. She waited as he moved around the front of the jeep.

'I think I saw you last night at the Trocadero,' he said, his hand on the door.

'Did you?' She wasn't listening.

If he was to continue this conversation it might be best to do so on her territory. He followed her up the steps, waiting for her to unlock the door and invite him inside.

The flat occupied the two front rooms and verandah of a weatherboard house. As he stepped into the closed-in verandah he imagined the sun boring through the corrugated tin roof onto the sloping yellow ceiling, the colour of fried egg. Windows on either side of the front door let in a feeble breeze and across the room, diagonal timber bracing crisscrossed the horizontal boards of what must once have been the front of the house. A geometric pattern of lines.

He glanced around. On every surface, leaning against the diagonal timbers, piled on the threadbare carpet, propped against the wall, were books. From a distance Joe checked the titles, names he recalled from high school, letters he didn't recognise — was that Greek? Could she know all these authors? These languages? Was it just for show? And if so, for whom?

'Were you there?' he said. The memory of the woman lingered.

'At the Troc? For a while,' she said. She sat balanced on the armrest of a stuffed chair and gestured toward a matching one opposite.

'With anyone?' He'd only gotten a brief look at the woman last night and couldn't reconcile the man beside her with the lifeless form he'd seen this morning.

'Just a Yank,' she said with a smile. 'It's not difficult finding one.'

'Where did you meet him? Who was he?'

A picture rail ran across the side wall. Leaning against the books, or lounging on the rail itself, were dolls. Just as Frank had said. Porcelain dolls, rag dolls, dolls dressed as elegant ladies with elaborate hairstyles and satin clothing, witch dolls dressed in rags. One, its raven hair slightly askew, as large as a toddler.

'Just around. Does it matter? It's not hard finding someone to go dancing with these days.' She leaned across the empty chair to reach for a cigarette case lying on the opposite arm. 'I got rid of him quickly.'

'Indeed. How?'

Rose stared out the window. A breeze ruffled the leaves of the tree outside but did nothing to relieve the temperature under the low ceiling. She looked directly at him.

'Why do you need to know all this?'

'What was his name?'

'Bobby,' she said. 'A sergeant on leave from New Guinea. It's what they all say.'

Bob. Bobby. Robert. It was possible.

'What were you doing at Leonard's place? Do you work for him?'

She rose, moved to a small brown suitcase that served as a low table in the centre of the room. It was the sort of case a child might carry to school, Joe thought. Identical to the one he'd seen at Leonard's. Rose lifted a zippo from the rounded surface and spun the flint wheel. She blew smoke toward the ceiling in a gesture she must have seen Bette Davis make.

'What's all this about?' she said.

'Why were you there?'

'I thought Alma would be there. She works for Leonard, not me. Looking after his syphilitic wife.'

'Who's Alma?'

'My sister. Well, half-sister actually, linked by the same mother. We lost touch long ago. I didn't know she was in Brisbane until I got here. She's being used, of course. I try to help but there's not much I can do.' She returned to perch on the armchair, her cigarette held in a raised arm.

'What can you tell me about this Leonard?' Joe asked.

'Why? He's a creep.'

'He drives taxis?'

'Owns them, yes,' she said. 'Three of them, in fact. And runs a book on the horses. He's into bootleg liquor and whatever scam is going. You Yanks are just another one as far as he's concerned — a more lucrative one.'

Joe remembered the stolen gas.

'Must take a lot of gas to run three cars,' he said. 'Would he have a source?'

'Leonard's got a source for everything,' Rose said. 'Everything and everyone.'

He decided to change tack. 'How do you know Frank Bischof?'

'Everyone knows Frank.' She reached down to flick ash into a glass ashtray on the floor.

'How does Leonard know Frank?'

'They're thick as thieves. Alma says Frank calls round every few weeks for a beer and a bet on the horses.'

'Does Frank know Alma, then?'

'No idea. She sees him visit but mostly Leonard keeps her out of the picture, makes sure his businesses remain separate. Frank prefers women in brothels. Not operating alone.' She got to her feet, moving the ashtray onto the suitcase beside the the cigarettes and lighter. 'Can we forget about those boring old men for a minute? Would you like a cup of coffee?'

'Java?' he said. 'Real coffee?'

She walked towards an alcove with a sink and gas upright, a kitchen cabinet painted white with yellow and blue leadlight windows.

'I brought this up from Adelaide,' she said, holding an Atomic coffee maker. Joe sighed. Perhaps he could, after all, be bought.

She closed the door to the kitchen and he heard the match flare as she lit the gas.

He got up, his feet silent on the faded carpet. He lifted the cigarettes and ashtray from the cardboard suitcase to place them on the floor. With the case on his lap and holding the brass lugs to deaden the sound, he slid open the two locks. No creak as he raised the lid to peer inside. A bundle of letters tied with a black ribbon. Underneath were ration coupons, dozens of them thrown in casually like confetti. He saw at least six different names. Beneath the coupons was a photo album with a dark blue cover of patterned cardboard. He opened the album, taking care not to tear the rice paper inserts between each page. Black-and-white photos of a young man in army uniform, arms around two elderly parents, both uncomfortable in front of the camera. Another, a studio shot of the sort he despised, of Rose and the same young man seated in front of an artificial landscape.

'Sugar?' she called out. The sound of the locks clicking back in place was lost under the gurgle of frothing milk and the final wheeze of steam.

'Depends how strong the coffee is,' Joe said, replacing the cigarettes and ashtray and resting his hand along the bookshelf. He reached for a volume of poetry that looked French. Baudelaire. Inside the front cover a signature in rounded letters of blue ink. James Mawinney.

'Here, try this.' Rose kicked open the door, carrying a metal tray which she balanced on the rounded surface of the closed suitcase.

Another volume caught Joe's eye, the same one he had on his desk at the Provost Office. 'Have you read this? What's it like? The army sends us books, I have this one.' He replaced the book and accepted the proffered cup. It tinkled on the saucer as he placed them together on the arm of his chair and sat.

'I'm not a fan of Hemingway's,' Rose said, 'sometimes they're just like boy's-own stories. But I do agree with the title.'

Joe didn't follow.

'For whom the bell tolls. It's a poem by John Donne. "No man is an island." You must you know it? "Any man's death diminishes me, because I am involved in Mankind; and therefore never send to know for whom the bell tolls; it tolls for thee." I suppose if you think about it, that's why we're at war. There are times when you have to take a stand and surely now is one of those times.'

Joe listened to the recited words, the declaration of

purpose. He'd wanted to fight this war. Why didn't he feel such purpose anymore? She made it sound so straightforward.

'Do you read all those languages, then?' Joe waved in the direction of the rows of books.

'Some. I studied classics at Adelaide, Latin and Greek. French at school, and I had a friend who was German. Not that anyone admits having German friends anymore. But I loved Goethe and don't see why he should be blamed for Hitler.'

Joe closed his eyes to test the coffee, hearing his mother's approval. Nice girl, she said, and knows how to make the crema right. A Catholic too, by the look of the medal on the wall.

'Perfect,' he said. 'No. Nor Dante for Mussolini. I don't know any Jap writers but it's probably the same.'

'Bashō. I read a translation of his poems once. They were deceptively simple, quite beautiful.'

'Where do you find coffee grounds in this town?' Joe said.

'I have friends.'

'So I gather. Who's Laurie? You said you caught the tram with him?'

'Oh, I love Laurie. Not like that, of course. That wouldn't work at all. He's going to be a painter, I just know he'll do well.'

'And Clem?'

'Clem Christesen and Nina,' Rose said. 'They keep me sane. He edits a journal, *Meanjin Papers*. Have you seen it? He writes most of it, actually, working out of his house. He's always having parties, gatherings of writers and would-be writers. Lots of people go there — even Americans. You could come and meet them if you like. Everyone interesting ends up there. There's a gathering tomorrow, why don't you come along?'

'Is that where you were last night?' Joe looked over the rim of his cup.

'Why do you keep going on about last night? What's this all about? Yes, I was at Clem's. Late.'

'After the Trocadero?'

'Yes.'

'Did you take the American? Bob, was it?'

'You're not serious,' she laughed. 'My lives don't overlap as easily as that! Clem and Nina are lovely — so are the others. But they're all so straitlaced. Even Thea's a good Catholic — although far too intelligent to accept all their hypocrisies. Is this all you do? Interrogate people? What a boring life you must lead.'

Joe found himself nodding. 'Some of it, yes. Writing reports no one reads, filling out forms and requisition orders. But no, it's not all boring.'

And it was true. He didn't have the words for why, only images. A black man slumped on the edge of his cell bed, a man longing to be a father but whose love would send him to jail. The white palings of a fence like a row of jagged teeth, a missing paling prised out to beat a man. A chinless woman trembling as she identified her attacker. He looked around at the books and dolls, the cardboard suitcase with its hidden histories, the woman seated opposite who quoted poetry with conviction.

'Sad, pathetic and often nasty,' he said. 'But people are seldom boring.'

Chapter Seven

The sun still hovered in the sky as Joe turned onto Vulture Street. Christ. What a name. As if the tramlines and overhead wires formed a vast web, trapping everything in its blackened net, swallowing things whole and leaving little but tatters and rags. Carrion. He parked in the open courtyard. He'd managed to avoid the place for over four hours. Almost a record.

For all its small-town self-importance, the Town Hall was a beautiful building, two storeys of red brickwork with terracotta and sandstone panelling; the stone arch over the entrance now sandbagged. He crossed the red and white mosaic vestibule onto the timber parquetry and up the steps.

At the top of the stairs he ran his hands along the rails of the internal staircase — looking into a rich burgundy, polished so it reflected his face. Mrs Lakursky, the cleaning lady, whose only son was in New Guinea, said it was red cedar. Rare now. All cut down.

Typical, thought Joe. We always kill what we love.

He slumped into his chair. He'd been on the go since

midnight and apart from coffee he'd eaten nothing all day. The sun glinted off the conning tower of a submarine at the dockyard, striking the window before landing like a thin blade across his desk.

'Where've you been? I'm still waiting on that report.' Major Mitchell strode toward his uncluttered desk, wiped his mouth with an ironed handkerchief and placed a plate smeared with what Joe knew to be mutton fat onto one corner. If that had been lunch he was glad to have missed it.

'I had to check on the murdered soldier.'

'And?'

'The police have questioned the other patient who was on day pass with him. Roughed him up a bit so I thought I should stay with him. Make sure they didn't get out of line.'

'How do you think they're going to solve a crime without crossing some sort of line? They've got a job to do. So have we. No point doubling up when we're short staffed.'

'But he's American, the soldier.'

'So are all of those.' Mitchell indicated the tower of folders on Joe's desk. 'You know as well as I that most of the courts martial are a waste of time, but it's important PR. The new Colonel, Braidwood, was stationed up north, says there's been lots of trouble there — MPs overstepping the mark, official complaints from the Police Commissioner. We can't afford that here so keep out of the way of the local CIB. They're the detectives. Not you.'

'Yes, sir.'

'And if that doesn't suit you I'm sure we can find something that does. I hear they need an investigator up in Batchelor.'

'Where?'

'You may yet find out. Meanwhile, I have a meeting with Braidwood at Base Headquarters. Make sure that report's on my desk by morning. And tell the cleaning lady to tidy up. The mess is in an appalling state.'

At the doorway the major came to an abrupt halt as Butt Monroe, his face as red as his birthmark, filled the doorway. Both men saluted and the major squeezed past.

Joe concentrated on the blade of sunlight. If only it were a stiletto, he thought as he forced his attention back to the room. A stiletto. Not something you'd expect a sergeant to wield, not even a military policeman. Even though he rarely carried a gun. More a woman's weapon, wasn't it, a blade of stealth and subtlety.

Subtlety wasn't a word you'd associate with the man who, wreathed in cigar smoke, fell into the chair opposite with the sound of a shovel mixing wet cement. Leaning back, pistol holster askew, he planted his legs on the desk, his enormous belly providing a platform on which to balance a glass ashtray. Given the size and distance to cover, Joe thought it something of a marvel that Monroe was able, even in this position, to scratch his crotch.

Corporal Butt Monroe was a hard-boiled sharecropper from Jackson, Mississippi, who'd escaped debt by enlisting — as he'd boasted more than once. He'd been in the army for only two months before sailing into a town whose sprawling houses reminded him of New Orleans, honeysuckle and all.

'Coons and no-good sons of bitches.' Monroe heaved a fistful of peanuts into his mouth. He finished chewing, placed the ashtray on Joe's desk and stubbed out his cigar.

Joe drew a pile of buff folders close and faced the boots. Monroe's conversation rarely changed.

'Called to the Carver Club again last night. White women there.'

So that's where Monroe had been when he should have been on duty. Hard to imagine it was a social call, although he'd heard Monroe reminisce about black velvet. Perhaps a stiletto was wasted on such a buffoon. If not a sword or rapier, a simple butcher's knife would do. A hunter's bowie knife, a machete, a cleaver, a hatchet. Given Monroe's size, a harpoon might not be out of the question.

Joe mulled over the possibilities, riffling through the folders, fingering the papers until he found what he wanted. Behind him, FDR looked down benevolently, firm jaw, steely eyes, no sign of the wheelchair. Joe knew photographs could lie as easily as words. Maybe better. Truth lay as much in the hands of the person behind the lens as the subject in front.

He slid a sheet of paper into the roller of the Remington, aligned it neatly and snapped back the lock.

'Disgusting,' Monroe said. 'White women.'

Joe began, eyes on the page. 'To the Provost Marshall. Point 1.'

'That Private Bryson's downstairs, the nigger we picked up in West End. Attacked those two white women with a fence paling. For Christ's sake. *White* women.'

Joe watched peanut skins float to the floor as Monroe brushed them from his dirty white puttees. At least Joe had been spared that sartorial indignity.

'He's in with the other nigger, Duke. The one knocked up the little girly. Better ways to deal with both of them than a court martial. Only gives them a way outta the army.'

Perhaps a pickaxe.

Monroe hawked toward the spittoon in the corner of the room and ground his cigar into the ashtray. The legs of the chair squealed as it tilted forward. He shoved a foot in Joe's direction. 'What's eating you?'

The pile of folders teetered and Joe adjusted the novel on top. After what Rose had said, maybe he'd find time to finish it. 'I expect they'll both get prison sentences,' he said, his fingers resting on the keys. Careful with his words. He knew even that wasn't for sure. Mitchell had said as much.

'No hanging rope here,' Monroe ploughed on.

Joe remembered the paratrooper Fernandez, a thin Hispanic, small as a jockey with a face like a ferret. He'd kicked a prostitute to death before raping her and boasting he wouldn't have done it if she'd been white. 'She made me look cheap,' he'd said. 'Asked me for money.'

'Wouldn't have happened in Mississippi,' Monroe said at the time. 'Helluva way to treat a GI, someone who's served his country. Been wounded. She was a slut, for Pete's sake. An Abo slut.'

They'd held Fernandez at Boggo Road before flying him to Port Moresby for the execution. A murderer taken to a murderous place so he could be hanged. The world was mad.

'Talk about a hick town,' Monroe went on, hauling himself up.

This, thought Joe, from someone who'd never been further than Alabama before enlisting. Had never ridden an elevator, was awed by the high ceilings of the municipal chambers of the Town Hall.

Monroe reached behind Joe and slipped the keys for the jeep from the hook on the wall. 'Gotta collect the ammo we ordered from the quartermaster,' he said.

Joe looked up, pictured the tip of a stiletto entering Monroe's body, the small point working through the regulation army fabric to the skin. Pale flesh with curls of ginger hair, the rubbery surface pushed inward until the surface tension broke, the pressure released with an explosion of entrails, blood, arteries and massive globs of waxy fat. Would Monroe cry out? Would he scream or swear or flail around? Or would he simply deflate like a balloon at a child's party?

When Monroe had stomped down the corridor, Joe upended the ashtray into the wastepaper basket and returned to the typewriter. The hours stretched out before him.

At least he was alone.

Chapter Eight

At five o'clock it was hard to find a quiet corner in the Terminus Hotel in South Brisbane. Wharfies and tradesmen surged to the front of the press of men, mostly off-duty sailors and soldiers gearing up for the evening. Across the road, queues were forming at the entrance to the dance hall.

Naval Shore Patrolman Gunther Hayden sat with his feet on the low table in front of him, the surface littered with half-eaten hot dogs, empty glasses and tall bottles of beer. A large kitchen knife skewered a thick sausage in the middle of the table. Hayden had a standing order for frankfurters at the PX.

From the minute he'd answered Uncle Sam's call and reported to the recruiting station at Colorado Springs, he knew he'd spend the war explaining his German name and awkward accent. Finally drafted early in '42, he was surprised to be posted to the Transport section of Naval Stores and wondered how his background as a boner at the meatworks in Tulsa, Oklahoma, might have led him there. Had anyone cared to find out about his prison term for assault they might have reconsidered, but organisation was sloppy and the need for police to accompany troops to the Pacific was urgent. He'd slept through a few lectures and basic training before finding himself guarding the naval victualling store in Spring Hill. They gave him a navy blue uniform, a white cap that made him look like a chef, a baton and little else. Brisbane was the biggest town he'd ever seen and he didn't like it. He didn't like the heat, he didn't like driving on the wrong side of the road, he didn't like sorting out pounds, shillings and pence. The only point he could see to it all was to leave with more money than he'd arrived.

He stared at the rat-faced man in front of him.

The war was the best thing to have happened to Eddie Ball since he'd been flung from his horse at the age of twenty. Now forty-three and limping from a shortened leg, he'd been saved from the call-up and the derision of women and young men alike. Too young for the first and protected from the second, he'd found himself in the best place possible. A city full of soldiers with more money than sense. Easy pickings.

Eddie knew all the games in town. This was his patch and he worked it no different from when he'd herded sheep out beyond Longreach, taking care to move them as a mob, watching for the one that would make a break, using the whistle to work the dogs that scrabbled over the sheep's backs to bark with irritation at their stupidity. It was, as now, so predictable. Piece of cake.

He sat down, poured beer into a glass and sucked on it. A line of foam hovered on his upper lip until he wiped it off and down the outside of his coat, where it mingled with older beer and snot.

Both men looked up as Butt Monroe lumbered in, a bottle in his hand. He sank into the chair beside Hayden.

'Here,' Eddie said, placing an envelope on the table. 'Fifty-fifty, like we agreed. You told me there'd be petrol as well, but Slim didn't know nothing about that. I need it if I'm to keep up with you blokes. Can't just keep driving across town every time someone wants more gin.'

'You know that's more complicated,' Monroe said. 'We'd need a truck and safe warehouse. It'd cost.'

'See what I can do,' Eddie said. 'Might be able to use a warehouse — I know someone works near the submarine base. It's good and central, close to the wharves.'

'Three more tallies, love.' Hayden winked at the matronly woman behind the bar who waddled toward the taps. He wiped beads of sweat and froth from his moustache and smiled at the poster above the bar — *The enemy is listening.*

'Anyone know why Mo rang?'

*

Cliff Stanaway lit a smoke and looked around the offices of *The Courier-Mail.* The newspaper occupied a two-storey building in Queen Street, conveniently close to MacArthur at Lennon's Hotel — 'Bataan' as the Yanks insisted on calling the building. It'd been a long day after a long night but he'd got a feel for things. Every night five cars patrolled the city, each covering about 100 miles, and last night he'd been in one of them. In spite of his initial suspicion, the detective assigned to him had proved an informative companion, explaining how the new wireless sets worked, going over the police codes.

The wireless cars certainly made quick work of trouble on the streets, police in patrol cars getting word almost as soon as the telephone operators in the depot at Petrie Terrace. It gave them the edge, made it easy to respond before things got out of hand. Last night they'd checked on a breach at the wharf — a cargo of beer was ransacked, no one caught — and although reports of an assault in Spring Hill turned out to be exaggerated, they'd been there almost as soon as it'd been reported.

Only one-way communication so far, from base to unit, not two-way. No doubt, Cliff thought with journalistic cynicism, this gave police a bit of leeway to act as they saw fit, get the job done and decide later what to report. Police knew everyone. They knew the men who picked up goods tossed from passing trains, the girls who worked the alleys around Elizabeth Street, the sly grog agent at Spring Hill who fixed up sales to the Yanks. A short step from policing to participating, and he'd got a glimpse of that side of things too.

He spun a sheet of foolscap into the typewriter, checked the ribbon still had some life and glanced at the clock on the wall.

'Wireless cars are one of the biggest factors in keeping down crime in a city which has been turned into a garrison town,' he tapped.

The call about the body had come through after midnight. Not the first murder this month. Probably wouldn't be the last. The detective had made sure Cliff was back at the newspaper before he heard much more, but his journalist's appetite was whetted. He'd rung around, checked with a few of his police contacts across the river. It'd taken most of the day.

The details were promising — the location, the placement of the body in the cemetery, the suggestion of a crime of passion — all of it elements he knew readers would love. Murder. Graveyards. Lipstick. Couldn't be better if it was fiction. And a Yank best of all. Much as everyone loved them in 1941 — had lined the streets in their thousands, waving flags, throwing kisses — the love was wearing thin. Too many of them still here even though the war had moved north.

A girl from the printery entered with a bundle of paper. 'Where were you last night?' she said.

'Spent the night in a police wireless car.'

'Wireless car? Why?'

The girl was only eighteen, just out of school, but with the confidence of someone double her age. What was the world coming to? All these young women working in munitions factories, driving trucks, even doing the dirty work of type-setting. Youngsters questioning their elders. He loved it.

'Where's Clem?' Cliff asked.

'He left early. Another of his literary meetings.'

Clem Christesen might plan a career in poetry, but for the moment he was doomed to life as an editor. Subeditor actually, the man who checked for typos, fiddled with grammar, worried at someone else's syntax. He was good at it. What was he thinking starting a literary journal in the middle of a war? Madness.

The girl placed a pile of newspaper cuttings on the high desk at the back of the room ready to be sorted and pinned onto the corkboard above. 'What about the wireless car, anyway?'

'Newest gadgetry. The police have a job on their hands these days, the streets teeming with soldiers and sailors even in the early hours of the morning. The police certainly know their haunts, all the dark laneways where people lurk.' Cliff warmed to his story. 'The new radio car means they get reports quickly and arrive sooner. They're certainly on the ball. No doubt about it. Although I must say a few of them seem more than a bit knowledgeable about what's going on — looked pretty chummy with a few of the crims too. But it's a messy place out there and for once I was glad to be on the right side of the law.'

'Well, it must make a change from warding off threats from the racketeers,' the girl said. She gave a knowing smile as she reached for the large scissors. Lowering her voice to a Marlene Dietrich growl, she looked up at the corkboard to read from the articles Cliff had pinned there, the ones documenting the threats he'd learned to live with. 'Keep your nose out of this business or you'll get bashed.' 'Lay off the gambling or you'll get your throat cut.'

Was she having a lend of him?

He turned back to his typewriter. Impossible to understand the young.

SUNDAY 10 OCTOBER 1943

Chapter Nine

Joe propped his wire-framed glasses onto the top of his head and looked down onto the bald head of a fat man in a baggy blue suit. A bullet head, the colour of brass. The angle gave a clear line of sight and from this height — the second floor of the Australasian Catholic Assurance building on Queen Street — he should have a clean shot from here. As the bald man turned to face the Royal Hotel, he pressed the shutter. He ratcheted the film forward and patted the strap roped around his wrist. From the seat beside an open window at the back of the room he alternated between watching groups of people take their seats in front of him and checking activity on the street. Professionals called the Argus C3 a brick but he liked the heft of it. It wasn't exactly unobtrusive but it was regulation issue now, the Provost Marshall having been persuaded of its usefulness. Joe had added the telescopic lens himself.

He adjusted the barrel and turned back to the window.

With the focus on the bald man on the steps of the hotel he took in the scene below: the limp palms outside the GPO, women in hats edging along the street as they avoided eye contact with soldiers milling at the hotel entrance. Overhead, tram cables sagged above the strip of melting bitumen that served as Brisbane's main street, a black line running back through town and down to the northern bank of the river. If he tilted the camera slightly and zoomed out he could see over the roofs to the river and across to the south side, to the grand house on the hill. Base Headquarters. He glimpsed the wharves and dry docks lining the riverbank. Swarms of men in overalls, welders and riveters, boilermakers and carpenters. Patching and mending the submarines and destroyers that limped down the Brisbane River.

Sometimes he had to remind himself why they were all here.

He swivelled the camera back to the street.

Dozens of men jostled as they pushed into the hotel's cool interior. The blue-suited man wiped sweat from a leathery skull and ran a finger around the inside of his collar. He must be waiting for someone. Not even locals stood in the sun for long without a hat, thought Joe. A taxi pulled into the sidewalk as an army jeep careened past. The MP leaning on the jeep's horn looked familiar, his beefy hands gripping the wheel, his helmet tipped low over his face as if to hide something.

Joe fired off a few quick shots.

Behind him the scrape of chairs dragging along the floor suggested the room was filling. The meeting was scheduled for one o'clock and he'd been sure to arrive early. He swivelled back, waiting as his eyes adjusted. Even indoors his skin freckled in the fierce sun, his mother's short stature and his father's colouring once again proving to be the worst combination. He fanned himself with his cap.

Joe had only sat in on a couple meetings, half-listening to the lectures while he staked out the hotel — in his own time, of course. Mitchell would be apoplectic if he knew. Joe wouldn't admit to having learned anything and had yet to make up his mind about the audience. Most of the lectures had bored him to the point of sleep — someone droning on about 'Nature Poetry', a paper on 'Our servicemen write verse' that made him wish they didn't — but he was amused by the young people who turned up. Teenagers most of them, just kids at school. Bubbling with enthusiasm, brimming with confidence. Joe guessed they'd run the show soon. Well, why not? Theirs was the new world, after all. Isn't that what it was all about?

For now, though, it was an elderly man with white hair and braces keeping his trousers aloft who moved to the lectern.

'Welcome, ladies and gentlemen. I trust you have made yourselves comfortable. Remember there will be refreshments at the end of our lecture and discussion, our thanks to the girls in the kitchen.'

In front of Joe, men and women sat in rows of chairs, seats too shallow for comfort, the chrome legs squealing on the linoleum floor as the audience settled. A tapestry of shapes and colours, woven together with the white, blue and khaki of uniforms from different countries and units. Joe had forgotten that clothes, like life itself, could be so varied.

Outside, the taxi had gone. A skinny man in a coat too heavy for this heat hid his face behind a wide-brimmed hat, a trail of cigarette smoke snaking above the brim. Like a character in a sepia gangster film, Joe thought, eyeing the soldiers as a hunter its prey. Briefly the blue-suited man looked up and Joe recognised the taxi driver. Leonard.

A woman wove through the crowd, her string of beads a rainbow of colours. Men whistled appreciatively and he recognised Rose, although an altogether more colourful version than the one he'd met yesterday. Brisbane was such a small town, he reminded himself, it was easy to run into people. But what were the chances of seeing both of them?

A door slammed against the wall and Rose smiled apologies as she wove between the row of chairs. Knees were pulled in, chairs pushed back, stern faces frowned. She settled into a chair between a boy with sandy hair and a small woman with bobbed dark hair. He recognised the boy from earlier meetings; you could rely on him to ask questions at the end. The woman he'd not seen. She was Rose's mirror image, dark to her blonde, homey to her swank, attentive where Rose was still fidgeting with her beads. Both wore lipstick, a dark blood red. It was the fashion, Joe knew, but if anything he thought it accentuated their youth, their lack of experience.

What was she doing here?

Over the last eighteen months Joe had come to realise that Brisbane society, like the tramlines that linked the outer suburbs to its centre, ran along parallel lines. One line passed through the saloons and cat houses of Albert Street and South Brisbane while the other followed a leisurely path, winding through the suburbs of Toowong and Ascot, the tea centres staffed by the Women's Auxiliary. Here, in the solid premises of the Lyceum Club, the Queensland Authors and Artists Association held its fortnightly meetings but Joe doubted that the earnest writers and artists in the room had any idea of the black-market dealings taking place in the Royal across the road. The parallel lines of Brisbane seldom crossed. Joe wondered what would happen if they did.

The man at the lectern tutted impatiently. 'I am delighted to welcome Dr Gertrude Langer,' he began, 'who will introduce us to the art of the surrealists. A movement, I'm sure we all agree, about which we hear much but understand very little.'

A short woman, stout with greying hair wound into a bun, stood and walked heavily to the front of the room, a sheaf of mismatched papers in her hand.

'Thank you,' she said, her accent thick. Not exactly his aunt Beata's but close, the same heavy consonants and odd syntax. Austrian, he guessed. 'And so, to art.'

Joe watched as she paused, her eyes closed. Was she seeing again the paintings themselves, in the homes of friends who had disappeared? In galleries and museums under Nazi control? She sighed as she began.

Joe followed her example, letting the voice take him back as he closed his eyes. Once, not long after they'd left Detroit, his mother had taken him on an outing across the Hudson and into the city, to the new Museum of Modern Art. He must have been nine he guessed, they'd only just moved from Detroit, but he remembered the paintings. Huge. Such colours. Vibrant blues and watery greens, the red of blood. Clocks melting over a dead tree branch beside a square table. The persistence of memory.

'They call this art?' his mother scoffed as she dragged him into the wintry air, his breath making clouds as he struggled to keep up. 'What the point, eh, Giuseppe? Nothing real you can see. How they get away with this? Raphael, Michelangelo, da Vinci. They can paint. But this? Pouf!'

He'd fallen asleep on the ferry home and remembered his father sitting in his chair on the stoop, waiting silently in the dark, a blanket over his knees.

A cough brought him back to the present. The blue-eyed boy glared at the culprit before leaning forward to listen. What had he missed?

Outside, the sky was bleached white. The MP had parked the jeep further up the street and now strode toward the man in the overcoat. He spun him around but their conversation was brief. Hard to tell from this angle, but it looked like Monroe. What was he doing in town on his day off? And why alone? He never went anywhere without the Shore Patrolman, the pair roaming the streets looking for trouble, mostly making things worse. Odd for Monroe to work solo without a big brother to hold his hand. Surreptitiously, Joe lifted the camera and aimed through the open window just as the MP moved under the awning. Damn.

'Painters work in two dimensions,' Dr Langer said as Joe lowered his camera, his attention back inside the room. 'Traditionally they manipulate these two dimensions — the flat paper and the single line of colour — to create a three-dimensional world. The world around us, what we see in nature. But in this period, at this time, painters like Pablo Picasso and Georges Braque unwrap the natural world, uncover the forms within, the planes and lines, the geometry of objects. They make us look at how the world is made and question what it is.'

A sort of detective work, Joe thought.

'Once you've liberated form from three dimensions,' she continued, 'few limits cannot be met. Surrealists have made this move. Dalí, Magritte, Man Ray. They find ways to show us our dreams, to paint our nightmares, to place a mirror in front of our desires. These painters draw the irrational, the things we cannot see but only feel. These emotions are a part of our world. Perhaps more now than ever before.'

He'd seen some of Man Ray's photos in a book once and had been shocked at the tricky techniques, how everything was staged and stylised. Joe had dismissed them as fakes — surely photos should report life accurately. But afterwards the images had stayed with him and he was no longer sure. Sometimes he wondered if you only really saw a photo when you closed your eyes.

He checked outside. The MP had gone but the man in the overcoat remained, leaning against the redbrick hotel wall. He flung a cigarette stub into the gutter as a large man barrelled toward him. Joe coughed to cover the sound of the shutter and took a few quick shots of the regulation suit with regulation white handkerchief. Regulation polished black shoes. Regulation hat. Regulation florid face and cauliflower ears. A dick by the look of him. Apart from soldiers no one else wore such predictable clothes. Were they onto it too?

The meeting seemed to have ended when he turned back towards the room, so he stood and threaded between the chairs, cap in hand, camera slung over one shoulder. He slipped a few biscuits into his pocket but excused himself before the mandatory cup of watery fluid that Aussies drank by the gallon and made for the stairs. He was on duty soon.

'See you tomorrow night? Eight o'clock? Judith will be there.'

Joe turned. The sandy-haired boy, rushing for the stairs, had addressed Rose and her friend.

'Where are you going?' Rose said.

'Got papers to sell,' the boy said. 'See you tomorrow?'

As the girls made for the stairs Rose saw him, showing a flicker of recognition before she turned to reply, 'Fine.'

The girls followed Joe down the stairs and onto a street baking under a bleached sky. He backed onto the sidewalk and waited. The expression on Rose's face was a warning — hadn't she told him she kept her lives separate? They joined him under the awning and she squinted, her gloved left hand a brim to an imaginary hat. She fingered the coloured beads that flashed in the sun. Red, blue, green, yellow.

'So what do you think?' she said. 'Are we interesting or simply provincial?'

The girls linked arms. A challenge. She proffered a hand.

'I'm Rose,' she said. 'Rose McAlister. This is Thea Astley.'

So it was a game. He moved the camera bag to his left shoulder and took her hand. The gloves explained the softness of the skin, the way she looked directly at him explained the steadiness of the handshake. Her hazel eyes flecked with gold around the edge of the iris, her perfume smelled of a flower. Was it lilac? Or rose for her name.

Thea's handshake was perfunctory.

'Sergeant Joe Washington, ma'am,' he said. 'Pleased to meet you both.'

'You didn't reply,' Rose said. 'What do you think of us?'

'I try not to make judgements too soon. Not before I have all the facts. That takes time.'

'Very sensible,' Rose said and frowned. 'But time is not something any of us have much of these days.' It sounded like a dismissal. She pointed at the bag slung over his shoulder. 'What's the camera for?'

'Mostly for work,' Joe said as he clipped on sunshades. 'And pleasure. I like taking photos, it makes me look at things closely.'

'Are you going to the newspaper, Thea?' Rose said.

'Yes, I'll run off now and check if Dad's ready to come home yet.' Thea slipped her hand free and raised it in farewell.

'And you?' Joe said when they were alone.

'I'm headed for the library,' Rose said.

'I'm making for North Quay myself.' Joe raised his cap and bowed slightly. 'If you'd permit me to accompany you.'

In his peripheral vision he saw the detective with the cauliflower ears muscle in on the man in the overcoat. No physical contact as far as he could see. He strained to hear the details of the exchange, but heard the threat in the tone.

Joe shepherded Rose around the square cement shelters on the street, past stacks of sandbags leaning like sagging bricks against the walls of banks and government buildings. Outside headquarters, two MPs from the 814th stood guard beside MacArthur's staff car waiting, Joe imagined, for the officers to return from their long lunch at Tattersalls. They'd fiddle with paperwork until cocktails this evening at Lennon's. Opposite, civilians sat on slatted seats eating lunchtime sandwiches out of paper bags. Rose pointed to the pigeons waiting expectantly for crumbs to fall, cooing as they competed for attention.

'They always remind me of Laurie,' she said. 'In full flight about the need to do more than write beautiful words. All that talk of ideas. Going on about *The Waste Land*. You'd think he was the first person to discover poetry.'

'Is that the boy you spoke with just now? The one you went to Clem's with? He looks very young.'

'Oh he's a boy alright, so full of energy it tires me sometimes. As much as I love him. He plans to be an artist, or a poet. Of course he's Jewish, so that explains a lot.'

Joe didn't want to admit he had no idea what she was talking about. What wasteland? Neither was he in the mood to discuss Jews right now. His mother had written a month ago, there was still no news. Nothing heard from his father's cousin for over a year.

'Did you enjoy the lecture?' he said. 'Are you a fan of modern art?'

Rose shook her head. 'No. I studied classics at university, I'm not up with modern art. The Pre-Raphaelites are about as modern as I get.'

'My ma would approve,' Joe said. 'She adores Raphael, but then in her eyes only Italians can paint. Or sing. Or write. Or cook for that matter.'

'She has a point. Not that the Pre-Raphaelites were either Renaissance painters or Italian,' Rose said, her smile making it clear that she knew he was out of his depth. 'And you? Your name's not Italian, you don't look Italian at all.'

'Only on my mother's side,' Joe said. 'My father's Polish. He changed his name as soon as he landed on Ellis Island. Well, you would, wouldn't you? Washington sounded patriotic and it's sure a lot easier to spell than Wawrzniakas.'

Rose laughed.

'If you didn't enjoy the lecture,' Joe said, 'why do you go?'

'Why do you?'

She had a point. Why did he? It was only partly to stake out the hotel, if he was honest. One part of him simply enjoyed being with people who were different, who weren't liars or crooks or spinning a line. People who were looking to the future, not stuck in the past.

'I like seeing the people there,' he said. 'Sometimes it's good to forget about the war, everyone in uniform.'

'Yes,' she said.

'Did you see Leonard outside the Royal? He seemed to be waiting for someone.'

'No,' Rose said. 'Should I have?'

'Seemed odd, that's all.'

At the entrance to the Regent Theatre, Rose stopped to peer into the mezzanine foyer, the interior cool in the midday heat. Joe watched her marvel at the gilded walls, the marble staircase, the murals on the vaulted ceiling.

'The air conditioning smells delicious, like ice cream,' she said and turned to face him. 'Tell me about somewhere else. Where do you come from? Somewhere interesting, I hope.'

'Nowhere special,' he said. 'Just a town in New Jersey that you won't ever have heard of. Five miles from New York. Cold in the winter. Hot in summer, but not like here. Just a place.'

'So you know New York. Is it wonderful?'

'Oh yes. And no. I guess.' Joe knew he had no words for these things. 'I like your town too. The Town Hall, the new iron bridge. It's a pretty nice place.'

'This isn't my town,' Rose said. 'I don't know my way around any more than you do. I came up from Adelaide two years ago and now I'm stuck.'

'Ah,' Joe said. 'I've heard a lot of people can't get back south. Not without permission. But there's no real threat now, not with the Japs on the run. Surely they'd let you go now?'

'But if I went back to Adelaide I'd be further away,' she said, walking out of the theatre foyer.

'From?' Joe didn't really have any reason to ask.

She turned toward him and he felt the intensity of her gaze.

'My brother was in Singapore. Now he's somewhere in Asia. No one knows where. But Brisbane feels closer. His friends are here.'

'At the meeting?'

'Yes.'

At the corner of Queen and George streets they veered left. Rose checked her watch and pirouetted. The beads took longer to come to rest, a dazzle of colours shimmering in the glare. How easily she slipped from mood to mood. She bit her lip, drawing a line though the crimson lipstick. Flecks of red remained on her front teeth when she smiled.

'Do you got to the Trocadero often?' he asked. The New York names amused him — the Trocadero, the Astoria Café, even a New York ice cream parlour in Queen Street. 'I heard there's a good band playing there tonight. Will you be there?'

'I often am.'

In normal times Joe imagined Queens Gardens would form a small green island between the ornate buildings, the Treasury on one side and the Parliament House that mirrored it. Now Joe watched Rose slip behind the cement bomb shelters and water pipes to run across what remained of the open space, looking neither left nor right until she reached the stone steps of the library. Before turning to face the CIB headquarters he noticed how in the humid air her cotton skirt clung to her thighs.

Chapter Ten

Joe passed through the archway of Morecombe House and turned left to descend to the basement. There'd be time for Frank later. The basement was Constable Tom Baty's domain. As a plain-clothes detective, Tom could wear whatever he liked, but Joe had only ever seen him in his off-white lab coat, artfully splashed with crimson and yellow.

Tom looked up from his desk as Joe entered unannounced, wiped his hands on the front of his coat and leaned back in his chair. 'Cuppa?'

Joe inspected the tannin interior of the chipped cup on the desk as he pulled out a wooden chair. 'Hell no. But thanks.' He'd avoided the obligatory mugs of weak tea at the Lyceum Club and refused to succumb to the ritual here.

Light filtering through narrow windows high up the wall did little to lift the gloom. Joe was grateful for the cool of the basement but not for the sour citric smell of chemicals emanating from behind Tom's desk. A steel bench held a row of test tubes, each hung by the neck in its wooden frame. A dozen pistols lay disembowelled on the table opposite, their cartridges extracted and laid out in neat rows. Joe envied Tom's photographic studio that took up the rest of the room; tripods propped against the stone walls, trays and bottles of developing fluid stacked on shelves. Usually Tom was happy to develop Joe's rolls of films, even the unofficial ones, his experiments with the patterning of light and shade.

'So, what can I do for you?' Tom crossed his arms, a smile playing with his toothbrush moustache.

Joe knew how much he loved a challenge.

Almost single-handedly Tom Baty had established a Technical Section in the Queensland Police, persuading reluctant officers that scientific solutions just might help to solve crimes. A simple firearm specialist with a firing range and a staff of two, he'd gone on to study science at university and when war arrived on his doorstep he was ready. Joe had heard older police complain, say it was all a waste of time, not real police work. But if the locals didn't appreciate it the Americans sure did, and were happy to pay. Joe had even helped rig up the ultraviolet and infrared equipment Uncle Sam bought for Tom so he could play with spectography and blood typing, fingerprinting and trace analysis. Tom was grateful for the support, but so were the Americans. It worked both ways.

Now Joe had a problem and he wanted Tom's help. Mitchell didn't have to know anything yet.

'How much do you know about gasoline?' Joe asked.

'Petrol? What's there to know? Not enough of it around.'

'And that's the problem.'

'Ah, and there's always people with limitless supplies,' Tom said. 'Is that what you mean?'

'Yes. The main source has to be the army. I've been trying to gather figures and this is what I've got. Every month the forces use about three hundred thousand gallons of petroleum blended with twenty per cent alcohol, even more of the high-octane gas. Oil companies deliver it in bulk to twenty US stations for distribution but after that it's anyone's guess. It's almost impossible to track and none of the depots want to cooperate.'

'Fancy that,' Tom said.

'Right. So, what I wanted to ask was, do you reckon it'd be possible to dope gas somehow? So we could track its movement? Identify where it's being used and by whom?'

Tom paused to think for a moment, spinning a pencil on his desk. 'Some sort of chemical tag, you mean, like fingerprinting? Took long enough to get police to take that seriously. Mind you, now so many soldiers are moving into Queensland and the crims are following the money, we've been using Sydney's Central Fingerprinting Bureau more and more. Even the old stagers are coming round. Who would have thought the war would be so good for crime?'

Tom placed his elbows on the desk, his fingers forming a triangle with the apex at his upper lip. Joe watched as he considered the idea, could see it appealed. Perhaps it would be possible to identify chemical markers and track them? What else, he wondered. Fingerprints had been a breakthrough, but what about other physical evidence left at a crime scene. Blood could be typed. What about sweat? Semen? Since the army had come to town there'd been a huge increase in the number of attacks on women. Often victims could identify their attackers but not always, and Joe knew that mistakes were made, identities confused. Wouldn't it be better to have scientific proof as well? But all that was for the future. He'd stick to gasoline for now.

'Might be possible,' Tom said. He reached behind and pulled a chemistry textbook from the shelf, opened it and began to read. Joe understood the conversation was at an end.

'I'll leave it with you, then,' Joe said. 'Oh, these too if it's okay.' He rewound the ratchet on the top of the Argus, clicked open the back and withdrew a roll of film that he placed on the desk. 'They're part of an investigation, I'd be glad if you kept it just between you and me for now.' He withdrew a second roll from his top pocket. 'And this one. Just a few experiments.'

Tom's eyes strayed upwards. He nodded, sweeping the film canisters into the top drawer of his desk before returning to the book.

Joe gave a mock salute as he pushed back the chair. 'Let me know how it goes. I'll be in touch.'

Tom grunted as Joe passed through the door and made for the stairwell.

*

Joe knocked on the dimpled glass window of the office at the top of the stairs and peered inside. 'Anyone around?'

The man he'd seen outside the hotel, flushed face and ears swollen into puckered lumps, rushed past. That detective's taken some hits in his day, Joe thought. Given some too, by the look of his hands. But he wasn't a boxer. Boxers knew how to strap them.

From behind his desk Frank Bischof looked up, leaned back in his chair, combed his hair with a chubby hand and straightened the cuffs of his shirt. Was it the piggy eyes in a puffy face and the hair resembling a bad toupee that made him look sinister? Light from the stained-glass windows formed spidery patterns that rippled across his forearms and cufflinks. This is how camouflage works, Joe thought. Creating confusion.

'Ah, Sergeant Washington. To what do we owe the pleasure?'

'I saw Leonard in town just now and thought to check if

you've got a statement from him yet, if we're any further along finding out what happened Friday night.'

'We?' Frank said. 'This is a police investigation for the moment. You know how it is. We'll inform you when a charge is laid. Assuming the perpetrator is one of yours.'

'Just remember that it was one of ours who got roughed up here yesterday,' Joe said. 'The major doesn't take kindly to that sort of thing.'

'You're privy to the major's views, are you? Not what I've heard. Anyway, the man fell. No one got "roughed up", as you put it.'

'Given that we both want the same thing,' Joe said, pulling out a chair without waiting for an invitation, 'I thought I'd update you on the assault at Highgate Hill. The negro Bryson is in custody and will be court martialled, charged with assault with intent to murder. Likely get a sentence statement. Probably happy to go home.'

Frank cracked his knuckles, leaned forward. The purple veins stood out against a red face. 'Two women assaulted.' He spat out the words. 'One with a wooden paling. Women simply going about their business, getting off the tram after a late night shift, working long hours at the munitions factory at Rocklea. Helping our noble allies. But it's those allies they have to fear. Soldiers too cheap to visit the houses along Montague Road, too tight to spend their lousy money on the girls who work for it.' From his pocket Frank withdrew a white handkerchief to wipe his lips.

Joe had no reply. He'd photographed the women, the young girl from the backwoods, the spinster in her thirties with heavy legs and a chin that slipped away into her neck. The colourless photos identified them but told nothing of the fear, the hand around the throat, the fingers pushing into the mouth, the sweet smell of whiskey breath on the back of the neck. What had the women done to warrant such an attack? The boarding houses overflowed with girls checking in the mirror the lipstick they'd earned the night before, straightening the seams of their nylons on the way to town, always on the lookout for a good time.

No wonder Frank was angry.

Frank pulled open a desk drawer and withdrew a sheet of paper. He slid it across to Joe and leaned back, arms folded. 'I take it you've seen this?'

Joe recognised the letterhead of the US Army, although the signature wasn't familiar. A new officer, Lieutenant Colonel Braidwood. Hadn't Mitchell mentioned him recently? The letter was addressed to the Queensland Commissioner of Police. Joe picked it up.

Could the Commissioner, Lieutenant Colonel Braidwood suggested in oily prose, ensure that goods now in the possession of the Queensland CIB be immediately returned to a Mrs Hamilton of Hoogley Street, West End. Her house had been raided a week ago but without justification. The Lieutenant Colonel, it transpired, took his evening meals with Mrs Hamilton, and the goods at her premises were simply those that he'd acquired from the GHQ Officers Club over the past eighteen months. If the Commissioner would be so good as to arrange their prompt return the matter would be taken no further. It would be a nuisance, wouldn't it, to involve higher authorities in such matters.

Joe scanned the list of confiscated goods, mentally sorting them into neat piles. In police custody were 2 cans of powdered milk, 36 cans of catsup, 42 small cans of condensed milk, a large tin of spaghetti (Joe imagined his mother recoiling in horror), 50 pounds of sugar, 13 bottles of vinegar, 9 tins of corned beef, 24 tins of assorted vegetables, 2 tins of powdered eggs, a large tin of army biscuits and 62 small tins of assorted food (beets, coffee, tomato soup, syrup, meats). Oh yes, and a new Electrice refrigerator.

Joe wondered what solace other than supper Lieutenant Colonel Braidwood found in the arms of Mrs Hamilton.

'There's no Mr Hamilton, of course,' Frank said as if reading Joe's mind. 'Who knows what delights she offers but it's hardly likely the goods are for nightly tea. Opportunities for graft are everywhere.'

Joe raised both hands in surrender. 'Nothing I can do about it, I'm afraid. Orders are orders.'

Frank tore the paper from Joe's hand and threw it into the open drawer. He slammed it shut. Case closed. 'What did you see Tom Baty about?'

Joe looked up. Did the man have spies in the basement too? 'Bootleg gasoline. Gotta get to the bottom of the racket. It's getting worse every day and now we have reports of gas so adulterated it's causing mechanical problems. Technically it's sabotage though I doubt the perpetrators are thinking about that.'

'Ah yes, there's a war on.' Frank smiled. 'I'm sure you'll keep me informed.'

'Of course,' Joe said. 'As you will, no doubt.'

*

Maureen was short, with puppy fat that everyone promised — given she was only twelve years old — wouldn't last, bright cheeks in a round face, eyes alert to what passed in the street. Most days she left her home in Spring Hill to walk along the edge of the park skirting Wickham Terrace, skipping down the steps toward the markets on Roma Street. Even on a Sunday the streets were strewn with stray cabbage leaves and split pine from the pallets offloaded at the markets.

As usual she stopped near the top of the hill to look over the town and out to sea. Two years ago she and Billy Smith had helped dig trenches at their school before it closed. Billy and most of her friends left for the country but she had no other relatives to go to, so she'd stayed behind with her mother. For a while she went to lessons in a big house at Spring Hill, but her school was open again now.

She remembered how excited everyone had been when the Yanks had sailed into Moreton Bay. She'd never seen a black man before, nor known what an accent was, nor seen men in so many shades of green and khaki, nor eaten so many lollies. Lots of her friends knew a Winston or a Denver. They all had such funny names.

Her mother told her to walk straight to the tram stop but she couldn't resist the soft voices, the men in neatly pressed uniforms and peaked caps who wandered the streets.

'Sure,' they would say when she asked if she could see the badges on their caps, or asked about their hometown. 'You're welcome, kid.'

They looked sad as they told her she reminded them of their daughters in Omaha or Nebraska. Yanks sometimes visited her family's small flat in the front half of a wooden cottage, leaving their coats on the back of the kitchen chairs while they helped with the washing up. It wasn't odd to have a Yank home for tea, for singalongs around the piano. Homesick young men singing, 'When You Wish Upon a Star'.

But she knew the ones to avoid, the ones with hands too familiar, eyes bleak, faces pinched. A lot of them lingered in the park near the public lavatories and she held her nose as she passed.

The Tower Mill stood on the highest point, neglected and forgotten. Billy said it was full of ghosts, the souls of convicts tortured on the rack. But she didn't always believe Billy.

Beside the stone tower, down the slope, were two wooden huts. Too low for anyone to stand inside, she thought. Squat structures with slatted windows and locked doors. Today she saw that the padlock on one of the huts was open. Gingerly she opened the door to peer into the darkness within, a dark vaulted space smelling of pee. She called out, hearing only her voice bounce back. A stack of old boxes was all she could make out against the round wall, but the hideaway looked well worth investigating. She wondered what she'd find when she came back later with a flashlight.

Chapter Eleven

Joe edged past passengers queuing in the middle of the street. A streetcar glided to a halt and people jostled aboard. Trams, he reminded himself. Through the open-sided carriage he scanned the dark interior where a conductress, her leather moneybag dragging to the right, collected coins from a corseted woman with a severe expression. Beads of sweat bubbled through face powder as she fanned herself with a copy of *The Women's Weekly*. Why did women even wear gloves in this weather? He climbed aboard. The conductress gave a deft tug on the leather strap and with a sharp 'ding ding' the tram edged forward between the iron semicircles of the Victoria Bridge.

In spite of his fastidious nature, Joe preferred the seedy southern side of town. Most of the area was poor. Ramshackle tin and wooden cottages with scratchy back-yards, warehouses and small factories strung out along the bank of the river. Billboards advertised the latest show at the Cremorne — Roy Rene and George Wallace were not to his taste but the jazz clubs and dance halls were. Untidy and messy certainly, but there was more life here than anything he'd seen in the genteel suburbs of Toowong or Hamilton on the north side of the river.

Crowds of sailors and soldiers crammed into the Ship Inn, jostling to get to the bar, elbowing each other, shouting insults. They called each other 'mate' but Joe knew they'd be quick to knee their 'mate' in the groin in the battle for a drink.

Joe nodded to the man on the door at Doctor Carver's Club, the large wooden building with triple awnings on Grey Street. He made his way past dormitories, the rec room, a barber's shop. A bit like the PX but less prosperous for sure. From somewhere came the rhythmic click of billiard balls and the low murmur of men lining up shots. Cool notes from a jazz trip — piano, bass, percussion — echoed in the empty dance hall. Swing bands had made the Carver Club famous. White soldiers weren't allowed in without an invitation but local white women happily flocked here to listen to bands and jitterbug. Monroe couldn't contain his horror. But hell, even Eleanor Roosevelt had visited only a few weeks ago.

Four negro MPs, the only ones in town, were based here and Joe needed advice.

'Anyone around?' he said, knocking on a door at the back of the complex.

'That Joe?' The voice was from the north — Detroit, the city of Joe's early years. In civilian life Sergeant Elmer McConachy worked in the auto industry, a machinist if Joe remembered right. He didn't remember much about Detroit, but he did remember the winter it snowed heavily — huge banks of it, dirty grey from the smokestacks, and treacherous if you got caught out. His father had showed him how to make a snowman, they'd carried clods of snow and packed them into a conical shape, topped with a red beret. Joe found buttons in his mother's sewing basket for eyes and his father got a corncob pipe from somewhere, just like MacArthur's.

Before they'd finished, his father was called away. He'd dragged Joe along to another interminable meeting where men with hollow cheeks stood around, hands in their pockets, listening to a speaker haranguing them. Not long afterwards the snowman melted into the sidewalk, his face slipping into a sad frown.

They shook, a firm handshake between equals. Joe liked that about Elmer.

'Let's go get ourselves a coffee,' Elmer said. He waved at a desk that looked remarkably like the one in the office Joe was avoiding. 'Must be time for a break from all this goddamned paperwork. I've had an earful of the quartermaster complaining about paper shortages. Lot of hooey. They could solve it easy if we didn't have to write every report in triplicate!'

Joe and Elmer had worked a few cases together and got along just fine despite their differences. Elmer was obsessed with baseball and able to recite the averages of every pitcher in the Major League; Joe couldn't tell the difference between a baseball and a football.

He followed Elmer to the cafeteria. Behind the counter a young woman — Joe knew she wasn't American, probably one of the local Aboriginal girls — poured coffee from a large urn. Beyond lay the kitchen, where cooks in white aprons stirred cauldrons and chopped mounds of vegetables for the evening meal. Joe was hungrier than he'd realised and lifted a plate from a stack to pile it with cookies, a poor substitute for lunch but that meal was long past.

Elmer balanced their cups on a tin tray and led the way. Around them conversations faltered, sentences broke off. From under heavy lids a dozen bloodshot eyes followed them to a table against the back wall. Joe had seen the expression before. White MPs were about as popular here as they were in Brisbane polite society. Understandable, given the likes of Monroe and his pals.

'You've come about Bryson,' Elmer said. 'Ain't nothing can be done for him.'

'No,' Joe said. 'He'll go to jail. But so will Dwight Duke from B Company Signals. It's him I've come about. Is there anything I can do?'

'They'll convict him, too. Send him home. Same as Bryson though they're nothing like each other. LeRoy Bryson's a thug. Always been a loose cannon and liquor just makes it worse. I feel bad about those ladies, real sorry. But Duke? No, he's on the level. Really loved that girl, used to write her from New Guinea, sent money for the kid. No idea if he knew how old she was, but if previous cases are anything to go by he'll get between five and ten. A bit rough but not as rough as it'd be in Mississippi. He'll survive.' He stared into this cup.

'Yeah,' Joe said. 'I'd like to help the girl, the baby too if possible. Maybe I could talk to the Red Cross? It's not as if she didn't know what she was doing, fifteen or no. And there's the kid to think of. He's half-American, after all.'

'We've talked to the grandmother. She don't want anything to do with us. So that's about the end of it. Can't do more than that. Duke won't be a father this time.' Elmer drank with a delicacy at odds with his roughened hands.

'Sad,' Joe said into his coffee. He reached for the sugar bowl, hesitating only slightly before emptying two heaped teaspoons into his mug. He stirred the white grains.

They savoured their coffee and cookies in a companionable silence. Joe had often thought about photographing Elmer, the furrows in his cheeks almost purple as he smiled, the ivory teeth. Difficult exposure levels, he thought, wondering if he'd be brave enough to ask.

'You were in New Guinea?' Joe seldom asked soldiers about their service, keenly aware of his own lack of it.

'Yes. Terrifying place for someone from the Midwest, gave me the heebie-jeebies. Never seen so much mud in my life. And the jungle. So thick you couldn't see more than a few yards in front of you and hardly ever the sky. Mind you,' he placed his cup into the saucer with a clink and looked toward the girl at the counter, 'it did some of the soldiers good to have to rely on black men. The Aussies too. They reckon they've never seen a black face but there's no shortage if you know where to look. The fuzzy wuzzies,' he added with a wistful smile. 'Short men most of them, hardly up to your chest and with hair almost as long. But they could climb the hills all day and night in mud up to your calves, carry loads of supplies across the mountains, and end every day laughing at a joke they made at each other's expense. Wonderful people.'

Joe had heard good reports from Oro Province, where Elmer served. MPs worked together without the sort of animosity that was brewing in this backwater. Why did quiet places produce the most vehement antagonisms? Almost as if boredom generated its own momentum.

'Were you on duty last night?' Joe said. 'Was Monroe around?'

'No idea. I was off-duty, spent the day at the Oasis lying under palm trees, floating in the big pool, pretending I was in California. About the only way to get cool in this heat. I can ask around if you want. Got a reputation, that one.'

'If you could, thanks,' Joe said. 'Don't be too obvious about it.'

They got up and Joe followed Elmer to the counter, where they deposited their metal trays. 'Who's playing tonight?' he said. Sometimes, if the band was good, he'd stand in the street outside. One day he'd get Elmer to invite him.

'No idea. I think most of the men will head for the Trocadero. Frank Couglan's playing again, with that sassy sax player.'

'Give us a hand, can you,' a voice decidedly not American called out, vowels broader than a Texan's. 'Got a delivery.' A scrawny man in overalls and a five o'clock shadow stood at the back door of the kitchen, sleeves pulled up to his bony elbows, a grease rag hanging from his back pocket. Behind, Joe saw a fancy car reversed up to the loading ramp with its boot open.

Joe watched as a contingent of soldiers unloaded boxes from the trunk and carried them into the kitchen. He heard the tinkle of glass as the delivery man directed privates to haul crates of tall brown bottles up the ramp. Inside, they stacked tins of fruit, stowed bags of sugar and flour, unloaded boxes of butter. Again he thought of the PX. It wasn't just gas that fuelled the army, but everything from buckets of ice cream to crates of beer.

*

At Memorial Park, Joe bent down and checked under the gun emplacement. He'd wrapped the cookies in a handkerchief and doubted she'd mind they were broken. When he'd first found the litter they'd been all bone and fur, kneading their mother relentlessly as she lay exhausted, her sides concave from the feeding. Now he found her lazing in the sun under the cannon, the kittens rolling and scratching each other in a heap. He left the biscuits and stroked the mother cat's white fur.

Across the road, the terracotta roofing of Base Headquarters baked under the afternoon sun, deep shadows forming on the ornately carved stone and brickwork. It must have made a grand home once, Joe thought, the driveway leading to broad stone steps, an arched entranceway, tall chimneys rising above peaked roofs. It would sit well on the set of *Gone with the Wind*. Now the verandah provided shade for two off-duty WRENs and a group of soldiers making a line.

On the roadway above the gardens Joe recognised a kid from the meeting, the one with all the questions. Laurie, was it? Dressed in shorts and long socks that made his white legs look even longer, the adolescent stood on the pavement waving roneoed sheafs of paper at bewildered passers-by.

'Read the latest, why don't you? Stories for the new world, poems and writing from the young set!'

'You got *Smith's Weekly*?' said a corporal with dark hair, cigarette held in his raised hand, as he searched in his trouser pocket for change.

'Not bloody likely. You ought to try something more up to date than that old magazine.' The boy squinted into the sun, his blond hair parted on the left, swept high on his forehead into a cock's comb.

'Suit yourself,' the soldier said, rejoining the group of Aussie soldiers heading for the Ship Inn, their slouch hats tilted at a rakish angle. He'd saved a few bob.

Intrigued, Joe walked over to the boy. 'How much?'

'A shilling. Hey, you were at the meeting, weren't you? You a writer? I'm Laurie. Laurie Collinson. Pleased to meet you.'

'Not a writer,' Joe said, his arm outstretched. 'But pleased to meet you. Joe, Joe Washington. What exactly are you selling? And why here?'

'It's our new journal. The latest in literary criticism, with poetry and prose, stories written *by* young people *for* young people.' The stress on the words made them a declaration. 'Have a read. It's our first proper edition.' He shoved a copy into Joe's hands.

'Is it *Meanjin Papers*?' Joe said, a handful of coins in his right hand. 'Someone told me about that.'

'No,' Laurie said, 'not Clem's paper. Oh it's alright as far as it goes, but too staid, not game to tackle real issues. We need to hear younger voices now. Most of us are at State High and we've made it a rule that we'll only publish writers under twenty-one. Of course it's much more than a school paper, or it will be. We call it *Barjai*.'

'I'll never understand the lingo,' Joe said. 'What on earth does that mean?'

'It's an Aboriginal word for a meeting place. And that's exactly what our paper will be, a meeting place for ideas. We need new ideas now. Look where all the old ones got us.'

'But why sell it on the street?'

'Old Waddle the principal doesn't approve, won't let us print it at school, doesn't want any talk of abortion or politics. But if we can't discuss things now — now that a new world is around the corner — what's the war been about? I told him to go to hell, I'd sell it on the street if he wouldn't help. And so you see me now.' Laurie flung his arms wide, a circus master welcoming Joe into his world.

'You know Clem?' Joe said. 'I've heard his name but gather he's not too keen on Americans. Especially the military police, which means me. Were you at his place last night? I heard there was a meeting.'

'Oh yes, what a bore it all was. I love Clem and Nina and all the others, but it's always the same old arguments, the same tired jokes. Fortunately some of our crowd was there so it wasn't a complete waste.'

'I met a couple of people after the meeting,' Joe said. 'Thea and Rose? Are they part of your crowd?'

'Thea couldn't make it, she's always studying. And Rose came but only briefly. Heaven knows where she'd been. I worry about her sometimes.' Laurie frowned.

Joe nodded at the gangly teenager with spindly legs in

short pants, impressed by his concern. It spoke well of him.

'Was there someone called Bob? She mentioned him, gather he's American.'

'She's got lots of friends,' Laurie said. 'Not my business.'

'Sure. Thanks,' Joe said, tucking the journal under his arm. 'Gotta get to work, I'm on duty soon. Good luck with all of this.'

'Would you like to meet Clem and Nina?' Laurie said. 'There's one of their do's on tomorrow evening if you want to come. They're really very welcoming to Yanks, even if wary of those in white helmets!'

'I'd like that, if you think it's okay. Where do they live?'

'Not far,' Laurie said. 'Rawnsley Street, Dutton Park, just opposite the cemetery.'

Joe made to leave but stopped as if with an afterthought. 'Oh, what time was it that Rose left?'

'Rose left with me, about ten o'clock, I guess. Why?' Joe noted the quizzical glance, the sensitive suspicion of the young.

'No real reason.' From the pocket of his trousers Joe withdrew a roll of notes and unpeeled a couple. 'I could buy a couple more of those papers, to pass around the Base if you like. Sure there'll be some people interested.'

Laurie's eyes widened. He counted out half a dozen copies and shoved the notes in his pocket. 'We'd print a lot more if we had the money, but paper's impossible to buy and costly. We only manage because Thea's father can get supplies from *The Courier-Mail*.'

'Perhaps I could help with that too,' Joe said, waving goodbye as he crossed Vulture Street. That was the second invitation in two days.

Chapter Twelve

Joe fingered the creased and crumpled corners of an ochre folder, neatening the loose papers and tucking stray slips inside. He placed his camera on top. He seemed fated to spend his life taking mugshots and documenting crime scenes. At least on Sundays, Major Mitchell could be relied upon to take the day off, which made life more tolerable. It gave him some leeway too.

At a rap on the door he lifted his head. Standing in the doorway, slouch hat squashed under his right arm, front pockets chunky with cigarettes, pencils and a flip notepad, stood an Australian sergeant. Archie Doyle was a provost Joe had crossed paths with a few times. He put Doyle in his forties, although it wasn't easy to tell from the weathered face of a man who had served in Africa and the Middle East.

'Sergeant Doyle, sir. You asked to see me.'

'Yes. Come in.'

Doyle stood to attention before agreeing to sit. He looked ill at ease and reluctant to meet Joe's gaze.

'The major has ordered an investigation into the arrest of

Corporal Duke, B Company Signals,' Joe said. 'I understand you know something of this?'

'The major?'

'Yes. What can you tell me?'

'Not a lot,' Doyle said, looking beyond Joe to the framed photo behind him. 'We had a report from the Children's Department, the grandmother worried her granddaughter had gone and got herself pregnant. She had a baby boy, I think. We got called in when the soldier got angry and refused to leave. A negro corporal. We called your men when we got him to Provost Headquarters.'

'Who came?' Joe said.

'A fat man — one of yours — and a pale fellow with an odd sort of accent. Naval Shore Patrolman.'

'Monroe and Hayden.' Not hard to guess.

'I believe that was their names, sir.' Doyle continued to interrogate the photo of FDR.

'What happened when they arrived?'

'They took the soldier away,' Doyle said. 'Apparently he needed medical attention.'

'Before or after they arrived?'

Finally Doyle looked at Joe. 'Is this necessary?'

'It is, I'm afraid,' Joe said. 'I've been tasked with investigating the incident. How did the MPs seem? Had they been drinking? We've had reports . . .' Joe reached for a sheet of pink paper, the text closely typed. Doyle needn't know it was just an article he'd written for the *Infantry Journal* to accompany photos he'd taken of Brisbane's unusual birdlife. Who would've guessed that a butcher bird would turn out to be a cheerful visitor happy to take pieces of sausage from your hand, and not the vulture he'd expected.

'Maybe Monroe. The fat one.'

'What happened?'

'Listen.' Doyle fixed Joe with his droopy eyes. 'I'm a military man, I've been in the army nearly twenty years, my father was at Gallipoli. It's my life and I don't like the way some people behave any more than you do, but I don't dob on people. Even Yanks.' He smiled an apology.

'Sometimes it's the only way,' Joe said. 'I may not have your military pedigree, would be the first to admit it, but I don't like the way some in this town look at us. Blaming us for everything that happens. We all live with the consequences of ill-discipline and we don't take kindly to bad behaviour . . . Well, it'll make things better for all of us. I'm an investigator. I like to solve problems when I can. And this is one of them.'

'Maybe you're right,' Doyle said, crossing his legs. 'You'll have to deal with Monroe one day. He was drunk alright, throwing his weight around. "Cocksucker, fucking coon." Not just out of control but vicious with it. I was shocked to see a uniformed MP behave like that. It was as if he thought he could do whatever he liked. I suppose that's often the case.'

'And it gives all of us a bad name,' Joe said.

'No doubt about it, sir.'

'Thanks. I appreciate this. Can you prepare a report for me, one that I can show the major? We've had quite enough trouble with Monroe and Hayden, and given what happened this time last year we've got to be vigilant. Stop things getting out of hand again.'

Doyle stood and saluted. Joe appreciated the unnecessary gesture. 'I'll get you a report,' Doyle said. 'And you're right. There's a lot of animosity building. You need to keep a lid on it.'

*

The sun scorched the cement pavements in the centre of town. Inside the reading room of the Public Library of Queensland,

Rose McAlister sat in the cool, almost funereal interior. Sombre wooden columns topped with faux Corinthian capitals, darkened binding on the spines of thousands of books ranged on unlit shelves. Rose liked that the library was small and unpretentious. A pity it was also sunless, poorly lit, and seldom busy. At the counter she paused to inhale the musky smells, the tang of glue, the rich chocolate leather, the acidic smell of books left too long unopened. A whiff of mould both predictable and almost comforting. Domestic. Beside her, an ungainly girl of about twelve, with pigtails and an ill-fitting dress, asked for a book on the Cathar conspiracy.

The librarian, his sleeves secured within a circle of metal, pointed her toward the correct row and frowned. 'Over there, Maureen. I'm surprised you don't know your way around by now. You're here often enough.'

'Even when she should be at school,' he said under his breath, handing Rose the volume she'd requested before silence settled once more over the room.

Rose moved to a large cedar reading table and placed her volume of *Childe Harold* under the pallid glow of a desk lamp. As she sat, she inspected her face in the richly polished surface, a ghostly yellow against the burgundy. Why had she mentioned James, however indirectly? There was no need. Her friends knew, the ones who mattered. She'd become used to the soft accents of the Yanks, no longer found their gentlemanly ways unusual. But there was something about this particular American. Joe wasn't handsome like so many of them. Too short for her liking and his face florid in the sun. Somehow he reminded her of the teddy bear she'd clung to when her mother died, and into whose soft yellow fur she'd cried herself to sleep. He lulled her into revealing more than she usually did.

Not a brother. James. *Her* James.

She closed her eyes and breathed deeply. There he was, cart-wheeling down the slope in the Botanic Gardens, dancing his way beneath the trailing branches of the weeping figs, stopping to honk at the swans, flinging himself onto the grass where she sat at the edge of the river. They'd met in Adelaide, had studied together at university. James read English literature, the Romantic poets. Partly, she was sure, to annoy his working-class parents who'd sailed from England hoping to escape a country polluted by the eccentricities of class. In Brisbane his parents had established a life of suburban solidity only to watch, bewildered, as their son — who'd escaped for a time to Adelaide — emulated the worst of public-school idiocy. All that talk of art for art's sake, playing at being Oscar Wilde. Rose smelled again the perfume from the rose garden and saw the irrepressible red hair, the scarf flung around his neck. She'd lain her head on his lap as he read Apollinaire aloud.

But the bourgeois values of patriotism shackled him in the end. Or was it just a wild attempt at glory — a Byronic affectation? He wasn't political. He hated fascism for its barbarism of ideas as much as the brutality of its ambitions. So he'd volunteered along with so many others, writing her long and passionate letters from Egypt full of the glories of the desert, the pyramids and the Sphinx.

He should have returned on leave, she was here to meet him. But his ship diverted and the last she'd heard was a brief card from Singapore. Then she heard that his parents had received a telegram. She visited them in their cottage at Sandgate, sat at the kitchen table as they clutched at the yellow paper. Missing, presumed lost. The worst kind of news.

Though their world collapsed, Jim went to the garage every day and Mabel kept knitting balaclavas for the Red Cross. But life was in limbo. Ghost-like, they inhabited a world that had been torn apart and neither could reach across the chasm.

When a further telegram came to tell them their only child was a prisoner, they cried with relief. Alive. At least he was alive.

Rose withdrew a precious sheet of notepaper from her bag. Her fountain pen was wrapped in an old glove in case it leaked in the heat. She liked the weight of it in her left hand, wrist and fingers curled so she wouldn't smudge the letters as she worked from left to right. Most days she wrote to James, sending letters through the Red Cross with little expectation they'd be read. Every day she visited the GPO but no replies came. Still, these rituals brought comfort, a sort of communion.

Today at least she had something to write about — the lecture and all their friends. Surrealism didn't appeal to her, she said, the paintings tried too hard, too much clashing colour. Perhaps that suited the times, but she wanted art to be restful, contemplative. Laurie had got hot under the collar and Thea was smoking too much. She'd see them again at Clem's tomorrow night. Would she mention the Americans? So polite, their accents amusing, harsh and nasal or soft and sibilant. So many varieties.

And Alma? Would she mention her? No. What was the point?

All his friends missed James, but none as she did.

She folded the page and slipped it into her bag.

*

In the basement of the Town Hall, Corporal Dwight Duke sat on the low bed, his back against the wall. He needed to think. On the other side of the cell LeRoy Bryson lay prone, asleep. Happy to go home, get out of the war.

Duke worried about the child. What would become of

him? A black kid in a country with so few black faces. How would Polly explain it to him as he grew up. Would the kids at school pester him, call him names? Would he wonder who his daddy had been, where he'd come from? Make up tall stories about an Indian prince or pirates? Pretend to be an Abo, like the men he'd seen in the park near the Carver Club. Eyes downcast, planted where they belonged, their gentle whispering mingling with the breeze. He'd tried to talk to one of the group, had asked him where he came from, what work he did.

Duke would be sent home to serve his sentence. He'd write to Polly, send money when he got out of jail. But his war was over, gone as quickly as his chance to be a father. How was he supposed to know she was only fifteen? And him only four years older. His sister was fifteen, had a baby girl, and no one worried nothing about it.

The hairs on the back of his neck stiffened as he heard the heavy boots of the fat MP who'd arrested him, the one with the red birthmark sliding down the left side of his face. He'd thumped Duke around in the back of the jeep, willing him to make an escape. Give him an excuse. Any excuse. Duke had seen his type before back home. Swaggering with pistols at their hip. Chewing gum as they ordered old men to shine their shoes, lift heavy bags down from the rack in their railway compartment. Come here, boy. Over there.

Duke sat still, studying the cell floor.

He heard a clank as the door of the adjoining cell opened. The MP moved heavily and he heard the sound of a man being dragged to his feet. Careful not to make a noise, Duke leaned backward. Through the thin prefab wall he could just make out words.

'What did you tell that pansy investigator?'

'Just what I remembered. Why?'

'What did he ask about?'

'Mostly just the fight. I don't remember too much.'

'What else?'

'He asked about the barrels and the Naval Patrolman.'

Duke heard a thump and a whisper full of menace. 'What did you say?'

'Nothing, nothing.'

'You're going to jail, you know. Murder clear and simple.'

Duke heard the creak of bedsprings as the MP sat.

'Mind you. There could be mitigating circumstances. Could have been self-defence if you get the story right. Perhaps we could talk to the Patrolman about it. He might be able to speak up for you. If you're sensible.'

'What would I have to do?' Duke heard the prisoner's feet shuffling. 'Just tell me.'

'Keep your mouth shut. No words with the investigator, right? Keep it just between us two. I'll look after you.'

*

The evening was sultry but not oppressive, the stars a splatter of lights across the darkened sky, a broad swathe that Joe was getting used to. The Southern Cross hung over his shoulder as he made his way to the river. He couldn't get the soldier out of his mind, the body abandoned in the cemetery, the black-and-white photo that took him back to his own childhood.

Why had he kept quiet about the Trocadero? He hadn't told the whole story. Not to Frank or to Rose, and he wasn't entirely sure why. There was something going on between Frank and Leonard, and he didn't know how Rose fitted in. They all seemed to know each other, that was clear. But how? The police knew most of the crooks in town, he understood that. They kept an eye on things, it made sense. But this felt different somehow. He didn't trust Frank. And what about

Rose? Just because you were a looker didn't mean you were honest and he knew she'd played him, that's for sure. This town was full of rackets and he was an outsider. He had to tread carefully.

He sat on a wooden pylon by the docks, tracing the swirls on the gnarled timbers. Similar spirals moved at the edge of the muddy river as the tide raced out against the iron dock. Metal clanged against metal and men called out. A welder lowered his helmet as he leaned toward the buckled grey hull of a destroyer, his flashlight hissing as the arc moved across the metal skin. The smell was bitter, somehow electric.

The brownout had been partially lifted last year but surely the glare from the dry docks would have attracted any passing Zero. Twenty-four hours a day they worked, welding and riveting. Repairing and mending, patching up. No different from the hospital in many ways. War was still the main game. Everything else — the brawls and murders, the gamblers and bootleggers — everything else was on the outfield.

Joe headed for the bridge and across to the north side of the river.

Normally he took the quickest route home, down the main street. But tonight he wanted to avoid the George Street soldiers at cocktail hour in Lennon's, the officers canoodling with girlfriends they'd brought up from Melbourne and gotten cushy jobs in administration. He clung to the river, turning right along North Quay past the *Mirimar*, moored peacefully, waiting for its weekly trip upstream packed with families and soldiers to see the koalas at Lone Pine. He passed the Commissariat building and turned left at Parliament House. He skirted the Botanic Gardens, leaving the sad young men to their evening rituals. He hoped the police would leave them be but knew it unlikely — he'd heard Frank laugh about 'poofters and perverts'. Like Monroe, he delighted in bringing charges of carnal knowledge. Against the order of nature, they said.

An urgent couple leaned against the iron railings, their faces locked, hands seeking openings in heavy dark material. But it was a skirt the sailor's hand lifted, white panties he slid his opened trousers toward. This couple was safe.

Joe followed the river, where other couples lay on the grassy slopes at the edge of the park, their limbs lit by the pale moon. He kept walking toward the iron bridge, beneath whose giant wings he knew he'd find relentless activity. Men moved along the great wooden wharves, injured ships lay waiting to be mended, their hulls cracked and swollen, their auxiliary engines gasping like the lungs of wounded animals gulping for air.

Along the clifftop at New Farm he looked back to where he'd started. Only a short distance 'as the crow flies', the Aussies would say. Below, the great greasy river wound its way toward the bay and out to sea, the same sea from where men and ships limped home to be patched up in hospitals and dockyards before being flung back into the maws of war.

But not Foster. Not now. Among so many deaths, did one individual matter? Who would miss him?

Joe turned his back on the river and headed for Brunswick Street and home. As he passed the Rialto Theatre he heard laughter as Thumper taught Bambi to speak. Rabbits and deer, he thought, made more sense than people.

Chapter Thirteen

Every Sunday afternoon Detective Senior Sergeant Frank Bischof circled the town centre in the CIB's only car, a black four-door Ford V8 convertible with metal funnels shading the front lights and sinister oriental slits that let through pricks of light to pierce the brownout. He was thankful he'd avoided those ugly gas converters that balanced on the sloping rear boot, although there was little enough petrol for routine patrols these days. Now he was in charge of the field work of all five squads, these regular tours of inspection were easy to arrange.

He'd told the constable to type up Leonard's formal statement, for what it was worth, and the technical boffins were checking Leonard's car, a cream-coloured Hudson sedan. He'd told them to be quick. Leonard had a business to run.

Frank glanced at the statue of the Old Lady, streaked with pigeon shit, as he crossed Queens Gardens, the pathetic patch of territory the Queen condescended to survey. The soldiers mooning with their girls on the park benches failed to pay homage, and the sandbags and brick barriers around the

Treasury building highlighted the beleaguered state of her Empire. But Frank had little interest in any empire but his own. He settled into the front seat, inhaling the leather polish. His immaculate white shirt was crumpled, the bow tie askew, his eyes puffy. He'd had a long day but it wasn't over yet.

Most of the establishments — or 'cat houses', as the Yanks called them — were small. A couple of girls on the day shift with more at night. Few of them lived in the houses but those who did knew to keep their douche cans under their bed, where police knew not to look. Elsie's on Albert Street was first on the list.

Frank parked against the kerb, just up from the green door where girls leaned against the wall, cigarettes dangling from hands raised in invitation. When they recognised him each girl reached inside her bodice for her slip of paper. He glanced briefly at each as he inspected the line, but doubted the certificates would be out of date. Every Wednesday the girls presented themselves at Hope Street, a pleasant enough visit to the woman doctor employed by the Health Department. It kept them out of the Lock Hospital.

He doffed his hat at Elsie, who lounged on a cane chair in the palm-fringed entrance. Her crimson evening dress clung to her body and shimmered as she moved.

'Beer? Wine?'

'No time for a chat.' Frank waved as he returned to the car, pocketing the envelope Elsie had discreetly pressed into his hand.

He turned into Ann Street past the live palms at the front of the Town Hall toward the crypt and walls of Duhig's great folly and into Fortitude Valley. He steered around an air raid shelter blocking part of the road in front of TC Beirne's, a Catholic shop he studiously avoided. The Royal George and the Empire, flanking Brunswick Street, were more his style.

He smirked as he passed the offices of *Truth*, a paper dedicated to anything but. He slammed on the brakes as a tram clanged to a stop in front of him. On either side, tiny houses huddled so close that their end walls almost touched, the timbers on their front verandahs sagging. Children in clothing stitched together from flour bags ran up front steps, abandoning the hopscotch squares they had etched with pebbles into the road-way. His job was to protect them, keep an eye on things. And this was the only way he knew.

A group of Yanks, all under the weather, staggered along the street. They whistled and leered at a young girl who scurried across the road. An elderly woman glared at the soldiers as she put her arm around the girl's shoulders. Frank pulled into the kerb and lowered the window to growl a warning. Bloody Yanks. Only last week a soldier had assaulted a five-year-old girl on Wickham Terrace. He shuddered as he recalled the testimony of the eighty-four-year-old widow from Boundary Street whose petticoat and bloomers he'd taken to the Technical Section, where they tested for the presence of semen. A young nurse walking home from the railway station after her late night shift — raped and sodomised.

And all we do is hand them back. Not one damn conviction.

The Yanks had changed his hometown in ways he was only slowing coming to terms with. You had to know how to move with the times. Adapt. Make the most of it. So now he kept it all under control, well managed, hygienic.

Of course the old crimes still paid. Booze, a flutter on the nags. But now thousands of Yanks wanted girls and had the money to pay. How much had Jones said they'd spent on Saturday night? More than a detective's weekly pay, that's for sure — or at least the one the taxman saw. Between three and twenty pounds a month, he calculated, multiplied a dozen times. No great loss to the public purse if not all the fines made their way into consolidated revenue. Best to keep the boys happy.

Over the years Frank had built the game into something with much better odds than the racetrack, but it would never be as much fun. He knew horses, loved the clamour and sweat of the track, but he was out of depth in this female world of sultry movements and sullen expressions, hands reaching out to hold the back of your head. Some of the men in the Consorting Squad took advantage of it all, but not him.

He liked the madams, though. Blowsy ladies with too many rings and cheap perfume; tough but honest. They knew how to do business and paid their dues without complaint. The real threat to the game were the sole operators. Delinquent girls or promiscuous amateurs, the loose women who danced all night at the Trocadero or drank at the Grand or the Royal. They lured Yanks home with cheap booze so their friends could ginger them while they lay drunk in bed. These good-time girls had no morals, no sense of right and wrong, no self-control. And no one managed them.

Evening descended as he crossed the Victoria Bridge into South Brisbane. Below lay the dark ropey coil of the river. Above, a flying fox flickered in the night sky, following the river's winding path to the paperbarks on the edge of Moreton Bay. Dirty squabbling beasts. As a kid he'd shot out the camp on his parents' dairy farm, dangling black fruit in the trees. He remembered the plop as one by one they fell to the ground. The stench lingered for a week.

The river divided Brisbane. It always had.

A thousand black soldiers were confined to the south side and it was Frank's job to keep things in order. He made sure the CIB kept tabs on the club at Red Hill some do-good Abo had started; as well as the other one, Doctor Carver's. People said it had the best music in town, and if it kept the negroes out of the white dance halls so much the better. But no one had expected white women would be drawn there, lured by jazz bands and the thrill of black skin. Brisbanites were scandalised but experience told him there were worse crimes. Unnatural acts he knew were widespread, especially among the negroes. Sometimes he found it hard to believe what the world was coming to. It was up to him to keep it all under control. All very well to rely on the hundreds of Yank MPs patrolling the streets in helmets and white puttees. Armed. Always armed. A bloody disgrace some of them. No discipline. No subtlety. Above all, no discretion. But this was his town and he'd make sure it was policed his way.

Frank turned into Montague Road, the reek of salt and blood from the fish markets mingling with the metallic odours from the gas works. Past the warehouses and soft drink factories he swerved to avoid a taxi full of soldiers. More happy customers.

The San Toy had been a smart boarding house once, the remnants of its backyard grandeur still visible — not just a bush lemon, a loquat and straggling banana clumped too close, but also a paved area around a central garden bed. Frank parked out of sight on a side street and locked the car door. Too bad about the tennis court. It'd seen better days, the ragged net now draped over the tin shed to provide shade for the half-dozen chooks that pecked at the edge of the weed-infested court.

Inside the main entrance, Frank headed directly to the office — or the folding counter and a single chair that served as one. The dining room had become a lounge bar, the tables and upright wooden chairs replaced with velvet armchairs, low tables bearing heavy glass ashtrays. Stairs led to another floor where the girls worked in private rooms. There'd be a bathroom with a stained toilet at the end of the corridor, like every boarding house he'd ever entered. Paint flaked off the walls, the furniture needed polishing. He noticed how the floral carpet that snaked up the stairs had been worn thin down the middle as the boots of countless soldiers traipsed up and down or stood waiting their turn. Six prostitutes worked here and only a fortnight ago police had recorded thirty-one American sailors and sixteen soldiers entering in just two short hours. 'The Manpower' would applaud the girl's diligence if nothing else.

At the counter, a woman grimaced as she twisted the rings on her fingers, the pudgy flesh on either side of the golden bands bulging. Betty Anderson was fat, her floral dress moulded to the hills and valleys of her body. Frank wondered if she ever prised the rings off, if it was still possible.

'Cup of tea?' she said. 'Beer?' She squeezed around the counter and led Frank to the armchairs at the bar. She nodded at a girl with auburn hair and a sprinkle of freckles who moved to the kitchen, returning with a silver tray on which balanced a teapot, plates and cups. She lowered it to the table and withdrew. Betty poured. The spoon clinked as Frank stirred three spoonfuls of sugar into the cup propped on a saucer on his chest. He lifted the cup to his lips, finger raised, remembering at the last minute not to blow on the hot tea.

'A slice of sponge cake perhaps? With real cream? Got to support our dairy farmers.' Betty gave a matronly smile as she proffered the large plate.

Frank placed his cup and saucer on the table before accepting a small plate that he set with reverence on the arm of his chair. Not a crumb fell as he lifted the moist yellow slice to his lips, closing his eyes as he compared the texture with his wife's sponge cake. He savoured the cream. How well he remembered those icy mornings, the fog as you breathed out, the steamy shit you slopped through as you walked to the bales, the soft rise and fall of the cows' bellies as you leaned into them, dragging on the leathery teats, the hiss of milk as it pinged against a metal bucket. His tongue found the stray streaks of cream and he smiled. He'd come a long way and was not going back.

He leaned back in the chair and withdrew an American Army identification photo from the inside of his coat. He slid it across the table. 'Ever seen this man?'

'A Yank. They all look the same after a while, don't they. Even sound the same.' Betty sipped her tea, her eyes on Frank.

'Are you sure? What if I asked the girls? Reckon they'd remember him?'

'He might have been here but it's difficult to remember them all.'

'You'd remember Slim. Tall. Well over six foot. He travels with a runt of a man, a pale shadow called Snow.'

'They could have been here. Why?'

'Last night?'

'No. We had a full house. He wasn't one of them.'

'Ask around,' Frank said, licking the fork before returning the plate to the tray. 'We'll be checking all the houses, asking the girls. Had any trouble lately?'

'Not from the punters,' Betty said. 'One thing you can say about the Yanks, they don't quibble over money and they treat the girls well.'

'Know someone called Alma?'

'The name doesn't ring a bell. Of course she might use another name for professional reasons, sometimes that happens. Is there more you can tell me?'

'Not a lot,' Frank said. 'She works for Leonard.'

'We don't allow boyfriends on the premises, and any other employment a girl might have must be kept strictly separate. So I don't think I can help you. We run a tight ship here.'

'Let's hope so.' Frank looked beyond the lounge area to the bar, where three girls sat sipping soda water. 'Must be expensive making sure they're all kitted out for the punters, nice clothes, stockings, that sort of thing. You wouldn't have any side interests, would you?'

'I don't know what you mean.' Betty narrowed her eyes, meeting Frank's gaze.

'Not what I hear around the traps,' Frank said. 'Perhaps you'd think about making a further contribution to the Police Youth Club. We can also do with some goods for the second-hand clothing sale.' He heaved himself up and brushed an errant crumb from the front of his coat as he leaned down to retrieve the photo. 'Donations always gratefully accepted,' he said as he made for the door.

MONDAY 11 OCTOBER 1943

Chapter Fourteen

Joe slipped his tie into his shirt, grabbed his cap from the bedside table and reached for his boots. He carried them down and sat on the bottom step to lace them. He hadn't worn them inside since the naval officer in the flat below had threatened to beat him to a pulp if he woke him one more time after an all-night shift. The book that Rose had talked about lay at the bottom of his shoulder bag, scarcely opened. He hadn't got the hang of it at all last night. This morning he'd ignore the tram, happy to walk into the Valley for a pale, milky coffee. He wondered how long before he'd taste coffee as good as Rose's.

New Farm was Italian, Joe had learned. A redbrick Catholic cathedral squatted atop the hill overlooking a few straggling shops along Merthyr Road with one service on Sundays still in Italian, in spite of Mussolini. Everyone knew someone who'd disappeared, and the fish and chip shop near the Astor Cinema flew a Greek flag although the proprietor's name was Alfonso. Joe wondered how things would change now Italy had declared war on Germany.

Coffee at the café on Brunswick Street was served by a disgruntled man called Marco whose brother was interned in a forestry camp near Dalby. Marco owed his continuing business, or so he claimed, to the good officers of the police. He knew to keep quiet when they came for their complimentary breakfast of fried eggs and bacon.

'Here.' The liquid spilled into the saucer as it and the cup were slammed onto the counter.

'Grazie,' Joe said with a nod and moved to a table overlooking the street. In spite of his mother's best intentions it was the only Italian he'd ever picked up.

Mornings were the best time of day, before the sun got too high, the humidity rose in clouds from the bitumen and the pubs opened to lonely soldiers full of bravado. On the street, milkmen loped from trucks to front porches with small metal crates of bottles clinking. Workmen clung to the sides of trams, ogling slender girls giggling their way to work at the submarine base or the warehouses along the wharves. Soldiers who'd slept the night off in the back room of hotels woke to lean out the window, their wolf whistles only half-hearted so early in the day. The town slept heavily and woke slowly as befitted the subtropics. Laziness suited it, thought Joe. He lifted his camera to photograph the scene. A soft focus might work, the depth of field diffuse.

Gradually the road woke up. Cars honked at people queued at the tram stop in the middle of the road, army trucks pounded along Brunswick Street with cargoes of machinery, military aircraft from Eagle Farm roared overhead. Among it all, children on bicycles wove their way through the melee on their way to school and officers and civilian workers streamed toward naval headquarters near the Powerhouse.

Joe stood, paid for the coffee, and headed out to join the madness.

Down the street he dropped coins on top of a metal stand and selected a copy of *The Courier-Mail* from the top of the pile. Curtin threatening coalminers; American landings near Rabaul; a man at West End charged with holding over three hundred petrol coupons. Business as usual. Frank would keep a lid on the murder until he'd made an arrest. On past experience that'd be soon. Frank loved a win, the speed of the investigation more important than its thoroughness.

Joe boarded the tram in Ann Street, surprised to find an empty seat.

There it was. On page seven, admittedly, but something. A body. Fairfield Road. The cemetery. American. You could always count on Cliff Stanaway to pull things out from under the woodpile. Gossip said it got him into lots of trouble.

*

In the vestibule of the grand house Joe waited like a penitent schoolboy, cap in hand. Early morning light filtered through the stained-glass windows on either side of the main entrance. He recognised characters from Shakespeare — Rosalind and Viola. He wondered what Portia would have made of it all. The Japs were in New Guinea, their bombs fell on Darwin and Townsville, no one worried too much about the quality of mercy.

Base Station 3 controlled US Army operations in all of southern Queensland. American technicians in the signal corps sat at functional wooden desks on mosaic floors in the ballroom, monitoring radio traffic across the South West Pacific. SWPA, he remembered. SWPA, PLUM. The military loved acronyms. A clatter of cutlery and laughter came from the wood-panelled dining room, together with the smell of fried eggs and bacon.

'Enter,' came a voice more resonant than seemed natural. Joe walked into the office to the side of the vestibule and saluted.

Lieutenant Bates of the Quartermaster Corps was a squat man with a hairless skull rubbed smooth. No neck. No chin. His head sat in the neat collar like a hardboiled egg in an eggcup. Joe wondered whether, if he knocked the lieutenant's head smartly from the side, it would tilt and topple sideways. Bates's face was of someone who'd spent his life finding fault with others' misdeeds, his cheeks etched with deep ruts pointing toward pursed lips. The lieutenant knew every regulation in the *Army Ordinance Manual* by heart, his tedious longwinded reports — famous in their way — redolent with language he imagined made him seem erudite. 'In respect of', 'in due course', 'in relation to'. Oh, how the army loved its ritual humiliations, the formalised brutality, the idiocy of rank and status. So many had found their niche in life after years of being bullied by someone else — the manager at the dime store, the owner of the milk bar, the wife or the mother-in-law. Joe imagined Bates wearing an apron, serving customers who ignored his attempts at courtesy, who scarcely saw him. Seething in silent rage and waiting for his moment. It had come.

'At ease,' Bates said. Joe's mind had never been anything else.

'Lieutenant Colonel Braidwood has informed me that yesterday you made requests for notepaper and carbon paper, well beyond the usual allowance. You must be aware that supplies of paper are low, strictly rationed. The US Army has better things to do with its supply vessels than carry stationery across the globe.'

Braidwood. That name again.

'I'm afraid the Lieutenant Colonel is correct,' Joe said. 'But if we are to provide detailed reports as requested, then we are left with no alternative but to use considerable quantities of paper. Photographic supplies are also needed.'

'Any deviation from agreed supplies of *matériel* is quite irregular.' The lieutenant emphasised the foreign word. 'You require authorisation from your direct supervisor.'

Joe nodded. 'I will be happy to prepare a preliminary report outlining the provost marshal's requirements and discussing all possible contingencies.' He couldn't help himself.

'Indeed.'

Joe stood, saluted, then coughed. 'I fear the preparation of such a report might exhaust the last of our current allocation of stationery. I assume you are in a position to authorise the provision of limited additional supplies, given these exigencies?' He guessed Laurie would be amused by the toadying. And it wasn't as if he was doing anything wrong, just a bit of creative redistribution. No one was hurt, were they?

'Very well.' Bates pulled a requisition book toward himself and Joe watched as he printed neatly, mouthing the words silently.

'I take it the extra ammunition supplies are not at issue?' Joe asked. 'From what Monroe says we have run short of that as well.'

'Not at all,' the lieutenant said, signing the pink paper with a flourish. 'Ammunition supplies are well up to date. Though we have had no requests from the provost section in the last month.'

'Thank you,' Joe said pocketing the slip of paper. He saluted again and turned sharply, a toy soldier enjoying the game for once.

*

Down the slope Joe passed the holding cells at the back of the Town Hall. He looked in on Duke who sat on his bunk, picking his teeth with a split match, a dirty bandage tied around his left hand. Opposite, Bryson slept noisily. With a glance and a nod, Duke indicated he wanted a word.

Joe worried again about the child, the baby son, but if the grandmother refused any help there was little he could do. It made no sense to charge Duke, to send him home to face a prison sentence. A boy needed a father, Joe knew that as well as anyone. He'd had one for a time; a normal father, one who took him to the zoo and carried him on his back. But that hadn't lasted long. Too many late night meetings, too many arguments. Joe could never understand why his father had got involved in the first place. They were never going to win. Why beat your head against the brick wall of vested interests? The shame hit his mother the hardest, having to go to the grocers to beg for last week's vegetables.

'Got a match?' Duke pulled out a cigarette and leaned close to the bars.

'Sure,' Joe said, taking out his lighter and moving closer to light the cigarette.

They stood together, separated only by bars.

'Your court martial's tomorrow, isn't it?' Joe said.

'Yes.'

'I spoke with Sergeant McConachy. Is there anything I can do? For you? Or the boy?'

'No. He's just a baby, maybe best to leave it be. Polly's grandmother never took to me, tried to stop her going steady with me, even threatened to call the Children's Department. Not cause Pol's too young — I didn't rightly know how old she was — but cause I'm black. Maybe if I'm sent home it's best for everyone. Best be forgotten.' Duke's voice faltered, the lines in his face etched deeper.

'I can visit if you think it'd help,' Joe said.

'No. Might make things worse for Pol. I'd reckon to write her, though. But I don't know if she'd get it.'

'I could take a letter,' Joe said. 'I doubt the grandmother would stop a policeman delivering a letter.'

'I'd appreciate that,' Duke said, a brief smile lightening his face. He glanced over his shoulder to where Bryson slept, looked Joe directly in the eye and whispered, 'Maybe I can give you something in return. You should talk to that fat MP, the one who hauled me in from Darra. Ask him how he knows the man in the cell next door.'

'Teague?'

'Yeah,' Duke said. 'I heard them talking, the fat one offering to help him, threatening him if he didn't do as he said. I don't know for sure what it was about but something's going on.'

Joe nodded. 'Well, you write that letter and I'll see about getting it to the girl.'

*

Joe almost collided with Mrs Lakursky's mop at the top of the stairs. 'Morning ma'am,' he said, skirting her metal bucket. 'Heard from Danny lately?'

Mrs Lakursky's two passions in life were gardening and her grandson Danny, now stationed in New Guinea. Joe knew more than he cared to about the boy's childhood ailments and adolescent successes.

'Not for a few days,' she said. 'He's a good boy, he always writes.'

Mitchell stood beside his desk, flicking through the written report on Teague that Joe had finished late yesterday. 'Is this all?' he said. 'All the witness statements?'

'They're appended,' Joe said, saluting as he slid into his chair.

'I had a call half an hour ago. From the CIB.'

'Any news on the dead soldier?'

'I thought you were warned. We want no trouble from the local police. Leave it alone.'

'Yes, sir. Was there a complaint?'

'The man in charge of homicide. A clerical name — Abbot? Bishop? He was most forceful, I thought. Certainly has the investigation in hand and has no need of your interference. Wait for someone to be charged.'

'Sir,' Joe said. No point arguing.

'And what's this about?' Mitchell lifted a sheet of paper from the desk and waved it in front of Joe's face.

Joe swivelled his head, trying to read the text. Had Doyle been as good as his word and got the report done already? Damn his efficiency.

'Who authorised you to consult with the Australians? Duke's been charged. You will not, I repeat not, interfere with due process. And leave Monroe alone. You may not get on with him, no one really gets along with Monroe, but he does his job and you could learn to do the same if you don't want to discover the pleasures of Batchelor. Hot as hell, I hear, and the crocodiles can be a nuisance.' Mitchell took the report on Teague to his desk and sat to read it through. He crossed out two words on each page before handing it back.

'You'll need to retype this,' he said. 'Make sure it's done by the time I get back.'

Smug bastard.

Chapter Fifteen

Since moving from Adelaide eighteen months earlier, Rose had grown fond of her new home. The tiny flat in the small weatherboard house near Roma Street was a long way from the Victorian brick home she'd left behind, with its heavy furniture and embroidered curtains imbued with the scent of her grandmother's Cashmere Bouquet talcum powder. Adelaide heat could be fierce, but nothing like the moist blanket that descended over Brisbane, smearing mould on her leather shoes and the spines of James's books. Even the pine table in the kitchen was covered in a thin film of grey on the days she didn't make it home. Yet she preferred the sultry weather to the icy winter mornings in Adelaide when her grandmother held her face in soft hands, tracing her lost daughter's features and not hers. She'd escaped her past now, had made a life of her own.

She stepped from the front verandah, only a few feet to the ground, and looked back. The blood-red tin awnings, each with a stencilled moon, the impermanence of the fibro walls, the sloping ceiling that felt like a ship's cabin, the simple kitchen with a gas cooker, an ice chest she seldom used, and a cabinet with mottled glass and broken headlight.

All of it beautiful.

As she walked toward Roma Street, she waved through the next-door neighbour's window to a woman seated in front of papers strewn in messy piles on her kitchen table. With a baby of eighteen months, a husband in New Guinea and no family in Brisbane to help if she went to work, Jill McDonald spent every morning in her kitchen, the breakfast dishes drying on the sink, a pile of papers and a red pencil before her. Censoring letters. Hundreds of women across Brisbane did the same. A simple job the Americans paid well for.

A tram pulled up and she climbed aboard. As it rocked from side to side Rose remembered the train trip eighteen months earlier. Lured by James and his poetry, she'd boarded a train in Adelaide, arriving in Brisbane to share his flat for a glorious month. She'd spent their last night lying beside him, folded into his arms, listening to him talk fiercely of poetry and freedom. But all too soon he was gone, letters and parcels their only contact. He sent her pottery shards from the desert, trinkets bought at the souk in Beirut. As the war came closer she awaited his return. At the last minute his company was diverted to Java. And then nothing. Finally a note arrived, written on soggy paper smuggled out by a native, handed on to another soldier. He was alive but captured.

Even if she'd been allowed to leave there was nothing for her in Adelaide. Her grandmother gone, her mother lost years ago. No job or family. Brisbane had in the end become a home by default.

She alighted the tram at the corner of Queen and Albert streets and climbed the steps of the T&G Building. At ten o'clock on a Monday morning the place was a scene of controlled chaos, the clatter of typists interspersed with the shrill ring of the telephone and the racket of the teletype machine. Neat stacks of letters sat on desks ready to be shovelled into large canvas bags and dumped at the back of the room. In a few hours couriers would load them onto trucks for delivery around the suburbs, into homes like Jill's. Rose had heard Rifkin boast that nearly one million letters passed through this office every month. She wondered what stories they told.

Fourteen staff worked in the United States Armed Forces Far East offices, which was also the headquarters of the small CIC — officers of the Counter Intelligence Corps. Rose only knew the name of one of them, if indeed it was his name.

'Enter.' Major Rifkin was neat and clean. From the Brylcreemed top of his short dark hair to the well-polished boots, he shone. Sleek, like an eel. Rose watched his hand slither across the desk as he pulled a paper toward him. No, perhaps a snake.

'Sit.'

'No need. I have little enough to report and can work while standing.'

'So I gather.' Rifkin's tongue glided over his upper lip, leaving it glistening.

'I went to their meeting yesterday,' Rose said. 'Just a talk about art. The only subversion these surrealists achieve is of reality.'

'Paul Grano there? Any of those Australia First loons?'

'No.'

'Clem Christesen? The communist with the Russian wife?'

'No,' Rose said. 'I was there on Friday.'

'And?'

'If he's a communist, he's an unusual one. Poets and writers were there, sure, but they only ever talk literature and art, not action. More symbolism.'

'What of your clients? Anyone of interest?'

'None.'

'Negroes? Jews?'

'Only the sad or the angry, or both. It's the Nips they want to fight, or each other. Nothing to interest you.'

'Black-marketeers? Any more details on the thefts of gasoline? It's subversion. And costly.'

Rose guessed which he thought more serious. 'I don't have many contacts with taxi drivers,' she said. 'I imagine the ones who own cars have most to gain. I can ask around, see what I can find out. But now it's my turn. What news from Java? You must have reports on the camps? I know the Red Cross pass information.'

'The Japs are not exactly cooperative,' Rifkin said, leaning back in his chair to smile, a poor attempt at sleaze. 'But like you, I'll see what I can find out.'

'Good. *Quid pro quo.*' She enjoyed watching his confusion, happy to remind him of her education. 'There's another get-together tonight,' she said, turning away. 'I doubt there'll be anything to report.'

She would walk on to Laurie's first, it wasn't far. Nothing in this town was, although the winding river confused distances, making everything oddly separate. Like wavy, parallel lines that never met.

*

William Dawes had only one passion . . . and everything he did was aimed at indulging it. He loved the variety of bodies, sleek or voluptuous, smooth or angular. Each with its own delights, its own idiosyncrasies. Each needing the attention only he could give, the petting and preening, the kneading of leather, the waxing and polishing. Fine sandpaper on the chrome work, the best chamois for the chassis. Cars were his life.

Most days after Dawes left work, he took the tram home to Mrs Bushel's boarding house on Dornoch Terrace where he spent the evenings working on the cream coupe — a Buick Series 60 — that he'd saved so many years to buy but that always needed fixing. First it was the carburettor, then the gearbox. Not that he minded. She was a beautiful machine, precision engineered. He polished the bonnet with a special chamois, cleaned the spare wheel perched on the running board and blackened its rubber, timed and adjusted the pistons until the engine purred. Maintenance cost more than his weekly wage but the work he did for Mrs Bushel's brother Sam made up the difference. Sam had the licence of the Mountain View Hotel, but now that grog — like most everything it seemed — was rationed, it made more sense not to sell it all to locals for a paltry threepence a glass. Much more could be made if he delivered any extra stock to the Carver Club, where even black soldiers paid a premium for limited supplies. Once a week Dawes collected the extra bottles, making enough as a deliveryman to cover the cost of those little extras — the Champion cleaner for the red-trimmed upholstery. Zip wax to make the dashboard gleam.

Mrs Bushel wandered into the room in an aqua chenille dressing-gown, a cigarette hanging from her lower lip, her eyes bleary.

Dawes sat at the dining room table, his singlet loose across a hairless chest, his stubble a tapestry of greys and browns. He ran his hand down the Golden Casket results on the back page of *The Worker*, a grease-stained finger in place as he lifted his eyes briefly to appraise the rounded bosom that hung over the table as Mrs Bushel laid a plate, cup and saucer before him. The sight usually brought more joy than the runny, tasteless jam that accompanied the stale toast, burned at the edges.

'Here's your breakfast, love. Sugar's running low.'

'Ta.' He reached for the bowl.

'Have a nice time last night? Didn't hear you get back.'

'Had some jobs to do for Sam,' Dawes said.

It had taken most of yesterday afternoon and evening to ferry and unload the goods, but the Carver Club was reliable.

A knock on the door surprised them both.

Mrs Bushel peered through the lace curtains before stubbing out her cigarette on the windowsill and opening the door. She stood with arms folded across the opening of her dressing-gown. 'What can we do for you?' she said. 'Something wrong?'

The plain-clothes detective tipped the brim of his hat as he retrieved his identification from his top pocket. 'Sorry to disturb you, ma'am. Can I come in?'

Mrs Bushel indicated a chair at the table in the lounge room. 'Cuppa?'

'No, thanks. This won't take long. I wonder if you'd leave me to speak with Mr Dawes for a moment. Just a couple of questions.'

She scowled but retreated to the kitchen.

'How can I help?' Dawes stood, the better to look the detective in the eye. He noted the blunt nose and cauliflower ears.

'Do you own a cream-coloured car used for transport?'

'A Buick, sure. A five-seater. It's not a taxi, though. What's this about? Registration's up to date.'

'We're investigating reports of a car of similar colour involved in an incident on Friday night. Can you tell me where you were between nine o'clock and midnight?'

'Friday? At a friend's place.'

'Who?'

'Sam Bushel, the landlady's brother. He lives out toward Greenslopes.'

'Must be expensive running a car like that,' the detective said. 'Uses a lot of petrol, I imagine. Where do you work?'

'What's that got to do with anything?' Dawes reached for a packet of cigarettes on the table. 'Is this Leonard again? I've told him I won't drive for him.'

'Just answer the question.'

'I'm a mechanic at the Austral Motor Company in New Farm.'

The detective paced the room, inspecting the photos on the sideboard, fingering the china ornaments. 'Pretty fancy car, even for a mechanic.'

'I do the mechanical work myself. Anyone'll tell you I'm good with cars.'

'And the petrol? Got your coupons here? Got an extra supply somewhere?' The detective lifted the lid of a wooden box on the low table in the middle of the room and rummaged inside. Buttons. Of all colours. 'This Sam Bushel. He's not the licensee of the Mountain View, by any chance? Wouldn't have need of a deliveryman, would he? Bit of extra money to be made from our faithful allies to help pay for all that fancy leatherwork?' The detective paused to smile, a shark spotting prey. Small fish.

'Sam gives me coupons sometimes, when I run errands or take her shopping.' Dawes nodded toward the kitchen. 'Nothing illegal in that.'

'I hear you're close with the darkies. Maybe got a bit of a tar brush yourself. Where were you on Friday between nine o'clock and midnight?' The detective leaned so close Dawes could see the individual hairs of his stubble.

'I told you. At Greenslopes.' He lit the cigarette and threw the dead match into the ashtray.

The detective held out his hand. 'If you'll give me the keys we'll just take your car in for a check. I have a constable waiting outside drive it to headquarters. You'll be alright for a day or two. Get some exercise, use the tram. Of course, carrying crates of beer might be tricky. Or drums of petrol. Still. You'll manage.'

*

As Rose crossed George Street a dumpy girl weighed down by a large cardboard suitcase passed her, heading in the opposite direction. Why wasn't she at school, Rose wondered, before recognising her as the girl from the library. The one who skips school. Where does she go each day? The librarian seemed keen to report her to the truancy officer but she doubted he'd do anything about it. Maybe the library was this girl's refuge, too.

'Hello,' Rose said, matching the girl's stride. 'Haven't I seen you at the library?'

The girl stopped to face Rose. 'Maybe. I like books.'

'Me too,' Rose said, looking into a pair of startlingly honest eyes, the trusting eyes of a child. Well, not quite a child, she guessed, the drab school blouse was beginning to pull tight across her chest. She lifted the girl's chin. Reaching into her shoulder bag, she drew out a handkerchief. 'Here, what's that on your face? You're far too young to wear lipstick.'

'Leave me alone,' the girl said, wriggling in her arms. 'I can if I want.'

'What would your mother think?' Rose couldn't believe she was sounding so censorious. As if she wouldn't have done the same thing when she was the same age. A city full of soldiers, who could blame her?

'She wouldn't know, wouldn't care,' the girl said. Rose saw her chin quiver, felt her own chest constrict, remembering how much she'd wanted to love a mother who'd abandoned her, who she pictured only as a blurred image in her grand-mother's bedroom, framed in silver.

'Fancy a milkshake or something?' Rose asked. She had time before the meeting. Why not? 'We could go to the Astoria, if you like.'

The girl beamed, full of a child's excitement at the promise of special treats. Rose doubted she had many.

'What's your name?'

'Maureen,' the girl said, licking the corner of the proffered handkerchief to wipe the lipstick from her mouth.

'Let's go then, Maureen. We'll share an ice cream sundae.' Rose retrieved her blotched handkerchief and linked arms with the girl. Her cardboard suitcase banged against her legs as they continued along George Street. At the entrance to the café Maureen wrapped her arms around the port, cradling it in front of her as they climbed the stairs. The Astoria served coffee; weak and with a layer overheated milk that regularly formed a skin on top, but coffee it was nonetheless. Groups of patrons sat in alcoves, chatting quietly so their conversations formed a gentle hum above the rattle of the milk refriger-ator. Rose knew the place would be full of Americans and half-expected to see Laurie or Thea. It was a favourite haunt; sometimes they held *Barjai* meetings here. She led Maureen to an alcove and sat her on the opposite bench. She checked her own lipstick in the scalloped mirrors on the wall before lifting her arm to a passing waitress.

'What would you like, Maureen?'

'Ice cream?'

'Coffee and cake for me,' Rose told the waitress. 'Ice cream for my girlfriend.' She winked at Maureen, who giggled. As she leaned back against the wood, she stubbed her toe on the heavy suitcase. 'I thought you didn't like school.'

'I don't. It's a waste of time. I'd rather be reading.'

'So why are you carrying around such an enormous school bag?'

Maureen leaned forward, low over the polished table. 'I've found something,' she said. 'Treasure.'

'Have you now? Can I have a look?'

'Not here. Someone'll see us.'

'Well, what is it?'

'Treasure's not treasure if you tell,' Maureen said.

'Surely you can tell me.'

'Well, maybe,' Maureen whispered, looking furtive. Heavens, she would never make an actress, thought Rose. Too much melodrama. 'There's all sorts of things. I found them near the Tower Mill. There's a big underground place there. It's where they used to keep the convicts in solitary confinement. Some of them died there. It's pretty spooky now but empty. Someone's using it to store things. Boxes and boxes of things. And drums.'

'So you stole this treasure?' Rose pretended to be shocked.

'Well, it's already stolen, isn't it? Why shouldn't I? No one was there. I only had a quick look. But there's lots of lovely things. Lipsticks and petticoats, lacy underwear.' She blushed. 'I thought my mother might like some.'

Back to the mother, thought Rose. She knew the agony of trying to please.

Maureen's eyes widened as the waitress arrived with a tray. Beside the coffee and cake sat a silver dish. Ice cream, a huge scoop with chocolate dripping down its side and a bright triangular wafer set in the middle. All of it melting slowly in the heat.

'You'd better eat that quickly,' Rose said as she sipped her coffee and crumbled a piece of cake. 'Can you show me the treasure? Perhaps I could meet you there?'

'Maybe,' Maureen said. 'Not now. Maybe later.'

'Of course,' Rose said. She knew not to push. The girl would show her when she was ready. 'Will I see you at the library tomorrow? I have to go now, but I've paid for two more ice creams. You'll be alright here?'

Maureen nodded, her eyes not moving from her plate.

Chapter Sixteen

I t was a perk of the job, Joe thought as he parked the jeep, and one of the few pleasures he and Monroe shared. He had the army to thank for teaching him to drive. Even though his father had built hundreds of vehicles, they'd never owned one, and by the time Joe was old enough to learn, his father had all but disappeared into the angry fog that had descended after the march. An uncle had tried to teach Joe, once, but there were so few opportunities to borrow a car that he'd given up learning to drive one at all. Now he was able to travel as far as investigations took him — once he'd gone up to Gympie to check on the assault of an elderly woman. Another time he'd driven down the coast, checking on soldiers gone AWL. At Lismore he'd had to placate locals who feared a moral decline with the arrival of soldiers on leave.

He'd finished retyping the report on Teague when the morgue rang to say Foster's body was ready to be released. As he entered for the second time in three days, he noticed that the smell of blood was now overlaid with the antiseptic scent of soapy water.

Seated at his desk and sucking a mint, the major reeked of aftershave. 'You didn't have to come in person although I appreciate your interest,' he said, indicating a chair opposite. 'We've been in touch with Brisbane General and the body will be transferred to the police pathologist tomorrow.'

Laid out on the table in front of him were photos of Foster's naked body. Joe swivelled one towards him. When he'd seen Foster on the mortuary slab on Saturday he thought it empty of life, the living planes flattened, with little resemblance to the man he might have seen at the Trocadero. But this photo — lit by bright lights, the shadows creating curves — brought the body to life.

'I know you'll prepare a report, but I'd like to hear your impressions,' Joe said. 'Unofficially.'

The major twisted a cigarette into a holder and slid three sheets of paper across the desk. 'I've prepared preliminary findings. The cause of death was haemorrhaging from the stab wound. The blow was fierce, forceful. The blade of the knife penetrated the cartilage to the left of the sternum, exactly at the spot to sever the right auricle of the heart and pierce the right lung. Ferocity and luck, that's what killed your soldier.'

'A right- or left-handed blow?'

'Definitely right-handed, the angle of entry is clear.'

'Any idea what type of knife?' Most Americans carried double-sided flick-knives. Joe had seen so many he'd become an expert.

'Anything with a blade about six inches long. Just a simple kitchen knife would do. Single-sided, nothing complicated. The wound was oblique but the outer margin is rough and red, suggesting considerable pressure. A fair degree of force would have been needed, he was a tall and fit man even if addled with drink. But a single knife wound rarely kills. In this case, either the knife thrust was exceptionally well aimed — not many people know how to locate the heart — or it was just luck.'

'Which do you think?'

'No idea. That's your job.'

'Could a woman do it?' Joe said.

'Depends. He was stabbed from below, so if Foster was standing at the time, the assailant must have been shorter. Foster's over six feet tall. A woman could do it if she was strong enough. Foster would have been dead before he hit the ground.'

'Any sign of a struggle?'

'There are a few other wounds, but nothing serious. Abrasions to the left side of the forehead, another cut on the left thigh, a slight wound on the right lower lip. I'd guess there was a fight, the cuts and abrasions look like there was a scuffle. But it was the knife to the heart that killed him.' The major leaned back and sucked on the cigarette holder. 'There was an older wound, to the under surface of the frontal lobes. Quite interesting. Do we know if he was a neuro-psych patient?'

Joe ignored the question. 'How drunk was he?'

'Blood alcohol 0.17 per cent. Drunk but not paralytic. He knew what he was doing.'

Joe thought back to the scene, the thin smear of crimson across the body like a bandolier from hip to shoulder. 'Why so little blood at the site? Had he been moved?'

'The internal haemorrhage was massive,' the major said. 'He would've lost three to four quarts fast, most of it into the body cavity. There would have been blood, but not a lot. The murderer wouldn't be covered in it, if that's what you're hoping.'

'Did he die where he fell?' Hadn't the old man said he heard something being dumped?

'Dependent lividity on the back and right side of the face is consistent with the way the body was found, but it's no proof he was killed there.'

'Thanks. You'll send a full report, will you?' Joe stood and glanced past the major's desk, his eyes drawn to the metal trolley, the buckets and mops, the jars lining the bench. 'What happened to his effects, by the way?'

'They're all here,' the major said, pointing to a cardboard box. 'They'll be returned to his unit. His family will get them in due course.'

'Why don't I drop them to the hospital now?' Joe said. 'It's on my way.'

*

Joe placed the cardboard box on the seat beside him and lifted the flap to check the contents. So this was all that remained of a life. At the bottom were Foster's boots; army regulation, muddied and scuffed. The sole of the right boot was worn down on the outside, so he'd walked with a roll. An injury perhaps? Foster's trousers and bloody shirt were folded into a neat pile. His dog tag lay on top, together with his wallet and a coin purse. Joe flipped the wallet open and looked again at the woman and small boy. Inside were a few dollar notes, two five-pound notes and his hospital pass. He put these to one side, withdrew the clothing and looked carefully at the ripped pocket, the blood, the smear of lipstick on the collar. Would it be possible to match the colour and brand? He must ask Baty about it.

He slipped the jeep into gear.

At the hospital entrance the same MP waved him through. Joe found his own way to the registrar's office and knocked. 'I've brought Sergeant Foster's personal effects,' he said. 'Can you deal with these?' He placed the box on the edge of the desk.

The lieutenant looked up. 'Anything more? Was it murder?'

'Looks like it. I've just come from the morgue. A single knife wound to the heart killed him, although there were also cuts to his head and leg. Lipstick on his collar.'

'Sounds like a song,' the lieutenant said with a smile. 'I must say paediatrics in North Carolina scarcely prepared me for all this. My only experience of trauma medicine was watching Hollywood movies and reading Upton Sinclair. But you learn on the job.'

'We all do,' Joe said. 'I need to check on a few things. Okay if I look around?'

'Help yourself,' the lieutenant waved him off, his head returning to a mound of paperwork.

Joe wandered alone in the direction they'd followed a day ago. The hospital had only occupied this site for six months but if you ignored the temporary appearance of the prefabricated buildings you could be forgiven for thinking it had been here much longer. Flowerbeds lined the pathways, a triangular garden bed rimmed with white stones outside the mess hall, petunias in neat circular gardens beside the neuro-psych ward. What was this impulse that impelled men to make a mark, to leave a record of their occupation, however transient? Nearly one thousand patients and countless staff had occupied the site for only a short time but their imprint was everywhere.

He passed a ward and the smell of antiseptic reminded him of the time he broke the bone in his right hand. Mr Mailer at the police club had told him to strap his hands. 'A boxer needs to look after his hands, Joey,' he'd said. 'They're your tools, remember. You gotta treat them with respect.' But at twelve years old Joe thought he knew it all, was used to making his own decisions. He'd learned the hard way. The doctor had wrapped his fist in heavy white plaster, set so he could still hold a pencil in class, and the class had laughed when they saw it.

Directed to the callisthenics area, he spoke now to the officer in charge and led Corporal Jones to a bench seat. He knew it'd be easier to talk sitting side by side than face to face.

'Feeling better today?' Joe asked, pulling the pack of cigarettes from his top pocket.

'Shouldn't,' Jones said, his shoulders hunched. 'Been told it's bad for the lungs. Good for the nerves, though. Thanks.'

'Thought any more about Friday night? Want to tell me what happened?'

'I keep thinking about Slim,' Jones said. He sucked on the cigarette, his left hand cupping the smoke. 'Not that he was a pal, really, we only met a couple of weeks ago in the ward. But he knew his way around the place, more than me. I've only been on day pass once before and didn't go further than the café up the road. Slim knew people, he knew where to go.'

'Where was that?'

'I told you already.'

'Were you with him all night?' Joe said.

'Like I said, I didn't go to the dance hall. I don't like crowds.'

'Is that all?'

'He met someone at the hotel, I think, went upstairs for a while.'

'Who, do you know?'

'No. I was talking to the barmaid, I didn't notice.'

'Tell me about the girl at Leonard's, the one you were with that night. Alma?'

'She was nice,' Jones said. 'She made us toast and eggs, she talked to us. Slim wanted to listen to music and she put on some records while we drank. I don't remember much of it.'

'What did she look like?'

'I was too drunk to notice much. Little she was, a waist you could circle with both hands real easy. And long legs.' For the first time since they'd sat down Jones smiled.

'Tall or short? Blonde? Brunette?'

'She was sitting down when we arrived, and then we were around the table, or in bed. She danced with Slim a while, only came up to his shoulder. She had a laugh, I remember, a high, peeling sort of laugh like a bell ringing.'

Joe remembered the dark-haired woman leaning into the tall man at the Trocadero that night, tucked under his arm. He replayed the walk with Rose to the library, how close the top of her head was to his eyes, the lemon scent of her blonde hair, the way she threw back her head as she laughed.

'Was there only one girl? For both of you?' He hoped he hid his disgust.

'Yes,' Jones said, dropping his head to look at the ground between his feet. 'We took turns.'

'Where was Leonard all this time? What about the other taxi driver, the one who took you there?'

'He left. Leonard went to get more gin.'

'So what happened to make you run?' Joe put his hand on Jones's leg, hoping to still it.

'When Leonard came back he wanted money but Slim wouldn't hand it over and they ended up fighting, rolling around the room bashing each other around the head. The girl got into it too.'

'Did Slim have a knife? Leonard?' he said, trying to keep the man's attention from wandering.

'Just fists and boots was all I saw. They shouted and screamed. I don't like noise.'

'How did you get back here? You said you don't know Brisbane.'

'I found one of those tramlines, just followed it for a while till I saw I was near the river, asked some soldiers and they put me on a tram.'

'Any names?'

'No.'

Joe turned to face Jones. 'Why should I believe any of this? How do I know you're not lying? Soldiers fight with knives all the time, why not you?'

Jones dropped the cigarette stub from his left hand and withdrew his other from the trouser pocket where, Joe now realised, it had been all along. Jones shoved his right hand into Joe's face. 'See.'

Why hadn't he noticed before? The skin of the man's hand was red, the patterns of scar tissue still raw, the fingers twisted into unnatural angles, the tips bent sideways, crushed and torn.

'Tambu, above Salamaua. Heard of it? A hand grenade backfired. It was a week before I got evacuated. I can't even feed myself properly.' Jones's shoulders were no longer hunched, the jiggling leg stopped. 'My war's over.'

*

The Mountain View Hotel served dinner meals to off-duty soldiers and civilian workers attached to the hospital from midday and Joe decided to join them. Men lined the bar, leaning on soggy strips of towelling while they flicked ash into the metal gutter at their feet. Sour beer smells mingled with the cigarette smoke. Joe ordered a drink — a pony, he'd heard the old men call the tiny glass of yellow liquid that landed with a thud on the counter in front of him.

Opposite, a small lizard-skinned man placed a similar glass down, took a leather pouch from his pocket and cradled paper and tobacco in adept fingers the colour of mustard. A tongue dripped spittle as he sealed the thin cigarette. 'Yanks,' he murmured, pinching the loose strings of tobacco. He hacked into the gutter beneath his feet.

Joe moved to a vacant table in the corner. With his back to the wall he looked around. A few soldiers looked in his direction, nudged each other and roared with laughter. A civilian in another corner table scanned the paper and Joe checked the headlines. 'The Red Army Has the Upper Hand', 'Ramu River Advance Maintained', 'Japs Give Up Two Solomon Islands'.

He waited, his beer going warm.

A skinny man with a freckled, leathery face walked through the door and made for a group of soldiers at the bar. The man in the overcoat, Joe realised, the one he'd seen outside the Royal. The barmaid pushed a small beer toward him but her expression wasn't welcoming. He slid along to get closer to the Americans. Out came a pack of cigarettes to share, an odd gesture given how cheap they were at the PX. The group leaned close, Joe saw two soldiers pass notes with a nod and a wink, but he couldn't make out any words. Soon the soldiers downed their drinks, whatever negotiations they'd made completed quickly. They followed the thin man to the door.

Joe stood up to order another beer. 'Another of these, ma'am,' he said, then nodded toward the door. 'Are they regulars?'

'What's it to you?' she said, placing his beer on the mat. She leaned against the bar, arms folded across an ample bosom. She'd seen it all before, heard the same stories.

Joe removed a card from his shirt pocket and held it for her to read. 'I'm looking into an incident on Friday. Was that man, the skinny one, here?'

'He's here all the time,' she said. 'Picks up soldiers in his cab, makes a quid driving them around town. No crime in that.'

Surprised by her antagonism, Joe lowered himself onto the stool. 'None at all,' he said, pushing his open pack of cigarettes toward her. 'I'm just checking who might have been here. Were you working Friday?'

'I'm always here. The Manpower never gives us a break.'

'Do you remember seeing two American soldiers? Patients from the hospital down the road, a tall one with a moustache and a shorter, fair one? They would have come in around about this time. I'm just wondering about their movements.'

'Why?'

'Because one of them died.'

'Good heavens. How?'

'Did they happen to go into town with the man who just left?'

'Yes,' she said, finally succumbing. She slipped a cigarette from the pack, reached across and took the lighter from his shirt pocket.

'What's his name? The taxi driver.'

'Eddie,' she said. 'Eddie Ball. He's a grubby little man but harmless. Into whatever the latest racket is but wouldn't harm a fly. Mind you, he'd fuck a flea if he thought there was a profit in it.' Her bosom shook as she laughed.

Behind the bar Joe noticed steps leading up to what he assumed were rooms for rent. Wire beds with thin mattresses and dirty sheets pushed up against each other to make space for extra tenants.

A tall man leaned through the doorway, a grease rag hanging from his back pocket. 'Sam around? I had to borrow a truck.'

Joe recognised the deliveryman he'd seen at the Carver Club. Small town.

Chapter Seventeen

In the lounge room of the Collinsons' flat, perched on the cliff above Kangaroo Point, Debussy's *Clair de Lune* drifted languidly from the record player. Mingling with smoke, the sound travelled to the bedroom where Rose had flung her sandals off and kneeled, drawing on a cigarette the way she imagined Katharine Hepburn would. Laurie Collinson sat in a cane chair with a book of Blake's poetry — open but unread — on his lap. On the floor below him Barrie Reid lay sprawled before a plate of biscuits. The carpet was strewn with coffee cups, papers and books.

'Will it ever stop!' Thea Astley rushed through the open door, threw her heavy briefcase down and propped herself on the bed beside Rose. 'Days at school and nights at university. Honestly, I love it all — the children are amusing, I adore the study — but it's wearing me down. It gives me wonderful ideas for stories but never enough time to write. Have you got tickets for the show?' She looked down at Barrie. 'I can't believe Eugene Ormandy's coming to Brisbane. Artie Shaw, John Wayne and now this. Sometimes I think it's heaven being at war. At least it's put us on the map.'

Rose stared at her hands.

'Oh,' Thea said, one hand to her mouth, the other touching Rose's shoulder. 'Of course I don't mean that. How thoughtless.'

'I know,' Rose said. 'You're right. We do live in exciting times.'

'Not yet,' Barrie answered Thea. 'I'm working on it. Some of the others have to be at the school's army training camp, but with luck they'll get leave and we can all get tickets.'

Laurie lifted a pile of paper, weighting it in purple-stained hands. 'Here, I've got the copies. Dad's duplicator's done a good job I think, and Mr Astley ran his eyes over to check for mistakes.' He smiled at Thea. 'It's definitely an improvement on anything State High could do.' He passed around the thin paper covered in closely typed text, a dozen or so pages stapled together. The front page featured a line drawing of a tree with no leaves, a road, and the words *Barjai* spelled out in winding letters along the track leading, Rose presumed, to the future.

Barrie flicked through the pages, smiling when he found the reproduction of his poem. 'It looks terrific,' he said. 'Have you sent Clem his copy yet? What does he think?'

'I'll give him a copy later tonight. But we're on our way, even without Clem. Our third edition. I'm not sure any of us thought we'd get this far with it. I'm pleased we agreed on the words of our statement,' Laurie intoned. '"We who are growing to maturity in war must not likewise refuse our challenge. This time is crisis. Either we can allow our world to go from crisis to chaos, or we can struggle to achieve a new world and regain for it a new moral sense."'

Rose smiled at the pompous words. Laurie was so serious and even though she agreed with the sentiments, for now she just wanted to live a little. She'd read articles on swing music before the New Australian voices of poetry.

'I'll send a copy to Jimmy, too,' Laurie said. 'He loaned me his copies of *Ulysses* and *Tropic of Capricorn* to share around. But you have to promise to keep them hidden. Next edition I'll write something on Havelock Ellis. Damn silly Waddle and his prudes, if we can't talk about sex sensibly there's no hope for any change.'

Thea said nothing but Rose knew her Catholic parents would agree with the school's headmaster. Her world was one of bourgeois conformity, no matter how hard she tried to escape it.

Laurie unfolded himself from the chair to lead Barrie in the direction of Debussy. 'Come and help get the rest of the copies, will you? And I think I may have come across another source of paper.'

Thea turned to Rose. 'Were you at Clem's on Friday?'

'Yes, although I always feel like a fish out of water. So many clever people trying to impress each other.'

'And Judith Wright? Did you meet her?'

'She was lovely, if a bit intimidating at first. I hope she'll read some of her poetry at our next meeting, although oh dear, what a voice. Someone said she's going deaf so she can't hear herself properly.'

'I was too busy marking earlier but I thought we might have seen you after, at the café,' Thea said. 'We waited until eleven o'clock, in case you turned up.'

'No. I had things to do. A pity.' She looked out the window, following the meandering river, the crowded wharves strung out under the Story Bridge. Grey naval vessels jostled for position while long queues of wharfies unloaded rough canvas and calico bags, wooden crates and metal drums. Working round the clock these days. MacArthur had beaten Trades Hall, after all.

*

Across Queen Victoria's broad shoulders the State Government's sandstone executive building faced its mirror image, the Treasury. While the buildings oversaw the political and financial interests of the state, the building that lurked in the corner of the park, the church turned CIB Headquarters, constituted a small but essential component of the arrangement.

The main Police Headquarters and lockup were further up the hill past the Town Hall but Frank dismissed it all — the Commissioner and his minions, the paper pushers and penny pinchers. All just part of history, like the Tower Mill itself, a structure used for an earlier, more barbaric, form of policing. Frank had no time for the past. He was content to make the most of the present and prepare for a future when Brisbane would return to its more familiar torpor. He'd be ready. This was where things happened. Here, at the centre of power. Just an easy stroll across the square, a bit of gossip over a lunchtime sandwich.

Frank watched Ned Hanlon, Deputy Premier, former Minister for Health and Home Affairs, settle into the chair opposite and withdraw a cigarette from the packet in his coat pocket. Hanlon was older than Frank by some seventeen years, a railwayman and Labor man, although Frank didn't hold it against him. They'd both delivered milk as schoolboys and in that, if little else, they had a point of contact.

'How's the wife?' Hanlon said with a smile.

'Fine,' Frank said. 'Still deaf as a post. We've been busy lately, not much time at home. Stanaway seemed impressed the other night. Might be able to keep his articles in check.'

Hanlon leaned over to lay a copy of this morning's *Courier-Mail* across Frank's desk. He turned it so the headlines were clear. 'The Case of the Body in the Cemetery,' it began.

'How in God's name? Bloody Stanaway must have heard something on the police radio. Damn. We planned to keep a lid on things until we have an arrest, which will be soon, I expect. Most of these deaths are from drunken brawls. I doubt this one'll be any different. Booze and sex almost every time.'

'I expect you to deal with this quickly.' Hanlon crossed his legs as he leaned back in the chair. 'We've got enough problems with brawls and rapes, out-of-control soldiers fighting each other or the military police. Parents afraid for their daughters. Any unsolved murder just adds to public anxiety, and the sex angle's a problem if the papers get hold of it. We've done a fair job of keeping things under control to date. There are health issues, of course. Alright to tolerate a few brothels but we need to put the abortionists out of business. Too many young girls have got a taste for the high life, they don't always reckon with the consequences. We've got to keep on top of this.'

'Should be quick sorting this one out,' Frank said. 'Although it sticks in my craw that we never get a conviction ourselves.'

'It's what's agreed. Can't be changed.' Hanlon stood. 'But I'll be glad when the war's over. Too many complaints — the bloody Yanks, the bloody petrol rationing, the bloody this and the bloody that. Anybody'd think the government had nothing better to do than deal with people's complaints!' He turned at the door. 'Quickly. We want this dealt with quickly.'

'You can rely on me,' Frank said. 'I'll see to it.'

The Big Fella was onto it.

*

At four o'clock Frank eased himself out of the car, collected his hat and coat from the back seat, and made for the entrance to the Terminus Hotel. With only limited racing at Albion Park, the SP bookies had to work that much harder, and Frank knew that Eddie would already have set up a table for the midday crowd in the back bar. The form guide and betting odds would be propped up on the counter, ready to be whipped away in the unlikely event that a conscientious policeman entered. Not likely. SP booking was the least of Frank's worries. No one got hurt and it was a nice little earner for men whose wives had to pay black-market prices for extra butter, or for those who liked to keep a bit on the side for themselves. Eddie knew the score and made no move to clean up the betting receipts and loose change as Frank pushed open the door. A dozen men clutching newspapers and pencils didn't bother to look up. Frank knew his horseflesh.

'A word?' Frank indicated a door at the side of the lounge bar.

Eddie stood waiting as Frank moved to a leather armchair in the adjoining room. He liked to place his bets in private, away from prying eyes. The men in the bar all knew what was being transacted but the fiction remained.

'Pretty Lady's looking good for the quarter-mile,' Eddie said. 'Not a lot of punters know her form, the odds are good.'

'What do you do for Leonard?' Frank crossed his legs and placed his neatened cuffs on his lap.

'Leonard? Been mates for a few years now. Do a bit of driving for him when the farm's not busy. Now there's only a couple of races a week there's not so much to do here.' He looked at the framed photos of racehorses that decorated the private bar. The publican had owned nags for years.

'The Yanks from the Mountain View,' Frank said. 'What happened?'

'When? I'm always collecting Yanks from that hotel, a never-ending stream of patients from the hospital. All of them wanting a good time. Can't be all that sick, is what I think.'

'Friday night. Two Yanks. A tall, thin streak and a short, fair one.'

'Yeah. Dropped them in the city and picked them up over the south side later that night. Spent too much time hanging around waiting while they drank. Why?'

'Did you take them to the San Toy?'

'No.'

'Leonard's?'

'In the end. Don't know where they went for a few hours but finally I got them to Leonard's, he's got a girl works for him on the side, if you know what I mean. Easier than queueing at the San Toy.'

'What girl?' Frank said.

'Never met her, Leonard's a bit possessive that way.'

So it could be Alma. Or maybe Rose. That would be useful.

'Did you take them back to the hospital?' Frank said.

'No. Had to get back to the farm or I'd never get up in time for the milking. Leonard said he'd take care of them.'

'Was there any trouble?'

'No more than any other drunks,' Eddie said, his finger finding a hard and loose piece of snot. 'They were both pretty far gone by the time I left Leonard's. Don't know how they managed to get it up at all.'

Grubby little man, Frank thought as he headed for the door.

*

Frank pulled up a chair at the small rectangular table in Leonard's kitchen, the sink full of dishes resting in soapy water, the smell of burned toast mingling with stale tobacco. He watched Leonard pick at the metal strip around the table that held the green-flecked laminex in place and gnaw at a loose cuticle. A sordid type, but a survivor. A reject from the slums of East London, he'd been transported as a child to the sunnier but no less squalid inner-city suburbs of Depression Brisbane, where he'd learned never to lose a fight. With a combination of mathematical genius and native cunning, his SP stand at the Albion Hotel became the haunt of punters from all over the northern suburbs. He gave better odds than most and kept the boys in blue happy.

Frank poured beer into a glass and placed the large brown bottle on the table. He leaned back as he sipped, a white line of foam lingering on his upper lip. Opposite, Leonard sucked at his fingers and fidgeted with the bottle opener. Against the side wall, the old woman Deidre lay motionless on the bed, the slow rise and fall of the crocheted blanket the only sign of life.

'So,' Frank said. 'Alma's gone?'

'Did a flit,' Leonard said. 'No one knows where.'

'I tried to help you. But there's a limit to my reach, you know. Can't be everywhere. So what now?'

'Dunno. Can't you pin it on the other bloke?'

'And hand it back to the Yanks?'

'Why not? Saves time.'

Their arrangement had progressed with the arrival of the Yanks. Leonard knew who was doping the horses and where the watered-down liquor could be bought. If you needed to move around town he ran a discreet taxi service. Girls were a complicated business — more trouble than horses but lucrative if kept under control. Bootleg liquor even more so. Leonard was Frank's eyes and ears. But it didn't make him likeable.

'What are we going to do?' Leonard said.

'I thought we had an agreement.'

'Yeah, well so did I.'

'No sidelines. Just stick to business.'

'Can't help if the girl goes off on her own,' Leonard said.

'You sure that's what happened? Doesn't sound all that likely. Sure you're not running her on the side?'

'What if I was? You don't want to lose my services, do you?' Leonard's voice held a threat.

Frank leaned across the table, grabbed Leonard by the shirtfront and reeled him in. 'Where's the girl now? Or was it Rose? Did she do the Yank? Which one? I can ignore a lot of things but murder's not so easy to sweep under the carpet. The Minister wants answers.'

Leonard shook himself as Frank flung him backwards.

'I don't need the details,' Frank said. 'Just how you plan to get out of this.'

'He was a problem,' Leonard said. 'Delivered the goods alright but too quick to spend the proceeds, probably skimmed a bit off the top as well. And he turned nasty. Fought with the girl, fought with me. Only just managed to get him to leave by agreeing to take him and his spineless friend back to the hospital. Can't help what happened to him once we dropped him off.'

'What about Jones?'

'He was drunk, what would he know.'

'Why should I believe you? You'd better find this girl, get her to corroborate your version. Where is she?'

'Gone. Like I said. She ran, don't know where.'

'And Rose?'

'The two of them are thick as thieves,' Leonard said.

'You'd better find her and bring her in,' Frank said, 'if you don't want to wear this yourself. I can only do so much. One way or another I need this sorted.'

'When's my taxi coming back? I've got a business to run and can't do that without a vehicle.'

'In due course,' Frank said. He lifted himself off the chair, buttoned his vest and pulled at the sleeves of his coat. 'Stay where you are Leonard.'

As he moved to the door Deidre jerked upright. The blanket fell away, exposing her bony shoulders as they shuddered, her body doubled over.

Frank turned back to the kitchen, where he found a clean glass in the overhead cupboard and filled it under the tap. He crouched beside the bed, lifting Deidre's head up as he put the glass to her lips. 'Here, Deidre. Have a drink. It'll help.'

She held the glass as he lifted it, her crippled fingers raking his hand. 'Thanks, Frank,' she wheezed. 'I know I can count on you. I always could.'

'Why don't you tell me what really happened that night?' Frank said. 'So we can work from there.'

Chapter Eighteen

At five o'clock on Monday afternoon Joe mounted the stairs of the house in Rawnsley Street, Dutton Park. Separately, both Laurie and Rose had invited him, but he felt awkward as he wiped his shoes on the coil mat, set down the suitcase, and removed his cap. Self-conscious, an impostor, and late.

'Sergeant Joseph Washington,' he said to the man who opened the door. Early thirties, moustache and glasses. 'I hope I'm not too late.'

'Welcome. Laurie said you might turn up. Delighted you could make it. Come, come.' Clem Christesen's handshake was welcoming although the expression on his face was reserved. 'Let me introduce you to everyone. Did you bring any of your writing? We like to share new work whenever possible.'

'I'm not a writer, I'm afraid. More of an interested bystander. I like photography.' Joe shook his head apologetically as he drew a bunch of flowers — roses and carnations — from under the brim of the cap he held in front of him. 'For Mrs Christesen.'

'Thank you. Please, come and meet everyone,' Clem said.

Leaving the case at the door, Joe stepped onto the polished yellow boards, his footsteps echoing as he followed Clem down the long hallway toward the back of the house. The route was an obstacle course. He skirted piles of books and magazines, ducked under the reaching hands of a philodendron in a colourful pot balanced on a wooden plinth. At the rear of the house he entered a room like a ship's cabin, the ceiling sloping toward windows at the rear and an enclosed porch like the one at Rose's apartment.

Joe passed the bunch of flowers to a woman he took to be Clem's wife, Nina.

'How kind,' she said. 'You Americans are all so considerate. And roses. Such a luxury.' She reached for a large pottery jar streaked with blues and greens, filled it with water from the tap and artfully arranged the flowers.

Clem beckoned Joe, encouraging him to join the conversation. An elderly man with a clipped white beard stooped over the back of a chair to chat with a woman in a flowered shawl. A gangly youth with ginger hair, his face sprinkled with freckles, sipped wine from a long-necked glass while he eyed a plate of cheese and crackers. Joe recognised some of them from the Lyceum Club. Clem made a round of introductions. Joe remembered Thea, nodded at Laurie.

'I didn't forgotten my promise,' Joe said when he got Laurie's attention. 'I'll show you.' Laurie followed Joe back down the hallway. At the front door Joe pointed to the cardboard suitcase. Laurie lifted it up and clicked open the latch.

'I really didn't think you'd remember,' Laurie said. 'This is tremendous. Is it alright? I don't want you to get into any trouble.'

'That should last a few editions,' Joe said. 'It's fine. Leave it now, let's go back inside. Just take the case when you go. No need to tell anyone.'

They sidled back, separating as they rejoined the guests. Joe collected a cup of tea from the table and slipped a pieroski into his mouth. Almost as good as Aunt Sophia's.

At the edge of the group he watched a woman with wavy brown hair parted down the middle, her clothing grey, the expression behind the glasses inward looking, reserved. Around his age, he guessed, but with an older demeanour. She sat still. Alert, it seemed, as much to the discussion between Clem and Laurie as to the butcherbird that had established itself within sight of the refrigerator door. It warbled insistently. A smile lit the woman's face as Joe moved to join her.

They shook hands. He was surprised at the gentle confidence of the handshake. She'd done more than hold a pen, he thought, reminded of his cousin Amy whose horsemanship was legendary in the family and whose handshake felt of leather and authority.

'Joe Washington. American, as no doubt you can hear,' he said.

'Judith Wright,' she said. 'My hearing's not my best attribute so thank you. I'm new to these circles, too.'

'You're not from here?'

'No. I've come up from the south to help Clem with the magazine. And for summers that are blue not grey.'

Joe couldn't imagine summers in Australia were ever grey, but then he'd seen so little of the country.

As Nina passed them, she held out the plate of pieroski. 'You seem to know what these are,' she said. 'Have some more.'

Joe raised his cup in a toast. 'They're perfect.'

Judith lifted one to her mouth to taste. 'I haven't eaten one of these for years. Not since I was in Hungary in '37. Delicious.'

'You were in Eastern Europe?'

'Mmm,' Judith said, her mouth full.

'My father's Polish, although he left a long time ago.'

'Does he still have family there?'

'Yes. We haven't heard anything for a long time. Could you see it all beginning?'

'Oh yes,' Judith said. 'I went travelling with a university friend — to Holland and Germany, Austria. All that sausage.' She laughed only briefly. 'And the fear. Etched in the faces of ordinary people on the street, worried mothers scolding their children, uncertain for the future. I keep thinking of the people we met that summer, where are they all now?'

She looked beyond the window to where the butcherbird sat on the windowsill, clacking its beak from side to side. The sombre mood silenced them both.

'Do you write?' she asked, smiling as she turned back to the room, the moment of reflection gone.

'No,' Joe said. 'I'm no good with words. I like watching people, it's the way I understand them. Perhaps I'll become a photographer one day, try to tell stories through pictures. I like the simplicity of photos.' But even as he said this he knew it was wrong. Hadn't Nancy said all along how photos could lie and distort? Wasn't it what he found so unsatisfactory about the photos he took at work — it was what they didn't show that was most interesting. He remembered what the speaker had said about Man Ray. Sometimes he thought you really only saw photos when you closed your eyes or looked away.

'I can't just look at things from the outside,' Judith said. 'We writers are far too emotional for that. I almost envy your detachment. We need to dig inside everything, like a surgeon or an archaeologist. Mucking about in the dirt, up to our arms in entrails. That's writers for you.' Again she laughed. 'Especially now, in these fearsome years. There are so many stories, so much happening, so many deaths — millions of crucifixions lining the road to whatever future we have. I can't stay aloof in a solitary tower now.'

Joe fiddled with his watchband, looking toward the door. Where was Rose? Would she turn up? He'd like to question her in front of others, see if her story changed.

'Forgive me,' Judith said. 'I didn't mean to criticise. I'm talking too much.' She made to get up, but he placed a hand on hers.

'No,' Joe said, his hand returned to his lap. 'Not at all. You're right of course. But I like things neat and tidy. It's my job to sort things out, to put things into place, to work out how things fit. I like photos for their simplicity, but I know they can be a deceit. Life's so messy sometimes.'

'What is it you do?'

'I'm with the military police,' Joe said, adding quickly, 'the investigative unit. There are surely no end of stories there, ma'am, but it would take more skill than I can muster to tell them. Often sad, sometimes funny, mostly banal.'

'Life often is. Who are you waiting for?'

'Rose McAlister said she might be here. Perhaps she's late.'

'She usually is,' Judith said in a tone of voice Joe found difficult to read. 'A butterfly, that one, not a moth. Jack finds her amusing and I imagine she is, but I have hardly exchanged a word. It's sad about James. It's so much worse not to know. Time stands still. Oh, here's Jack.'

Joe turned to see a much older man, his short grey beard forming a neat triangle, his eyes merry behind glasses slightly bent out of shape. He looked rough around the edges some-how, not like someone you'd expect in these circles, and more curious because of it. Joe watched Judith, fascinated to see her transformation from wallflower to exotic orchid. Well, that was an interesting pairing.

'Jack McKinney,' Judith said. 'Have you two met?'

'No,' Joe said, shaking the older man's hand, feeling the rough knuckles. 'Joe Washington. Pleased to meet you, sir.'

*

Rose turned her back on the shadowy emptiness of the cemetery, its wrought iron gates gaping. It was half past five on a hot afternoon in October but she shivered as she made her way down the street toward the house at the end of the road.

She held the rail lightly as she mounted the rickety wooden steps. Fuchsia bougainvillea spilled over the railing, its multiple arms threaded through the squares of the lattice screen to overhang a cane table and chairs on the wide front verandah. Papers strewn across the table were held in check by a large dappled cowrie shell. A small black and white bird eyed her quizzically.

Through the open door she leaned into the darkened hallway, searching for Clem or Nina among the cluster of people in the light at the far end. 'Sorry I'm late,' she called. Nina glanced up, placed her glass on the sideboard and wove her way toward the door.

'Hello, Rose. Welcome.' The remnants of a Russian accent remained although it was almost twenty years since she'd arrived in Brisbane. 'Come in. Everyone's out the back. Clem and Barrie are arguing about the role of art in the Soviet Union, Jack's come in from the country to buy shovels and talk philosophy, Thea's insisting on the need for educational reform and Laurie's quoting Auden and lisping Oscar Wilde. Clem's in his element, of course, he adores a good fight.'

A teacher, thought Rose, she misses nothing.

'You look wonderful, by the way. How do you manage with all the shortages? New shoes and what looks like a new frock. And lipstick. Heavens, I haven't seen lipstick in the shops for ages.'

She followed Nina to the enclosed verandah at the rear of the house. Tables laid with canapés and cocktail sausages, a teapot with cups and saucers. Rose selected a devilled egg and moved to join a group of men and women laughing at, or perhaps with, Laurie.

'Hello,' she said, threading her arm through Laurie's and smiling at Thea on his right. Of the two helmsmen of the *Barjai* group, she liked Laurie the best, perhaps because he reminded her of James, their unruly hair and gentle manners, both of them determined to be avant-garde yet too polite to really succeed at it. Laurie liked women but loved men, she could relax with him.

'Where's Barrie?' she asked.

'Trying to persuade Clem to sponsor our magazine. It's going well enough, but if Clem supports us it'd help. It might become a real meeting place, after all.'

Rose looked around the room. Judith sat beside Jack, her glasses and serious expression matched by the colour of her dowdy cardigan. Seated, her heavy legs firmly planted on the ground, she looked a picture of solid conservatism. But the eyes, Rose thought. Something in the intensity of her eyes spoke of much more.

Beside them sat Joe Washington. So he'd arranged to come, after all. He listened to Judith intently, his face earnest in a way she found intriguing. When he'd questioned her yesterday he seemed simply sardonic, glib in the way Yanks often were, open-faced and courteous but somehow superior, looking with amusement at the antics of the locals. But if he found Judith's conversation arresting, perhaps there was more to him than she'd thought. She moved to join the group.

'I'm sorry, I didn't get time to meet you properly on Friday night. Welcome to Brisbane. I'm Rose.' She held her hand to Judith, not surprised to receive a warm but confident handshake in return.

'Thank you,' Judith said. 'I'm looking forward to it, a bit of summer is always a pleasant change, and Clem and Nina have found me somewhere to live. I had no idea it would be so difficult finding accommodation, the flats are all full of soldiers and people coming and going. Do you write?'

'Heavens no,' Rose said. 'I'm more of a hanger-on, really. Hello, Jack. You're back in town?'

'For a short while. I'll be out at the camp tonight. I must say you're looking like a peacock, all bright and shining. Dressed for something special?'

'I've come from work,' Rose said.

'You've met Joe, I gather,' Judith said with a knowing smile.

'Yes. We met at the Lyceum Club, didn't we? Good to see you again.'

'Those old fogeys,' Jack said. Did he not realise he was older than most of the Lyceum Club members?

'Ma'am,' Joe said and shook her hand.

'Have I interrupted something?' Rose said. 'You all look so serious.'

'We are just talking about how important it is to live in the moment,' Judith said. 'Especially now that the world is so bleak, the armies of the night drawing in, the failure of old certainties.'

'Bleak? Yes, I suppose it is.'

'Perhaps we need companionship in troubled times, people we trust, the simple life. The company of lovers even,' Judith said.

'Epicurus knew all about happiness,' Jack said, 'and the simple life. We could do well to adopt his ideas, it seems to me. In fact, all the advances in Western philosophy have done little to improve on the Greeks. You're a classicist, aren't you, Rose?'

What a bore he was, with all his tedious talk of ideas and philosophy. Why did he bother? The earnestness and introspection was all very worthy but it irritated her. No one needed to tell her about the armies of the night, she knew the loneliness that came with not knowing, the terror and the nightmares. All of a sudden she was angry. None of them had lost anyone, yet all they could do was complain about the housing shortages, the rationing, scoff at the cultural desert of the Lyceum Club meetings. Small-town worries.

'What do you think, Joe?' she said. 'What do you live for?'

'Peace, I guess. The future. A better world at the end of all this.'

More platitudes, she thought. Did anyone bother to look around? Of course the world was bleak, but not all of it. Since coming to Brisbane she'd heard jazz, danced until midnight, met people from all over the world. You just had to live a little, take a chance.

She turned away wearily but met Judith's gaze as she did. 'I couldn't agree more about the company of lovers,' she said. 'Bodies are quite valuable these days, worth remarkably more than the paltry wage you get at the munitions factories. And it's easy money. A whiff of danger every now and then, but not often. The Greeks called them *hetaera* if I'm not mistaken,' she said to Jack.

Jack made no reply. He's an old man, she thought. He went through the last war and Laurie said it had changed him. Maybe this one would change James as well. Perhaps James would return — if he did return — another man.

'Does it interest you to know I'm a prostitute?' she said.

'Not particularly,' Jack said. He wasn't shocked at all, she realised, feeling childish. 'But it interests me that you want to tell me.'

TUESDAY 12 OCTOBER 1943

Chapter Nineteen

Although he'd seen the lines on the street, and had interviewed soldiers in brawls with queue jumpers, Joe had never before entered the San Toy on Montague Road. He wasn't a prude. Brothels were part of life on this side of town, just not a part of his. Mind you, if he was about to be shipped out to Guadalcanal he couldn't vouch for what he'd do. It couldn't hurt to check, he thought, as he parked in a back alley. Had Leonard told the truth about the men leaving? Was Jones lying about avoiding a brothel? And why did Frank keep bringing the San Toy up in interviews?

He assumed the place would be quiet this early. Should he knock on the door or call out? Simply push the door open? He had no idea what the protocols were but the house had the feel of a private home, so he knocked and waited on the doorstep.

A woman with all the appeal of a spinster aunt opened the door. Thin to the point of gaunt, greying hair tied in a bun, shapeless beige dress and flat shoes. Had he made a mistake?

'I'll get madam,' the woman said, ushering him into the front room.

He stood waiting, cap in hand.

A large woman, more grandmother than maiden aunt, entered from an adjoining room, a fan held in pudgy fingers. She looked to be poured into her lilac dress, the horizontal lines of violet marking the sweaty valleys of her body from the more than ample bust to the triangular valley beneath an overhanging belly.

'I'm Betty,' she said, splaying the fan to cool herself. 'How can we help? We don't open for a few hours but we like to be flexible. So many of our girls live elsewhere, so you may have less choice, I'm afraid. But we always accommodate.'

'No, thank you,' Joe said, willing his face not to flush. 'I'm here on official business. Sergeant Joseph Washington, Criminal Investigation Division, Base Headquarters Military Police.'

'I see.' The woman sat heavily on a floral chair and ushered Joe to its partner on the other side of a low table. She waited for him to sit, fanned herself, then smiled. 'My question remains, then. How can we help?'

'I'm checking on two soldiers who may have visited here on Friday night. A tall sergeant with a thin moustache and receding hair, and a shorter, fairer man. A bit slow.'

'To be honest, I can't tell one uniform from another. Our clients come in all shapes and sizes, we don't discriminate.'

'And two girls,' he said. 'Alma and Rose. Do you know either of them?'

'Our girls don't always use their real names, you know.'

'No. I suppose not. But have you heard of them?'

'I'm not familiar with anyone with those names, I'm afraid. Of course, sometimes the girls find it convenient to adopt *noms de plume*.'

'Do any MPs come here? Perhaps a fat one with a fair-haired shore patrolman?'

'Maybe we've had MPs as clients, I can't be sure. Once or twice there've been fights on the street outside, the MPs come to break them up, but I have to say they're more brutal than I'd expect from a proper policeman. Perhaps there are different standards in your country.' She snapped her fan shut.

Joe knew that the people of Brisbane were shocked at the propensity of American MPs to use their weapons. Local police had nothing but batons and fists and their powers of persuasion, although recently the Commissioner had allowed detectives to carry pistols.

'And the soldiers? Is there anyone I can ask? Someone who worked on Friday who might remember?' Joe persevered.

'No one's here now, and I doubt if they'd remember. Neither man sounds remarkable.'

Joe was inclined to agree, and in any case there was no money in talking to the police.

'Do you get deliveries sometimes?' he said. 'Personal items for the girls, perhaps?'

'Most of the girls don't live here. Why would they get mail delivered? Personal items, you say. What sort of things?'

Joe struggled for details, knew this was a fishing expedition. 'Well, you know. Nylons. Lipstick. That sort of thing.'

'Who's put you up to this?' she said. 'Is it Frank?'

'Frank?'

'Bischof,' she said, the fan gripped in her fist.

'Frank Bischof? Why would he be interested?'

'Are you serious? He's interested in everything, surely you've learned that by now.' Her face was stern but fixed. 'No pie gets baked in this town without his little pinky finding its way into the crust.'

*

Dawes sat on a box of tinned food at the back of the Austral Motor Company's warehouse off Brunswick Street. He sucked on a stale Anzac biscuit and washed it down with a cup of tea from Mrs Bushel's thermos. The walls on all sides were lined with wooden pallets, cardboard boxes, metal drums and coils of rope. Close to the Teneriffe wharves, the warehouse served as a transit point and, although only employed as a general handyman, it was Dawes' mechanical skills that kept the trucks moving day and night from wharf to warehouse. His skills had made him an asset, gave him ease of entry. He'd told Eddie about the warehouse, had let him use it from time to time — for a fee — as one of his own transit points. It was a simple matter to let Eddie know when the owner was having dinner, easy to open the gate for another van. There was so much stuff packed into the shed that a bit more wasn't noticed.

Daylight shone through the entrance as a door opened and two large men entered, an MP and a naval shore patrolman. Both Yanks. He'd seen them before. Dawes crouched low against the back wall, wedged between sacks of sugar and a pile of empty butter boxes.

'So what really happened at the wharf on Thursday then?' The fat MP sat on a chair and plonked his legs on the table. He stared at the patrolman who paced the table's perimeter.

'When there's a delivery, there must be someone to keep an eye on things.' The shore patrolman spoke in a voice Dawes recognised from the movies — the hard nasal sounds of the Nazis in *Man Hunt*. White hair, blue eyes, squashed nose.

'Yeah, but you got involved in some sort of brawl? A soldier was knifed. He's dead and a couple of others are in hospital.'

'I was there with a dozen other patrolmen. I wasn't the only one.'

'Why'd you get involved? It's put everything at risk. And now that poxy investigator is talking to the soldier they've charged. We have to hope he doesn't say too much. I've warned him off, told him you might speak up for him if he sticks to the story. But I don't trust him, he's tricky.'

The door slammed and a third Yank arrived, a sergeant with a cigar clamped between his teeth. He sat across from the MP. 'Anyone know what happened to Bob?' He ignored the big blond patrolman.

'Apart from that he's dead?' the fat MP said. 'Nothing so far. Knifed. Found Saturday morning in the cemetery.'

The tall, thin sergeant chewed on his cigar and spat. 'He owed me for the last delivery, a big one, too.'

'What happened?' The shore patrolman prowled around the table, rolling his shoulders as he cracked his knuckles. The hair on the back of Dawes' neck twitched.

'Not clear yet,' the cigar smoker said. 'But it might be as well to lie low for a while. Goody-Two-Shoes was sniffing around the hospital again yesterday. On his own this time.'

'I can handle him,' the fat MP said, wiping sweat from his forehead before quickly replacing the helmet to cover his birth stain.

'Yeah, well,' the sergeant said. 'Bit of a ponce if you ask me.' He chewed on the butt of his cigar and stabbed the wet end toward the patrolman. 'But where's the money gone? That's what I want to know. Know anything about it, Kraut?'

In a single movement the blond man reached forward, grabbed the sergeant's shirt and dragged him to his feet. He snarled as he shoved the thin sergeant up again the wall, a hand clamped around his neck. Both men were red in the face but only one struggled for breath, the cigar clenched tight in his jaw.

'Easy, boys.' The fat MP lumbered to his feet, placing his bulk between them. 'Keep a lid on it till things settle. We'll sort it.'

'Where's Eddie?' The man who'd been pushed against the wall moved back to the table, righting his fallen chair.

'Lying low.'

'Wouldn't be hard. A snake if ever I saw one. Maybe he knows what happened to Bob.'

In the back of the warehouse Dawes stayed crouched, waiting for the men to leave. He swallowed nervously. This was all meant to have been a sideline, one of many ways he'd found to finance his hobby. But it was becoming dangerous. He wanted nothing to do with these people anymore.

He'd have to talk to Eddie.

*

'Morning, Frank.' Joe leaned through the open door. 'Just checking on the Foster case.' To hell with Major Mitchell.

Frank looked up but made no move, simply nodded at the chair opposite. 'Nothing to interest you — and I thought you were warned off.'

'Well, I am interested. The body was transferred to your people a day ago. When will it be released? His family can't be notified before then. So, what have you got? Is anyone going to be charged?'

'Where's the autopsy report?'

Joe dropped a folder on the desk. 'This is only preliminary — your people will confirm it, no doubt. Death was caused by a single knife wound to the heart, a single-sided knife, not a flick-knife. The coroner can't be sure Foster was killed at the cemetery but he was drunk not paralytic. He was a fit young soldier, so whoever killed him was skilful or just plain lucky. I'm guessing lucky. What about Leonard? What's his story?'

'A bit of this and a bit of that,' Frank said, his face expressionless. 'Makes money from his taxi business but my guess is he's involved in a bit of black-marketeering on the side.'

'What did he say about the woman? The one the soldiers had sex with.'

'Alma,' Frank said. 'He called her Alma. Wanted for soliciting, drunk and disorderly, offensive behaviour, stealing. You name it. She seems to have conned Leonard into taking her on as a domestic but has turned his place into a private brothel. Leonard's a businessman but he's not the type to be a bludger.'

'Bludger?' Joe said.

'A pimp, I think you call them. What did you get from Rose? That one's trouble. She's not what you think, you know. Her boyfriend's a POW; no good comes of playing around with a floozie like that.'

'Why does Rose rile you so much? Or is it Leonard she riles? What's he to you? Why are you protecting him?'

Frank leaned across the desk. Joe smelled stale beer and noticed veins on his neck pulse, but he was the first to look away.

'You're out of line here,' Frank said. 'I can report you, that's the easy part. The major'll be happy to have you out of the way and a transfer's easy to arrange. Far better than the alternative.'

'Which is?'

'You can get into trouble if you rub people up the wrong way in this town. You don't want to end up in the drink.'

'Are you threatening me?'

Frank leaned back, arms crossed, a crocodile smile. 'Me? Threaten a soldier like you? Where've you served, by the way? Seen much action?'

Joe had asked himself the question so many times he was beginning to doubt his war would amount to anything much. But for Frank to ask it? What a hypocrite. 'Have you?' he said.

'You'd be surprised how much action I've seen,' Frank said. 'Especially now you bloody Yanks think you own the place.'

*

At the bottom of the steps Joe knocked on Tom Baty's door. Without waiting for a response he entered and found Baty and his assistant inspecting a dozen dismantled guns laid out on a table in the middle of the room.

'G'day,' Baty said. 'How easy do you think it'd be to manufacture your own dumdum bullets? I can't think what else could have caused such appalling injuries.' He waved at a line of photos across the end of the table.

'No idea,' Joe said. 'Seems to me people make do with almost anything these days. Very inventive, you Aussies.'

'Hmm. What can I do for you?'

'Just checking on the film,' Joe said.

Baty nodded. He left his assistant with the guns and beckoned Joe to follow him into a side alcove. He slid a black curtain aside, ushering Joe inside. A forest of half-curled negatives hung like seaweed from a wire strung along the back wall. He unlocked a cupboard to the right and withdrew an envelope.

'Not sure where you're going with these but you may want to keep them out of general sight.' Baty gestured beyond the curtain. 'I developed them myself. No one else has seen them.'

'Thanks,' Joe said. 'I really appreciate this.' He slipped the envelope into his shirt pocket.

'It's not like you haven't helped me out. Wouldn't have been able to get most of this equipment without you persuading your bosses. But you should be careful who sees those.'

Chapter Twenty

It was nearly two o'clock by the time Joe entered the Provost Office, the smell of cigar smoke reminding him of the smoke house where his grandfather made sausages in every possible shape and size.

Monroe blew smoke rings and smirked, nicotine hands folded over his belly. Joe moved to the window, opening it to encourage a breeze.

'Too hot for you?' Monroe hauled himself upright and headed for the door. Buddies in the mess room were of more interest.

Joe sat down behind the towers of folders on his desk. They still bulged with sad stories awaiting his attention. He was grateful for the solitude. Last night had been pleasant; he liked the enthusiasm of Clem's group although he doubted they'd ever cross paths with the likes of Leonard, or meet people like Betty down the road. How could they begin to understand Joe's world?

Even Rose was more actor than participant. He'd learned nothing more from her, still couldn't even be certain he'd seen her that night at the Trocadero. What game was she playing? She liked to shock, that was obvious. Playing at being a good-time girl, the dark challenging lipstick. But she was no fool, easily conversing about poetry or drama, casually switching between groups all evening, never the centre of attention but always near the inner circle. He'd got nothing from her, no further details about Friday night. Finally she'd slipped away, no one in the group surprised that she'd left without a backward glance.

Still, in a small way, Jack had turned the tables on her. She'd wanted to shock them but it was Jack who'd surprised her. Joe had watched Rose's reaction, saw how embarrassed she'd been, not quite the sophisticate she played at. He enjoyed seeing the change.

When he left he'd made sure Laurie took the suitcase, and had asked about her. 'Rose?' Laurie said. 'She's wild, untamed. Like Kipling's cat, she walks alone.'

Joe pulled open the drawer to check its contents. Doyle's preliminary report was tucked under a bunch of papers but now that Mitchell had read it he doubted there'd be a final one. Hayden and Monroe were vicious thugs. It wasn't unusual; 'provos' had a reputation and many felt obliged to live up to it. He'd seen too many batons wielded against soldiers' bare heads, too many beatings in the cells. Nothing his colleagues did surprised him anymore.

Beside the report were two envelopes, both unopened. He felt the weight of the first one, knew his mother would have taken time over it, her arthritic fingers struggling with the pen as she mouthed the still foreign words. She'd been to school in Italy but only until the age of ten, when she'd had to leave to help her mother at home. The bottom envelope was long and thin, the script precise, letters perfectly angled. Nancy prided herself on her writing, her way with words. He'd not replied to her yet, there seemed no easy way to explain his gloomy letters. She kept saying how lucky he was to be out of the fighting, at least he'd escaped the horrors of the Pacific War. But surely there was more to life than playing safe. He dreaded the thought of returning to the life she gushed over — gossip at work, drinks on a Friday night, a show on Saturday.

Until now, he'd dismissed this job, complained about the banal crimes, his pointless reports. But in the last few days he'd got a glimpse of what life might be like as a real detective, unwrapping the layers of a crime, peeling away the lies and deceits to reveal the truth. This town was a puzzle that he couldn't stop thinking about. Soldiers had something to fight for, could be proud of what they accomplished. Perhaps in time he would feel the same.

Absently he patted his pockets. He'd almost forgotten the photos. What had Tom warned him about? He withdrew the envelope and spilled the contents onto the desk, over twenty black and white images, some disappointingly out of focus. The bald man had his back to the photographer but Joe had seen enough of Leonard to recognise the stance, hands in pockets, hunched over. Joe pushed the photos around, hoping to form a complete picture. One photo showed Monroe, his helmet pulled down over his birthmark. In another he recognised the detective who'd been with Frank at the CIB, the one with cauliflower ears.

Who did he dislike most? At least Monroe had the excuse that he'd been raised in the backwoods, in a place where Joe guessed even the mayor and chamber of commerce thought lynching a normal state of affairs. Joe had visited the Deep South only once, after the strike and its aftermath. He'd been sent to visit a distant cousin while his mother arranged the move to New Jersey. He knew now that he should have stayed, could have supported his mother. But at the time he'd been so grateful to leave behind the arguments and the angry, hollowed-out man his father had become. His cousin didn't see the 'Whites Only' signs, didn't register the open talk of negroes shot in broad daylight, didn't care about the pinched faces of white children living in tents along the railroad, or in squalid vans on the edge of town. But Joe did. The army must have been an eye-opener for someone like Monroe. Regular meals and clothes provided, a gun you didn't have to pay for. For someone with an ounce of smarts it was an opportunity.

But Frank. He had no cause so far as Joe could see, other than greed and vanity; the desire for power that gripped so many men. And control. Frank loved to be in control, to watch others squirm.

A photo caught his attention. Also blurred, it must have been taken rushed, just as the lecture began. The detective appeared to be moving toward someone off camera, a flounce of skirt and a brief swirl of beads all there was to indicate the woman who held his attention.

He swept the photos into the drawer as Monroe clomped in.

'Court martial begins soon,' he said. 'Prisoners are in the mess.'

Joe rose, lifted the top two folders from the pile; the evidence needed for his cases. Monroe followed him through the door.

At the end of the corridor, a group of prisoners — two privates, a corporal and staff sergeant — followed the guard toward the mess, where they'd eat an early lunch brought over from the base's main kitchen. The smell of overcooked vegetables and greasy lamb turned his stomach. Aussies were addicted to it, but no American thought sheep worth farming let alone eating. He caught a glimpse of Corporal Duke and remembered that he'd promised to collect the letter he was writing to the girl Polly. Maybe he could persuade Duke to make a formal complaint about Monroe and Hayden. He'd enlist Elmer's help, but even Elmer would be wary. Black men knew not to trust anyone more than necessary, that sometimes it paid to lie low.

'I'll see you after this,' he said to Duke. 'Like I promised.'

The floorboards creaked and Joe felt Monroe's stale breath at his neck. 'Move your asses,' he said. 'No time to talk.'

Joe took the stairs to the top floor, where the elegant council chambers served as the setting for military courts. He sat outside the door, listening to the steady hum of charge and response, waiting to be called.

Four soldiers faced court this afternoon. First up was a forty-two-year-old staff sergeant charged with indecent assault on a nine-year-old girl, followed by a twenty-two-year-old private charged with unlawful carnal knowledge of a male person. Joe wasn't involved in the first case and Monroe would give evidence for the second; he'd caught the man in one of his regular forays into the Botanic Gardens on the lookout for perverts.

Although every soldier was provided with counsel at his trial, proceedings were often perfunctory. There was little time for unnecessary argument, no need to delay sentencing. Joe didn't expect any of the cases to take long. The Queensland Police had found the nine-year-old girl hiding under the staff sergeant's bed, a bag of sweets in his wardrobe awaiting the next child. The young private had been caught with his trousers at his feet, a young man kneeling before him.

Bryson and Duke were Joe's cases. Bryson's posed few problems, the women he'd attacked had identified him easily in the roll call; he'd be found guilty of assault. Duke didn't deny he'd fathered a child, only that he hadn't known the girl's true age. The fact that he'd supported Polly and the baby might go in his favour, but Joe doubted he'd escape a sentence.

So many of the cases involved sex. Brisbane swarmed with young men with too much time on their hands and an uncertain future. Judith was right — it was no surprise they looked for the company of lovers, even if military law took a dim view of their appetites.

A guard opened the door and escorted a prematurely aged man, stooped and grey, toward the stairs. The first case was over already. 'Got twenty-two years,' the guard said. Staff Sergeant Jacobsen's career was over.

In a short while the guard returned with the second prisoner, a pale and frightened private with a face so smooth Joe wondered if he was even old enough to shave. The man shuddered involuntarily.

Joe didn't have long to wait, but enough for his thoughts to return to the cemetery. Why did Foster's murder so unsettle him? He couldn't decide. Perhaps it was because he didn't know who to trust. By all accounts Frank was a thorough detective, but Joe saw how he strayed close to the criminals, eager to get the conviction he wanted. Foster gave him the opportunity for a win in the courts, something he rarely got now that so many perpetrators ended up in military courts. But what had Foster been doing all day? And where? Leonard was weak and sly — did he really have it in him to drive a knife into the chest of a strong young soldier, however drunk? And Eddie — just another taxi driver doubling as a small-time crook? On the lookout for a quick buck and another chance. Neither struck him as murderers. It wasn't good for business.

In any case, there was no weapon, almost no evidence, no motive as far as he could tell. And Jones, the only witness, was drunk and crippled. Mind you, he'd seen how often a simple brawl could get out of hand. Look at Teague, he could hardly remember throwing the knife, could barely recall details of the fight. Yet he'd killed a man and would go to jail.

And then there was Rose. Or Alma. Were they one and the same? How innocent was she really, playing games with writers and artists, pretending to be something she wasn't?

'Next,' said the guard. He gave Joe a wry look as he led the boy soldier down the stairs. 'Six years.'

Joe walked into the chambers where once the South Brisbane councillors had voted to raise levies and open public libraries. Today's court dispensed with the frippery of gowns and decorative cushions; three American officers sat in a line behind a prosaic wooden trestle table, upright chairs arranged before them. The high ceilings and ornate plasterwork gave the proceedings an air of formality that the simple furniture belied. Joe took a seat as the guard ushered LeRoy Bryson to a seat in the middle of the semicircle.

'Accused, state your rank and serial number for the court.' It was a colonel who spoke, a lawyer with the soft voice of authority.

Bryson stood to attention. 'Private LeRoy Bryson, 35240112.'

'You have been arraigned on the charge of aggravated assault. In particular it is charged that at eleven o'clock on the night of 2 October you assaulted two women on two separate occasions, both attacks taking place in the vicinity of Dornoch Terrace, West End. How do you plead?'

'Guilty, sir.'

The colonel directed his attention to the defence counsel, a lieutenant seated at the end of the row. 'Does the defendant understand the charge?' the colonel said.

'He does,' the lieutenant said. 'He's been advised of the consequences of a guilty plea and is aware that he is likely to receive a custodial sentence given the gravity of the case. Sergeant Washington can detail the case.'

Joe nodded, stood and saluted.

'Go ahead.'

'This office was contacted on the evening of the second of October by the Woolloongabba Police, who had been called to a disturbance on Dornoch Terrace sometime after eleven o'clock. The police found the defendant and an American sergeant, Sergeant Jimmy Pierog, who had apprehended Private Bryson after witnessing the attack. The victim, a Miss Whittington, aged thirty-three, was accompanied to the police station to provide a statement. Further to this, a second woman came forward to report an attack. Both women identified the defendant.'

The officers shuffled papers, leaning to left and right to confer with their fellows. From outside, suddenly, came the sound of gunshot. The silence that followed was pierced by a woman's scream and the crash of metal.

Afterwards, Joe wondered how long they'd all sat there, how long it was before the officers leaped to their feet and the guards reached for their weapons before racing to the door. He guessed there were three seconds between each of the three shots, the sound ricocheting along the corridor and up the stairwell. Joe raced forward, taking the steps two at a time followed by the guards, guns held at the ready, the major shouting orders.

Below, in the corridor, Mrs Lakursky's face was parchment, her hands clasped to her mouth. A metal tray lay at her feet, the white china smashed into the spreading stain of lumpy brown stew. Behind her, in the kitchen, Joe saw Monroe's white helmet lying on the table beside a plate of half-eaten lamingtons.

At the end of the corridor Corporal Duke lay facedown, the back of his head a mess of blood and bone, his arms flung to either side, his body almost cut in half. The guards lowered their weapons.

No one moved. Joe heard the clock ticking in the hallway, Mrs Lakursky's stifled sobs. The air smelled of sulphur.

'He ran,' Monroe said, sliding a 9 millimetre pistol back into the holster at his hip. 'Tried to escape.'

Chapter Twenty-One

'Hello again.' The woman at the entrance punched the ticket and rang up coins in the heavy cash register on the counter.

Rose pocketed the slip of cardboard before moving into the familiar darkness of the theatrette on Queen Street. It made no sense to keep coming, it didn't help. Made it worse if anything, but she found it impossible to pass, the welcoming darkness drawing her in, the flickering on the screen, the optimistic tone of the newsreader, the images of young men laughing as they boarded ships and planes, waving to their mates. A great adventure.

She'd made such a fool of herself with Jack. Why? Was it to shock Joe?

Soon the screen clouded over, planes flying in formation, bombs cascading silently to the jungle below, black smoke exploding into the sky. The seas churned with oil and stricken ships. Men in ripped boots or bare feet struggled through muddy rivers, skidding down slopes, arms encircling each other, bandages loose around heads or arms. Stretcher-bearers staggered, tipping their patients at precarious angles. In dirty rags, the wounded lay inert, tossed from side to side.

Every day the newsreel cycled, repeated endlessly as the day progressed. Boys sat transfixed, naming each machine one by one — the tanks rolling over the desert, the bombers rumbling through the skies. Women held lace handkerchiefs to their open mouths.

The Cine Sound logo appeared as the lights came up. Soon the national anthem would play and the newsreel, rewound, would begin again.

Just once more, she thought, sliding further into her seat, tucking her bag safely under her feet.

*

The sky, laden with dark bruised clouds, mirrored Joe's mood. as he descended the stairway onto Vulture Street. Opposite the tram stop, the front page of the *Telegraph*, held vice-like in a flat metal cage, screamed its news: 'Nazi Air Losses.' 'Portugal Prepares for War.' 'Japs Fail in Ramu River Push.' In small print at the bottom corner a notice announced that the United Auto Workers had reaffirmed its no-strike pledge.

Brisbane lay before him, a muddle of wooden houses and backyards, a mosaic of trees and tin roofs becoming more scattered as the town spread half-heartedly north. In the distance, the Glass House Mountains loomed over the coastline. When they'd first sailed into Moreton Bay he'd marvelled at the strange peaks, their smoke-blue shapes against the sky, like misshapen ghosts from another world.

He crossed the street to the park, drawn to the river. Abandoned beside the gun emplacement, a kitten lay preening itself, slicking its fur as it washed away the grime and dirt of the street. Nearby, the picked bones of a small bird were already swarming with ants. The kittens might not need the food, after all, although perhaps the birds did.

At the river's edge men swarmed over the wharves, their ceaseless hammering pounding in his brain. Refuelling and refitting, welding and riveting. On the riverbank oily slicks swirled in eddies, painting wheels of colour where none should be. The patterns of red and orange, yellow and green, blurred under the pale dockyard lights. The clang of metal on metal rang out like the tolling of a massive bell.

Was it self-indulgent to care about a single death? Did one more matter?

He imagined two women, each standing on their front steps, Duke's mother and Foster's wife. They'd open the door to a telegram boy with red cheeks and pimply chin. Two women, one black, one white, with nothing in common but grief. The fate of women across the globe. Two deaths, two murders. A son, a husband. Each man had survived months aboard vessels in the South Pacific, near escapes from Jap raids, camps in muddy malarial swamps, nightly strafing. What had brought them here to die? Why Brisbane?

Joe passed the Ship Inn where a group of Aussie soldiers hung from the windows, their glasses raised. They yelled a curse but he looked away. He was an MP, after all, a figure of fun, the 'provo' all soldiers despised. And a Yank. The war had flattened the uncertainties and subtleties of civil society into the hard billboards of fear and patriotism — the Japs, the Nips, the Jerries and I-ties. Now the threat of invasion had receded, the occupation of their hometown tasted increasingly bitter. He guessed he'd have felt the same had Australian men come in such vast numbers to New Jersey, imposing their odd ways of speaking and clumsy joviality on the peaceful residents of his hometown.

A wolf whistle pierced his thoughts. Three girls squealed in delight at the effect their passing parade had on the drinkers.

'Hello, angel, where did you drop from?' So there were Yanks in the hotel as well.

'Whatcha looking at?' The bold redhead sashayed ahead of her friends, swinging her hips so her dress flounced. 'I've got a boyfriend already.'

And the Aussies threw their arms around their mates, feigning indifference.

'Another bloody Yank,' one of them spat.

Joe walked on, not caring to hear the reply.

Two boys ran past swooping a model aeroplane made of strips of wood glued together with paper. *Akk-akk. Akk-akk.* Spitfires always downed Messerschmitts, he noticed, the boys spiralling their precious planes into the dirt, always careful not to wreck them. Their short pants were patched and torn, their faces grubby as they looked up at him as he passed.

'Got any chewing gum? Candy? Comic books? Superman?'

Joe carried strips of gum along with cigarettes, so he handed them around as he made for the bridge.

By five o'clock a steady stream of men flowed across the iron bridge, seeking out the rougher side of town, the jitterbug and bands, the girls, the sex. Beside the door of a wooden house on Stanley Street, Joe watched a madam check the potential. Her black cocktail dress clung to curves that had been clutched by countless men, although Joe thought some of the curves outlined so clearly were probably best savoured in private. What passed for a waist was now much wider than her hips and as she moved toward a group of soldiers the hills and valleys rolled and bobbed, as if the earth moved.

Under the Victoria Bridge the tide was on the turn, the oily waters carrying half-sunken logs and scraps of timber out into the bay. Joe turned his back on the river. Maybe the music would make sense. Little else did.

＊

Rose stepped inside, smiled at the insouciant frilled lizard sitting snug on its rock in a glass aquarium, pushed open the swing doors at the end of a darkened passageway and peered into the dim light. She needed company. If not the company of lovers then the sound of people laughing at silly jokes, making plans for tonight or tomorrow. Talk of music or poetry, something to black out the images that rolled incessantly through her head. She replayed them as an alcoholic reaches for the next drink, desperate for the very thing she knew would never give release.

Tuesday at six o'clock but already the Emerald Iguana heaved with men and women squeezed into the smokey, windowless room in the basement of a building opposite the Customs House. Most sat at tables laid with checked tablecloths strewn with crumbs from raisin toast and melted cheese. Candles dripped onto saucers. Thea waved at Rose from the back of the room, where she sat with a group of girls from the Cremorne, their primped hair matching their glittering gowns. The bandleader from a show at the Blue Moon sat nearby, his red vest loud against the deep navy suit. Laurie sat further along, at a table apart, deep in conversation with an older man whose long fingers drew circles in the air as he spoke. Neither noticed her as she draped her bag over the chair she fell into.

'Hello, I'm Rose.' She held out a hand to an Australian soldier. His handshake was reticent and he looked to Laurie for explanation.

'This is Joshua, from Sydney,' Laurie said. 'Joshua, Rose. Rose is an old friend.'

Joshua stood and bowed, moving to another part of the room.

'Sorry,' Rose said. 'I didn't mean to interrupt.'

'There wasn't anything to interrupt,' Laurie said. He sighed as he searched the room, at last finding Joshua beside a man dressed in an elegant suit. They laughed, the suited man punctuating each point with his cigarette holder.

Poor sweet Laurie. Of all the people Rose had met since arriving in Brisbane it was Laurie she loved the most. So intense and committed she could listen to him talk for hours, about love and socialism, art and beauty. He read his poetry to her — children scraped from their mother's wombs, every possible mood of love. She remembered his trenchant criticisms of the local art scene. 'Year after year the same pretty still life, the same pretty landscapes, the same pretty figure studies disgorged by the hundreds. Brisbane favours pretty.' She wondered at his power to clutch at experience, and thought that the only thing he feared was loneliness.

Rose placed a hand on his arm. 'Drink?'

At the counter she ordered two strong coffees, waiting until the bottle of Scotch was hidden back under the counter before collecting two anodised cups.

A woman brushed past, knocking a cup from her hand. She threw her hands up then kneeled to retrieve the cup that clinked to the floor. 'No. I didn't mean to. What have I done? I'm sorry,' she said, wiping whiskey and coffee from the hem of Rose's skirt. Flustered, she kept wiping Rose's shoes, eager to please, whimpering as she looked up with hangdog eyes. Rose met the woman's gaze and watched as her eyes widened, her mouth open. 'Oh.'

Rose had told her sister stories of the café, of the women in feathered boas, the shimmering dresses, the slim men in neat trousers and waistcoats. Now, seeing her struggle to get up, Rose knew how out of place she must feel, Alma's rich raven hair unbrushed, her black court shoes scuffed, her cotton shift ill-fitting. Rose steered her toward the table, introducing Laurie as she set down one of the cups.

'What are you doing here?' Rose said.

'I've run away. Can you help? I can't go back.'

'From Leonard?'

'Yes. I tried to get away but he came after me, he's threatened to have me locked away again — in the hospital.'

'You can't be locked in a hospital against your will, silly girl,' Laurie said. His scepticism was natural, widespread even. How little he knew.

'The Lock Hospital,' Rose said. 'It's behind Boggo Road, easy to see if you know what to look for. But most people don't want to. You can be sent there for up to three months for a venereal disease, although I've known lots of people sent there without. Only women, of course.'

'Don't let them take me back,' Alma said. 'Please.'

Alma wrapped her arms around her small frame, rocked gently, and Rose nodded to Laurie to leave them. She held Alma's hands, stroking them as she would a puppy's.

'Just tell me what I can do,' she said.

Alma's shivering subsided, shoulders softening as she relaxed. Finally she raised her head, wiped her eyes with the back of one hand and smiled.

Chapter Twenty-Two

Joe paid at the entrance to the Trocadero and propped himself against the bar, craning to see the orchestra. The bandleader tonight was the Australian, Frank Coughlan. He'd played dixie with the 9th Division in the Solomons and New Guinea, but always returned to the Trocadero when in Brisbane. Tall, slim, with white tails and spats, Coughlan lowered his trombone to reach for the baton. Joe held his breath as a woman with chestnut hair to her waist, dressed in a flapper shift with no back to speak of, moved to the microphone, horn in hand.

A cacophony of wolf whistles accompanied the musicians as men reached for their partners. Soon jitterbugging couples jumped and jived like demented insects, their arms and legs jerking in all directions. Behind their writhing bodies he saw Coughlan lift his instrument to his lips, the mournful wail of a trombone joining the sorrowful notes of the saxophone to soar over the dance floor.

The music matched Joe's mood. He knew nothing would happen. Monroe and his buddies, the thugs who roamed the

streets beating up negroes, Jim Crowing them across to the
south side, were safe. No one would rock the boat. Not Major
Mitchell or any of those higher up. There was a war to win,
and as it moved northward, officials were too preoccupied to
bother about provosts like Monroe. There'd be no justice for
Duke, not from the army, at any rate.

As the band finished their first set, couples moved to tables
at the periphery. Waiters glided past with trays of drinks, hard
and soft. Clusters of young women eyed the men who circled
the room, checking the talent, considering who they might
ask for the next dance. The choice was theirs to make. Never
enough girls to go around.

Joe made no move. Beer bloated him, he'd never gotten
the taste for the fizzy stuff the Aussies drank by the gallon.
Maybe it helped digest all that greasy mutton. But he knew
how to get whiskey so, although his glass held looked like it
held stale beer, it was in fact some of the best bourbon he'd
ever tasted. He slipped the hip flask back into the inside pocket
of his jacket and waited for the second set.

Two years before he'd enlisted he'd scandalised his
mother by visiting the Apollo Theater in Harlem, but Lionel
Hampton's sixteen-piece band had been well worth her displeasure. None of the orchestras here was as good, but jazz at
the dance halls was improving.

A group of negro servicemen entered quietly, making for
the back of the hall. Joe noticed Elmer among them, willed
him to look the other way. What would he tell him? How
would he confront all those bloodshot eyes in the canteen? No
one would be surprised, most of the men were brutalised by
battle or the mindless cruelties of the armed forces. He'd tried
to help Duke but instead he'd made him an easy target.

A private wearing the distinctive kookaburra and boo-
merang tag of the 7th Division wove through the crowd, his

drunken mates encouraging him as they edged toward an American naval officer with a young girl whose bobbed hair and floral outfit made a splash of colour among the khaki and beige. A corsage of orchids accenting the pink of her blouse.

'Hey, honey,' the private said. 'Want a pretty flower to pin on your boobies? Why don't you get a proper man, not a pansy.'

The Aussies draped arms across each other's shoulders and roared with laughter.

'A mob of bloody desk johnnies, that's what you are.' The private poked his finger in the American officer's face. 'Where were you at Milne Bay?'

The naval officer moved his partner toward a stool at the bar, standing beside her and turning his back on the group.

'Yella. That's what you are. Yella.' The Aussies jostled their way to the bar, ordered a round of beers. Mother's milk.

Joe moved further away from a scene whose ending he'd seen so often.

Perched now on a stool, the officer pulled a pack of cigarettes from his pocket, offering them to the woman who slid one out and put it to her lips. The Australian private leaned across with a light but was pushed aside.

'Take your hands off me, you bastard,' the Aussie said. He was a cockerel in a barnyard, steadying himself against the alcohol, buoyed by his mates. He raised his fists.

'Let's go,' the officer said. He reached for his partner's arm as he picked up his glass.

The private leaned over to grab the half-empty bottle and cracked the base on the edge of the bar. A pool of silence spread around the tableau, a scene Joe wished he could capture. His photo would show the cocky expression of the private reflected in the glass, the flinty stare of the officer, the trembling lip of the girl with her eyes on the neck of jagged glass.

The officer's eyes glowed against the white incandescence

of his face, narrowed onto the private, all sight reduced to a single focus. Some of the men around him knew to give him space. Joe remembered back to Mr Mailer's instructions as he watched the officer roll up his sleeves and set his stance to establish a base from which to move. Rock solid.

When it came the fist flew with more speed than anyone could have expected. Even Joe. A right forearm that Joe now saw was solid as an iron rope, and just as wiry. The captain's rigid fist left its imprint on the private's face, as would a child smacking its fist into a ball of plasticine. It was over in one punch. The Australian private crumpled, rolled over, and was unconscious in a single move. The captain turned back to his girl, her face white as she stared at the body on the floor.

Joe sat still. Just another fight among many, he thought. The Australians hauled their mate to his feet and dragged him between their linked arms.

The audience, distracted, hadn't noticed the orchestra return. Now Frank Coughlan moved to the microphone, lifted his baton and let it fall. A middle-aged woman, no looker, sat at the piano. She punched the ivories with ferocity as the twelve members of the 9th Division Band raised their instruments as one, a sound to raise the roof, to lift Joe's spirits. As Frank Coughlan lifted his clarinet to his lips, Joe remembered that some things, like music, were worth fighting for.

He gulped his drink at each solo. A toast to life.

*

Suddenly Rose realised that the rabble of overlapping conversations had stalled and an unnatural quiet had descended over the café. Looking toward the entrance, she found the cause. In the doorway stood two squarely built men in overcoats, pork pie hats and suits they'd clearly bought from the same store but with no thought for fashion. Two plain-clothes police from the National next door, the usual police watering hole. She recognised the man with the boxer's cauliflower ears but not the one with the punch-blunted nose. Fine red lines of broken capillaries mapped two lives devoted to alcohol. Neither removed hat or overcoat as they strode into the café, muscling their way through the crowd to glare at the man behind the counter.

'Two beers.'

The bartender, checked apron over black trousers, shook his head. 'We have coffee or tea. Soft drinks, if you prefer. Lemon squash is good in this heat and we always add a sprig of mint but not everyone likes the taste, a bit like toothpaste if you're not used to it.'

Rose watched him falter, willed him to stop babbling.

Cauliflower ears leaned forward to pluck the straps of the bartender's apron. 'That's not what we hear,' he said. Even from across the room Rose could smell the stale beer.

'Perhaps you'd like to talk to Mr Friend,' the bartender said, searching for help from the closed door behind him.

The men began to circle the room. 'Poofters and perverts,' they roared as patrons scurried for dark corners or made for the light of the exit.

Rose saw Laurie move toward the police but Joshua grabbed him by the shirttails and pulled him back. Laurie wrestled free, hurling himself at the two detectives. Blunt Nose rounded on the boy and they stood eye to eye.

'And you are?'

'Laurence Collinson.'

'You'll do.' The detective grabbed Laurie by the shirt front. 'Bloody underage drinkers.' He pushed Laurie ahead, holding him from behind by the top of his trousers, a beefy arm around his neck. Joshua made to intervene but Laurie shook his head. Rose leaped from the chair and ran toward the large man as Thea jumped up to join her.

'Pick on someone your own size,' Rose said, Thea resolute behind her.

For a moment the detective paused but it was the man with cauliflower ears who reacted first. He swung around to face Rose, then smiled as he recognised her face. He'd seen her the other day, leaving the meeting with that stunted little Yank. She was one of them sole operators, the ones who refused to be part of the trick. He looked past her, hoping to find her friend, the one who'd run away. Leonard wasn't happy about it and nor was Frank.

Rose tried not to look in Alma's direction, to where she sat low in her chair, head in her hands.

'Leave him,' Cauliflower Ears said, noticing Rose's aborted glance. 'Here's something much more interesting.'

Blunt Nose flung Laurie aside. The two men moved toward Alma but Rose came from behind, striking out with her fists. Leaving Alma to his partner, the man with cauliflower ears turned. He raised his hand to catch Rose's arm and she cried out as his grip tightened, letting her know how easily he could snap it.

'I know you,' he said, his face thrust into hers. 'Filthy whores both of you.' He flung her away and turned to face Alma, now held fast by the other detective, arms pinned behind her back, her cotton dress straining against her beating chest.

'You should know,' she said. 'You've had me enough times.' With what Rose knew took great courage, Alma spat.

The detective wiped away the spittle, his cauliflower ears reddened with fury. 'We have reason to believe,' he began, with all the pomposity he could muster, 'that you are operating as a prostitute using the premises of a person whose wife you are employed to nurse. I am arresting you under the provisions of the Suppression of Contagious Diseases Act. You will be taken from here to an appropriate facility where you will be detained for the protection of public health.'

'Once a copper, never a man,' Alma said as the detectives held her between them, one with his hand low on her buttocks.

'Fuck you!' Rose screamed, rubbing her wrist to bring the circulation back. Four purple prints circled her upper arm. 'Fuck Minister Hanlon and fuck that pious bastard Cilento!' She watched the two detectives manhandle Alma through the door into the long passage. Neither she nor Laurie followed. Thea, her face a mixture of shock and bewilderment, came to stand beside them.

The three stood in impotent rage as the noise in the room returned to a steady hum.

The police were in control, she'd known it for a long time. She'd seen the way they worked the streets, demanding kickbacks from the black-marketeers, heavying working girls while skimming money off the top. Fat cats who licked cream from their paws before dunking them in again. She'd seen the way the Big Fella lined his pockets at night while spending the daytime toadying up to the crusaders from Ascot and Hamilton who folded their gloved hands over their heavily corseted laps, disapproval etched in their faces. She was sick of it all.

The good-time girls from the Cremorne were already up and dancing, the whole incident put behind them and forgotten. Laurie and Thea returned to their table. The Movietone newsreel replayed in Rose's head as she joined them.

'James wouldn't have taken it lying down,' she said. 'What is he fighting for if not for the right to live the way we choose?'

'It'll be a long time before I'll be able to live as I choose,' Laurie said. Rose reached across to him, held his hand. She knew he had friends who'd appeared in court, their only sin to find love in the shadowy pathways of the Botanic Gardens.

Thea banged the table with her fist. 'It isn't right. How can they get away with it? Why doesn't anyone do anything? Look at all these people.' She swept the crowd with narrowed eyes. 'Just look at them. If it doesn't affect them they're happy to go back to their drinks. Hypocrites.' She stroked the crucifix at her throat. 'Come on, let's go see Dad. See what Cliff can do about it. He's always banging on about corruption, let him tell the story as it really is.'

Thea and Laurie got to their feet, but Rose held back. 'You go,' she said at last. 'I might try another angle.'

*

In the darkness Queen Street slumbered fitfully but inside the newsroom of *The Courier-Mail* no one slept. Desks were piled with papers and typewriters, coats slung over chairs, men and women rushing from one side of the room to another. Cliff Stanaway lived for this — the smell of ink and paper, the roar of machines rolling out news at midnight, the certainty of being at the centre of things.

He raised his head as Thea burst through the doors of the newsroom, Laurie Collinson in tow. Hair and clothes awry, faces flushed, they came to a stop in front of his desk.

'You need to come with us,' Thea said, hands on hips. 'They've raided the Emerald Iguana. Police thugs everywhere, out of control. Come with us. You need to report on this.' She turned, dragging Laurie with her, expecting Cliff to follow.

Cliff pushed his shirtsleeves above his elbows, placed inky fingers on the keys of his Remington and checked the time on the wall clock. Nearly ten o'clock. 'Nothing unusual about that,' he said, lining up the ribbon.

Thea spun around, furious. Laurie paced.

'They've taken a woman,' Laurie said. 'Dragged her away, threatened her with the Lock Hospital as punishment for running away from her pimp. She's not even charged with anything, they're all just in cahoots. Clem says you're a campaigner. Now's the time to do something.' Laurie stopped his pacing to direct his attention at Cliff. 'It's about time we shook this town out of its complacency, dragged it into the present. We have to make people confront the facts on the street. Isn't it about time they knew what the police are up to?'

Laurie looked flushed, exhausted by his proclamation. Thea stood her ground.

Cliff concentrated on the last few words on the page in front of him. He swung the carriage to the left when he'd finished. 'They get to do pretty much what they like in this town, as far as I can see,' he said. 'Nothing new there. Mostly they keep a lid on things, although of course it's getting harder now, with all the soldiers and money flooding in. Not everything's the fault of the Yanks but they've become the scapegoats. Always simpler to blame others than take the time to look in the mirror. What do you think I can do?'

With a flourish he ripped the sheet of paper from the machine, enjoying, as always, the zipping sound of completion. 'And anyway,' he said. 'What are you two doing here at this time of night? You should be home getting ready for bed.'

Thea hated being treated like a child but Cliff had known both of them for so long he'd forgotten they'd grown up. He looked from one to the other. He'd been a mate of Laurie's father for years — had often shared supper at the family flat. Knishes and blintzes washed down with wine and argument. He was still at school, Laurie, but old before his years and becoming something of a trifecta — not just a Jew, but a communist and a poofter to boot. Not that Cliff had a problem with any of that, but he didn't want the boy to get into trouble. And Cliff knew the editor. Although they'd run a few of Laurie's art reviews once or twice, he doubted the paper would run a story on police corruption. Thea was older, less of a child. But he didn't think the chief subeditor would thank Cliff for getting his daughter involved in anything radical. Although he'd written articles on black-marketeering and gambling, pilfering on the railways and wharves, Cliff knew how far he could go. Death threats were only a part of it. It wasn't time to push the boundaries. Not yet.

'Sit down,' he said. 'You're both making me giddy. Look, the Lock Hospital's operated for years. No story there. I know sometimes the cops use it as a threat and a halfway house, but can you blame them for trying to keep girls out of the slammer? And everyone knows the plain-clothes blokes get a bit out of hand after a few beers, but given what they have to put up with, who can blame them?'

'Doesn't justify their behaviour.' Thea folded her arms over her chest and dared Cliff to disagree.

A knock on the door interrupted their conversation. A gaunt man in a dark suit and white shirt entered, pork pie hat in hand. 'Ready to go? The radio car's outside.'

'Sure,' Cliff said, grabbing a notebook from his desk. 'Laurie Collinson and Thea Astley, meet Detective Holmes. I'm riding around town with the police again tonight. It gives you an idea what they're up against, how they deal with it.' Standing, he slapped Laurie on the shoulder and patted Thea on the head. 'What say we give these two a lift home? Bit late to be walking the streets.'

Chapter Twenty-Three

Rose couldn't be sure he'd even be there, and in any case it was a long shot. Would he help? Could he? She struggled through the crowd at the entrance, ignoring the wolf whistles, glowering at groups of soldiers dishevelled with drink. When she saw the poster and heard the sound of the band she knew she was in luck. At the entrance she paid, entered and scanned the crowd until she spied him at the end of the bar, concentrating on the piano solo, fiddling with a half-empty glass of beer. He'd been drinking, she saw, his uniform no longer neatly pressed, his tie askew; slumped on the bar as he watched the orchestra, his face redder than usual, his sandy hair glistening. He was not the handsomest man in the room, but he was the most intense. His hands drummed the beat on his thigh. She willed him to turn and when he did she registered the play of emotions. An inward smile, a gentle sigh, a concerned frown. Or doubt. Why was he always so suspicious?

He walked toward her, taking care as he skirted tables and chairs, each foot set down in front of the other with deliberation. Careful not to tip the glass.

'Hello,' Joe said. He shook her hand then held it gently. 'Where've you been?'

'In town with friends. I need your help.'

'Help? I can't even help all the people I'm supposed to.' He waved his arms, marshalling imaginary rows of men. 'Drink?' he asked with a lopsided smile.

She lifted his glass from the bar. Not beer, after all. 'Not for me,' she said. She set the whiskey onto a nearby table, threaded her right arm through his, her shoulder bag dangling. She felt him lean into her. 'Let's dance,' she said and led him onto the floor. She slid her arms around his neck, his hands resting lightly on her waist. When she laid her head on his shoulder she wondered why girls favoured taller men. They merged with the crowd, just another couple among the hundreds. He lifted her hand from around his neck, held it lightly as he gazed into her face. Such melancholy eyes, she thought. His eyebrows met in a querulous frown, the expression on his face grave. What had happened?

The notes of the piano solo faded, the band acknowledged the solo with a nod and took up their instruments. The drummer lifted his sticks and brushes. With a crash the musical mood moved up a notch, the pianist now duelling with trombone and clarinet, fingers pummelling the keyboard as they raced up the keys. Around them couples pulled apart, bodies jumped and spun around, legs flung out in all directions. A naval officer pulled his partner toward him, swinging her between his open legs. She squealed with delight as he hauled her back to her feet. Couples followed their lead, jerking and jiving, arms held out to each other, bodies flailing.

Joe stood still, his arm around Rose's shoulder, his mind on the music. They separated and she studied him. Listening to each beat, tapping his foot in time, moving his arms on each upbeat, stepping from side to side with each bar. Even after so much alcohol he analysed the orchestration, responding with his head not his heart. If only he would give himself to the melody, let her show him. She spun around, moving to the syncopation, ignoring his methodical pace. She let the sound take hold, filling her body with its beat, the rhythm matching the pumping of her blood. Invaded by sound, pure and unsullied.

She would make him dance.

She held his hand then tossed her head, swung away, waiting at the point of the turn, cajoling him, willing him to see how it was done if only he'd let it happen. Hoping he'd catch her on the return. And there he was. His arms outspread, amused at his audacity as much as hers, he laughed as she fell into his arms.

At last.

The pianist accelerated, a series of rapid-fire ascending chords as the saxophonist raised the pitch higher and higher in search of the perfect cadence, blowing as if her lungs would burst, the blood vessels split. She soared to a climax of body and sound, an exquisite culmination ending in a piercing cry into the night. Sweaty bodies clung to each other, laughing at the music's denouement, before drawing apart in surprise at their boldness.

Rose felt her heart pound against Joe's chest as he rested his chin on the top of her head, both exhausted.

Back at the bar he gulped for air, reached for the now empty glass.

'No,' Rose said. 'Let's go outside.' She pulled him to her, linking arms. 'You look like you need company.'

They moved along the alley, finding a quiet spot between two parked cars. No one was around, the night felt still. She reached for a cigarette, held it for Joe to light, a scene from a

---

movie. Faint strains of music mingled with the clang of the trams, the *bump-bump* as a solitary car crossed the tracks. As she lifted the cigarette to her mouth Joe reached for her arm. Under the pale light of the moon he traced four purple bruises.

'What happened?' Joe said.

'Oh. What do you know about Frank?'

'Did he do this?' Joe said, his voice loud in the quiet alleyway.

'No. Well, not directly. You work with him, don't you?'

'On and off,' Joe said. 'He's always in on the big cases. He's meant to be pretty thorough.'

'Who says that?'

'Mostly the other detectives, I guess,' Joe said.

'They've taken Alma. She ran away but they've taken her, the coppers. They'll throw her in the Lock Hospital where they can keep tabs on her. Why does he want her out of the way like that? What's she done?'

'Maybe they want her safe. Somewhere they can find her.'

He moved away from her, leaning against a railing. The dancing had sobered him. The sadness was there still but no longer directed inward. Now it was aimed at her.

'How well did you know the tall Yank you met on Friday night?' he said.

'Why? He's just someone I met, only briefly. No one special.'

'Where did you meet him?'

'Here,' she said. 'Well, near here. We crossed the bridge together and started chatting. He was with another soldier, a funny, nervous man who didn't want to go dancing. He was angry about something. I was happy to get away, to be honest. I don't mind when they're just homesick but some of them can be strange. Scary.'

'Them? What happened after you left here?'

'I went to Clem's. You've been there. You know where it is, South Brisbane.'

'Near the cemetery,' Joe said.

'Yes.' Why was he going on like this? Rose had come for his help, not to be interrogated. Was he even going to ask her what she wanted?

'What time did you get there? And leave? Can anyone vouch for you?'

'What's this all about?' Rose said. She dropped the cigarette butt and ground it out. 'I came to ask for your help, but all you want is to ask questions.'

'He's dead. Did you know that?' Joe said. 'Your tall sergeant Bob is dead. Now what do you have to say?'

Her hand covered her mouth. 'How? Where?'

'His body was found in the South Brisbane cemetery on Saturday evening. He was murdered. The cemetery right by Clem Christesen's. You may have been one of the last people to see him alive.'

WEDNESDAY 13 OCTOBER 1943

Chapter Twenty-Four

Joe rolled over and carefully extracted his left arm, sliding it along the sheet so as not to wake Rose, her breath soft and regular, warm against his chest. She curled at the edge of the narrow bed, the band of purple bruises like an armband above her elbow, her hand shielding her eyes from the moonlight filtering through the shutters. She'd wake at any moment, stretch her limbs languorously and turn over and return to sleep. Her mouth twitched.

His apartment was little more than a single room with a short galley-like kitchen and a tiny bathroom he sometimes used for enlarging photos. Tall ceilings, picture rails, scrubbed pine floors covered with a shag rug worn thin. The numbering amused him. The Avalon had twenty-six flats, each with its unique letter — his was number 'G'. Down the hallway lived two other officers and a transvestite who spent most of her days wistfully pacing outside the officer's club on Moray Street. There was something of the feel of New York here, something trying to be modern.

He pulled on his discarded trousers and sat, bare-chested,

at the desk. A jug, a pottery cup, pencils and a fountain pen, his folded glasses. He held his camera. A shaft of moonlight struck the table like a blade and another ran its sharp edge across his forehead as he remembered the flask of whiskey. He reached for the jug of water and his leg knocked the heavy bag Rose had slung over the round back of the chair. A dull clank, as of metal against wood. Turning, he saw her eyes on him, lids lowered. Feline.

He put the camera down, lifted the bag onto his lap and opened the clasp. Before she could react, he swept aside the papers and upended everything onto the table. Handkerchiefs and cosmetics, a hardback book of what looked like poetry, a roll of notes, a bottle of expensive perfume, and a black leather purse heavy with coins. He picked up a cloth bundle, feeling something solid inside.

'Should I open this?'

At last she stretched. Sensuous. 'If you like,' she said, curling back into a ball.

Joe unwrapped the cloth, a tea towel of thin blue and white checked cotton. Inside was an ornate knife. Brass at both ends, with a loop at one to attach to a belt and two tangs at the other to protect the hand. He weighed it in his right hand. The handle was covered in patterned leather and the blade, when he flicked it open, was stainless steel. He placed his thumb against the edge to test it before laying it on the table.

'Shouldn't you have told me about this?' he said.

Rose rolled towards him and sat up, sheet held lightly at her waist. 'James sent it to me from Syria. It's beautiful, isn't it? Usually I don't like knives.'

'Then why carry it?'

'It makes me feel safe walking home from the tram at night. Clearly you don't approve but honestly, most of the Americans carry them. What's the problem?'

'Rob Foster — Slim — was killed with a knife,' Joe said, watching as she responded with nothing more than mild annoyance.

'Well, it wasn't me. I wish I hadn't taken it to the Iguana but I couldn't easily get rid of it earlier, could I?' She smiled, pulling back the sheets. He moved to sit on the edge of the bed.

'It doesn't look good,' said Joe.

She ruffled his hair, soft as a teddy bear's fur, and leaned forward to kiss him on the chest. He found himself sliding lower. 'If you're looking for someone keen to knife the Yank, I'd choose Leonard,' Rose said. 'If he was going to drive the men back to the hospital he wouldn't have let Slim go without paying. He's greedy.'

Joe felt her lips lick the soft depression at the base of his throat. 'And Alma?' Her ear was too close to ignore.

'You haven't met her. She has been beaten so many times she's got no strength to fight back anymore. She's easy money for a pimp.' Her knee moved below the sheet, pushing up between his legs.

'Pimp?' Joe was confused, his attention diverted.

'A bludger, pimp. You know. Someone who runs girls, for sex. It's not as if the girls make any money,' Rose continued, purring ever so slightly as she fiddled with the zip. So much easier than buttons. 'Most of it goes to their men.'

'You don't mean the ones in the cat houses, do you? You mean the street walkers.' He rocked from side to side as she slid his trousers lower.

'Alma's not a street walker. She'd make more money if she were. She's just a poor sad girl who ran away from her foster family in Newcastle and ended up looking after Leonard's wife. The sex is better money than most jobs but she doesn't get to pick and choose.' Rose found what she was looking for and Joe found it difficult to concentrate.

'What's all this got to do with Frank? I thought he was big on keeping the cat houses under control.' He reached the hidden part, behind the soft earlobe, with his tongue.

'Yes, but only the girls in the brothels he controls, the ones who pay him to keep things sweet. He hates the single operators, the girls he can't make money from. Like Alma.'

He held his breath as she increased her pace. 'And you?' Joe rolled on top, no longer listening to Rose and caring nothing at all for Frank and his minions.

*

Rose slipped her dress over her head and bent to retrieve her sandals from under the bed. The moonlight illuminated her stockings lying ribbon-like on the scuffed rug. On the table her life lay before her — Blake's *Songs of Innocence*, a Syrian flick-knife, perfume and more money than she could earn honestly. She bent to retrieve her stockings, crushed them in her hand and stuffed them into her bag together with everything else.

She looked at Joe lying on his back with arms askew, like a child fallen suddenly into a deep sleep. She liked him. She'd seen the way he handed out lollies to the kids on the street or listened with head cocked when Laurie spoke of the problems of modern art. Sure, he was a military policeman, here to keep a lid on troubles and smooth over problems, but when he'd questioned her last night he'd seemed willing to listen, genuinely keen to find the truth, to right the wrongs. Not attributes likely to endear him to the Queensland Police. Last night she'd seen his other side, one loosened with whiskey that was true, but no less real for that.

She hadn't meant to use him, or at least not in this way. She knew she must leave before he woke, before he confronted her again with the contents of the bag she now draped over her shoulder, the sordid reality that her life would appear in the sober light of day. Joe turned in his sleep, one arm across the bed, his fingers loosely pointing toward her in accusation. Such an innocent he was, she thought, as she closed the door gently and tiptoed along the corridor to the stairs. Better to let him cling to the myth a bit longer.

At two in the morning New Farm Park slept fitfully. Snores from the rows of camp tents around the perimeter of the park combined with the deep throbbing of engines from the submarine base at Teneriffe where dark shapes rose out of the river like round-backed sea monsters, awaiting their time to dive once more into the deep black waters of the Pacific. Two men in naval bell-bottom trousers lurched out of the dark, each with a tall brown bottle in a raised hand, their vacant eyes more used to an underwater world. They leered at Rose, moving to either side, herding her away from the roadway. But she held her breath as James had taught her when they sank into the deep end of the pool at the Oasis, her heart rate slowing, calming her. The men stumbled away as she kept moving.

On the southern side of the river, around the bend, the shipyards at Kangaroo Point were never truly still. Judith's landlord complained of sleepless nights followed by the dawn whistle of the shift change. The relentless loading and unloading, repairing, revictualling, crews going on leave and returning, aircraft dismantled and reassembled on the wharves at Hamilton. Rose knew that soon the streets would pulse with booted men in overalls heading to the woolstores and sugar refinery; women in neat skirts and blouses would jump from the tram off to work at the Naval Barracks or the Austral Motor Company.

She made quickly for the river. From the farther side of the park came the hiss of the Powerhouse letting off steam. She'd come to love the jacarandas. Their blossoms, crushed and flattened underfoot, formed a purple carpet spreading down the slope, splattering the path beside the muddy river. Each flower a bell, velvet to the touch, hollow, the colour iridescent. She'd heard one of Laurie's friends say how impossible the colour was to paint — too rich for lilac, not red enough to be a true purple. At night she half-expected it would light her way along the unlit pathways through the park. But in the dark, the newly laid carpet of flowers became a deceit, a thin and treacherous slime that caught you unawares. She slipped and reached out to steady herself. Treachery and danger so often lay below the fickle veneer of beauty.

This was becoming a dangerous game and she couldn't remember when it had begun. Was it when she discovered work difficult to find and rent so expensive in a town already bursting at the seams, or was it when loneliness turned bleak and oppressive?

Brisbane had been just a country town when she first arrived. How quickly it changed. Rose remembered the first time she'd seen a sign for waffles and ice cream, posters advertising shows at the Cremorne, jazz at the Trocadero, John Wayne and Eleanor Roosevelt. Hollywood came to town and everyone was starstruck. Brisbane's women danced at the City Hall, earned their own money at jobs in the textile factories or the munitions factory at Rocklea. Money they could spend on themselves for once. We all discovered zips, accents and gentlemanly behaviour, she thought with a smile.

She had few qualms about the morality of her life. James had shown her the bourgeois hypocrisy, the gossamer-thin film of respectability over the deep wells of human desire. No, she knew who she was and why. But how and when had she changed? That she couldn't remember.

Above her the moon shone and she wondered if James could see it too. In Singapore, or wherever he was. Surely the walls of the prison would not be so high, the jungle not so thick, the skies not so clouded.

Her bag bumped along the ground. At the river's edge she opened it, pulled out the flick-knife and flung it into the centre of the oily current, watching as it sank, the circular ripple contracting to nothing.

*

On mornings when he woke to the magpie's lyrical song and the sweet smell of orange blossom from the hedges lining the streets of New Farm, Joe wondered if he was acclimatising. When his battalion had first arrived he'd been billeted, together with a dozen other men, in a boarding house at Spring Hill. One night he was deafened by a thunderstorm drumming rain on the tin roof, expecting at any minute to be swept away in the torrent pouring from the rusty gutters. The house shook. It felt as if the building itself, like the timber floorboards and rounded tree stumps that propped them up, was a part of the natural world — yet alien. He missed old buildings, the granite of his hometown, but he'd come to love the Avalon, this brickwork and stucco edifice with its neat lettering on the gable, its solidity and predictability. Above all, he was grateful to have found a room of his own. Here, lying in bed in this sturdy structure, he could feel almost at home.

He felt the empty space in the bed, the sheet cold now the sweat had dried.

Chapter Twenty-Five

An army jeep beeped a cheeky greeting as Rose crossed George Street at nine o'clock on Wednesday morning. She stepped aside as two men spat into the gutters while they unloaded sacks of what smelled like sugar. From before dawn, trucks backed into the Roma Street markets laden with bags of flour from the mills at Albion, wooden pallets of vegetables from Redland Bay. Rose wasn't the only newcomer. Brisbane's population had doubled in two years and business was brisk.

She'd chosen her most demure outfit today, the better to fit the role of chaste sister visiting a sadly fallen sibling. Dark skirt, white blouse, sensible black court shoes, hat and gloves. No jewellery. At the last minute she lifted the raven wig from the porcelain doll which eyed her reproachfully, its white head now naked. She slipped the wig over her head. A glance in the mirror to check the effect. With only a few hours' sleep she prickled with energy as she boarded the tram at North Quay.

Near Boggo Road she alighted at the entrance to the hospital. Typical of the authorities to place the ward so close to a prison, she thought, as if infection were a crime. She looked up at the unmarked entrance, the heavy door set into a featureless redbrick façade with windows high enough to allow light to enter but not the prying eyes of the general public. She trotted up the stairs. Hasten slowly, she remembered, flattening her skirt, taking time to breathe. Through the door and into the main vestibule, she navigated a series of corridors.

Beyond the door's dappled glass she could make out blurred shapes moving slowly. Adjusting her focus, she checked herself in the glass, making sure no blonde curls were escaping. Sometimes she thought she looked better as a brunette, although that might be because she usually matched it with finer clothes.

'You are?'

Rose faced a gaunt woman in a white uniform, the stiff lines of her cap and collar matching those that etched her face in prim disapproval.

'I've come to visit my sister,' Rose said, speaking to her feet.

'And she is?'

'Alma. Alma Smith. She came in last night, I believe.'

As her eyes lifted, Rose met a face soft as dough, two black eyes like currants pinched into the folds. A pert mouth smiled above a chin decorated with fine lines and a single errant black hair.

'Humph. Doctor's just seen her.'

The matron — if such she were — slid aside metal bolts and Rose followed the broad expanse of white buttock toward another frosted glass door. As this door opened, the impression was of entering a church. Not that Rose had been inside a church since she'd turned fifteen, when the ministrations of the reverend father had finally became intolerable. She remembered the sweet smell of wine as he kissed her on the edge of her lips, his hands creeping up her back to slide around and come to rest under her budding breasts. When she refused to go to confession, her grandmother hadn't spoken to her for days.

High ceilings, white walls, a ghostly light filtering through a row of dirty clerestory louvres set at such a height that only a long-handled pole with a hook at the end could hope to reach them. This was a room that imposed passivity, if not reverence.

The matron waddled down the aisle of a long ward. Metal beds tinged with rust lined the walls. Some were empty and unmade, others had their sheets tossed aside. Girls and women lay or sat, dressed in hospital gowns, well-laundered white cotton shifts of no particular shape but ill-fitting nonetheless. On bedside tables Rose saw out-of-date copies of the *Women's Weekly*. The antiseptic smell of Lysol mingled with the rich tang of overripe bananas on bed stands beside tubs of face cream. Rose knew that over a hundred girls were housed and treated here — most of them after falling foul of the police, their families, or both. 'Delinquents and moral degenerates', Cilento called them. Never mind the men, she thought.

'Your sister's come to see you.' The nurse paused at a bed at the end of the row before returning to her station by the door. Alma lay on her side, her back toward them, her hair dishevelled, her gown crumpled. She made no move to turn.

'Who?'

Rose placed a hand on her shoulder as she leaned forward. 'It's me,' she whispered.

Alma turned slowly, her eyes widening above a slackened mouth. 'What are you doing here? Did they take you, too?'

'No,' Rose said. 'And they never will.'

'How did you get in?'

'It's not a question of how I got in, but how we get you out. You're not going to stay where Frank or Leonard can collect you as and when they choose.'

Alma made no move to rise, her limbs heavy or limp, her mind fogged. Rose wondered what drugs they'd injected her with.

To their left, a teenaged girl in a cotton nightie flicked through a magazine.

'Where's the bathroom?' Rose asked. The girl tilted her head to the end of the aisle, her eyes glued to the page.

'Follow me,' Rose said. She hauled Alma upright. With her handbag slung over one arm Rose shepherded Alma with the other.

Communal bathrooms were situated at the end of the corridor — white and black tiles, open cubicles, overhead showers. Beyond, there were two rows of toilet doors. Although the girls would shower together, no one — even here — could expect them to share a toilet. Not given their 'diseases'. In spite of evidence proving you couldn't catch the pox off toilet seats, Rose guessed even the nursing staff would think twice about barging in. So the toilet was a private place, the one place you'd be sure no one would enter.

Rose pushed Alma inside. She pulled her nightie over her shivering body, shocked at her bony knees and elbows, her sunken chest. From her handbag she drew out a dark skirt and white blouse, black court shoes exactly the same as the ones she wore. She brushed Alma's hair, making sure it sat neat in a bob. They were close enough to the same height; from a distance Alma would pass. Rose folded the discarded gown before shoving it behind the toilet pipe leading to the cistern.

'That should do. Just walk out the front door, don't look at anyone, just go. You can find your way to the station? Dutton Park. I'll meet you there.'

Alma nodded, collected the handbag, less cumbersome now, and moved with purpose toward the door. Nobody would bother her as she walked out into the sunlight, picking up pace as she headed for Cornwall Street.

*

The Lock Hospital was anything but. A couple of girls in the ward showed Rose the loose window in the bathroom they used to go out for a night with their boyfriends. Then it was a simple shimmy over the wall into the yard, made simpler because the carpenters working on the hospital left their ladders propped against the brickwork. Yet another hypocrisy, she thought. Looks good in government statistics, gives the police a useful threat and satisfies the moral outrage of locals. What a farce.

Rose followed Cornwall Street over the hill, down onto the platform at Dutton Park. At first she thought Alma seemed subdued, head down, face expressionless. But Rose knew enough of her half-sister to recognise the fury below the placid surface.

'This is where I came that night, you know,' she whispered. 'After the fight with Slim. Leonard made me help, made me drag him into the cemetery. But I scarpered as soon as I could. If only I'd kept going.' The knuckles of her right hand were white as she clenched and unclenched her fist.

'You tried,' Rose said, putting her arm across Alma's shoulders as they moved to the steps.

Not that Rose could judge. She'd made pretty poor decisions herself. She'd do what she could for Alma, and if it thwarted Frank's plans, well so much the better.

'They'll track us down,' Alma said. 'You know that. There's nowhere to go in this town.'

'I'm not so sure about that,' Rose said, shielding her as they climbed the stairs to the road.

A few hundred yards from the railway station they passed the turn into Rawnsley Street. Rose paused. Nina would be teaching, but Clem or Judith would be there, working on proofs, editing. She could almost hear them now, discussing poetry and politics, laughing at the grammatical errors of careless writers, the faulty arguments. Much as she loved them both, she thought how little they knew of the struggles taking place just down their street. But that was Brisbane, parallel worlds inhabiting the same space. Public and private. Night and day. Like the mice and cockroaches behind the skirting boards, living in the same house but only appearing at night. She'd been wise to keep her lives separate.

Rose pointed to the end of the street, to the house on wooden stumps with a wide-open front verandah. 'If you ever need to find me,' Rose said, 'ask the people in that house. They know me, they're good people, they'll always help you.'

She led Alma up the hill past the cemetery. Ahead lay the dirty river. Beyond, the Town Hall shimmered in the cloud-less heat. Always hide something in full view. Isn't that what they say?

'You know the San Toy?' she said, guiding Alma down the slope toward West End. 'Betty's one of the few people prepared to stand up to Bischof, even if it does mean she finds herself in court most months. I'm sure she'll help.'

They walked through the back streets, quiet in the mid-morning, the pubs shut, most men at work in the factories lining the river, children safely lined up at desks in the redbrick school on Vulture Street.

Alma followed Rose up the steps of the house on Montague Road. Girls sat in groups in the foyer, gossiping and smoking cigarettes. Most had flats or took rooms in boarding houses nearby, but a few lived in, the convenience outweighing the long hours on call. Clad in daytime clothes, each could easily pass for clerical staff having a quick fag on their way to dinner, but their underwear was silk and the way they moved gave away a confidence that came from money and independence. Betty treated them well.

Rose led her sister across the foyer to the office. Alma slumped in a chair, a sparrow among a flock of peacocks. Rose knew she'd be safe here, but she certainly wouldn't feel at home.

'Is Betty around?' Rose said.

'She's out back with Ricardo. Who's this?'

'Sit here,' Rose told Alma. 'I'll find Betty. You'll be safe. I'll be back as soon as I can, but first I have things to do in town.'

*

Frank Bischof pulled open the desk drawer and retrieved his bronze letter opener, a gift from a grateful customer. He rarely received personal mail at work but this hadn't looked official. He didn't recognise the script and there was no return address.

Even before Hanlon's little visit he'd been considering how to deal with the situation. Leonard was useful and he didn't want to lose him. Far better if the girl could be implicated. They'd all been so drunk he doubted anyone remembered much. The courts wouldn't find any of the testimony reliable unless he presented the case as cut and dried. It could be done.

He could pin it on the other soldier, of course, it'd be expected. But he had no intention of just handing it over to the Yanks. Not this one. Not if he could help it. It was high time he got a conviction, kept Hanlon on side. Newspapers and police ministers were one thing but his reputation was another. He'd never lost a case and he wasn't going to lose this one. This could be a real opportunity if he worked it right. But it had to be quick.

He unfolded the stationery and read slowly. So. Rose and Joe. Slimy Yank bastard.

Interesting. Maybe there was a solution.

Chapter Twenty-Six

Things had become complicated, Rose thought as she stepped off the tram. She needed to work out her next move. She had to protect Alma, but there were so many balls skittering in the air, she wasn't sure she could keep them from falling. Alma, Leonard, Frank, Joe. Not to mention Bob, or Rob, the tall Yank who'd been looking for a fight but had clearly got more than he'd bargained for. Or deserved. Had it really been only a few days since he'd whistled as she crossed the bridge?

She removed her gloves as she stood at the entrance, noting the grime from the railing outside. How suitable, she thought, as she headed once more into the office of the Counter Intelligence Corps.

'Enter.'

Rose opened the door and stood facing Major Rifkin, his hair newly oiled, his indoors complexion colourless.

'Sit.'

This time she did. She crossed her stockinged legs, placed her hands neatly on her lap and waited. It was a skill she'd perfected at her grandmother's, seated at the dining table or in the sitting room, waiting for conversations that never started. She'd learned not to look up expectantly as her grandmother entered the room, not to smile in anticipation of a question directed her way. In the end she'd found what she needed in books, but she'd never lost the capacity for stillness. She was surprised how easily it unsettled people.

'So?' Rifkin said at last. 'To what do we owe the pleasure so soon after your last visit?'

'Frank Bischof. I presume you know him,' Rose said. 'Queensland CIB.'

Rose knew the Counter Intelligence Corps had dealings with the Queensland Police. It was inevitable really, given so many of their cases covered common ground — black-market issues sliding into security concerns, national security regulations involving communists or Jehovah's Witnesses, alien internments.

'Yes, I know him,' Rifkin said, his voice as unctuous as his hair. 'The Queensland police are so amateur, so inept. Bischof's just a big toad in a small pond. A nuisance.'

Rose marvelled at how apt the image was, how easily it could be turned 180 degrees to face its creator. 'Takes one to know one,' her grandmother's cleaning lady always said.

'I keep hearing rumours about him,' Rose said, 'that he's in with the black market. A man called Leonard features a lot in what I hear.'

'And where do you hear this?' Rifkin leaned forward. He loved rumours, the more elaborate the better.

'From an American sergeant, a patient at the 42nd hospital. He boasted about how he was dealing in stolen PX goods, told me his contact was called Leonard. He said it was all sweet, that even if the police found out they wouldn't prosecute because they were all in on it.'

'And where is this sergeant now? Can you arrange an interview?'

'Actually no. He's dead. Murdered.'

Rifkin slid a sheet of paper across the desk, and placed a pen slowly on top. 'We'll need details. Sergeant's name and the names of others involved. I can't promise anything.'

You never do, Rose reflected, beginning to write.

*

Not a cloud smudged the sky as Joe swung from the step of the tram and crossed Vulture Street. At the top of the stone stairs under the archway he bent to pinch the purple flowers of a basil plant. He crushed them between his fingers, smiling at the memory of his mother's kitchen. The scent lingered as he laid his briefcase on the desk where the tower of folders had toppled, the avalanche barely held in place by a cup of stale coffee. He whistled a Benny Goodman tune as he pushed through papers, pencils, a box of matches, until he found the file.

'You must have had a good night,' Monroe said, a sneer spreading over his face.

'Great band,' Joe said. 'Almost worth putting up with the crowd.' Determined not to let Monroe spoil his mood, he selected a pink sheet of paper and waved it at Monroe. 'Here's the requisition chit I signed for the ammunition you said you had to collect from the quartermaster. Lieutenant Bates wants a full accounting. Something about the last one being incomplete? Take your time. Get some coffee from the canteen while you're up the hill. I've got phone calls to make.'

The wooden floors creaked with the weight of Monroe's boots, responding to his movements the sea to a ship. Nothing stayed still in this flimsy town, its endless creaks and groans.

With a backward glance at FDR, Joe pulled the Bakelite

phone toward him, picked up a pencil, dialled and listened. Frank's wheezing was phlegmy, and Joe idly wondered about the man's blood pressure.

'CIB. Detective Inspector Frank Bischof here.'

'Sergeant Washington, Base Station 3,' Joe said. 'It's time for an update on the Foster case. What news of the weapon? The car? When do you expect an arrest?'

'Hold on, hold on. What makes you think we've got enough evidence for an arrest?' Frank said.

'The Provost Marshall's pretty agitated about the murder of one of our men. The press are calling for action. So are we.' Joe propped his legs on the desk, enjoying himself.

'One thing at a time,' Frank said. Joe could hear the procedural cogs shift into gear. 'Investigations are continuing as we follow certain leads.'

'Have you questioned Leonard again? What about the other taxi driver — Eddie? Have you searched the house for the murder weapon? Spoken to the wife? There's been no request to re-interview Jones.'

'We're still looking for the girl. Leonard's been told to find her. And quick.'

'I don't believe anyone can go missing in this small town. I've never known a place with so many people minding everyone else's business,' Joe said, recalling the way WRENs on the signals desk at the big house gossiped all day. 'You seem to know Leonard's place pretty well, fitted in just fine the other day. Is he one of your contacts? Maybe you know more than you're letting on.'

'That's the pot calling the kettle black,' Frank said. 'Would have helped if you'd mentioned that you recognised the deceased. Seen him at a dance hall just a few hours earlier. Or so my sources indicate.' He paused, waiting to see if Joe would react. 'Let me give you some fatherly advice, Joe, there's no point protecting that filly. She'll give you a run for your money but you'll never saddle her.'

Joe sat with the phone to his hear. Who'd blabbed? Who knew he'd been there?

'Right. I'd be grateful if you'd prepare a briefing,' he said.

'In due course, young man. In due course. Don't go thinking you can keep information from me. This is my investigation and I pull the strings. You wouldn't want to get tangled up in them.'

Joe placed the phone back on its cradle.

Damn.

*

Joe turned the jeep into the street, pulled up against the kerb, dragged on the brake and swung himself over the door. It was clear that Frank had no intention of investigating. He'd simply lock Alma up until he could charge her, with or without any evidence. To hell with Frank, and Mitchell, he thought as he walked past the mound of cigarette butts at the front door.

'Anyone here?' He looked past the half-opened door into an empty living room.

From within, a woman's weak voice replied. 'He's out. No one's here.'

Joe stepped into the living room. Beyond the lounge, through an open door to the kitchen, a woman who must be Leonard's wife lay on a day bed, a crocheted rug pulled tight under her chin. She stared at Joe with wide eyes as he moved toward her. Her mouth hung open, spittle dribbling onto the coloured threads. As the rug fell away he saw the tumours, misshapen lumps, mottled and puckered. What was her illness?

'Can I sit here?' Joe closed the door quietly. He lowered himself onto a kitchen chair he brought close to the bed. She nodded. He folded his hands on his lap. 'My name's Joe. I'm sorry to interrupt. Can I make you a cup of tea or something? Get you a glass of water?'

She shook her head, her eyes never leaving his face.

'I suppose you've guessed I'm an American soldier.'

She nodded.

'Do you remember the other soldiers who came here? On Friday night?'

She closed her eyes as she rolled into a huddle against the wall.

'Slim and Snow, they called themselves. Two soldiers, tall and short. Sure, you must remember? Alma was here as well, wasn't she? I guess they had a bit of a party.'

She seemed to nod, but he couldn't see her face.

'You see,' he continued, 'we need to find out what happened. Were you here all the time? In the kitchen?'

He heard the front door open and footsteps.

The woman put her finger to her lips.

They waited in silence. Joe heard someone — it must be Leonard — settle into a chair. He heard the pop as the top was prised off a bottle, a click as he turned on the radio. A call of today's form at Albion filled the room.

The old woman rolled towards Joe but her eyes never left the doorway. She whispered so softly Joe had to lean close. 'They were here,' she said, her voice a rasp. 'Drinking. Sex. It's what they all want. Nothing else.'

'Not all soldiers,' Joe said before he caught himself. What a hypocrite. 'Can you tell me what happened that night?'

'They drank. They fucked. They fought.'

As a summary of the world, Joe couldn't fault it.

'What did they fight about? Do you remember what happened? Was there a knife?'

'Dunno,' she said. 'Anyway, who cares? Alma's a good girl

but she needs the money.' She was drifting. Joe leaned closer.

'Was she here all night? With Leonard? Where is she now?'

'She's a good girl,' she said, 'a good girl.' Joe watched as she fell into a torpor, her eyes closed, breath rasping, fingers working at the rug she may once have made. He knew he would get nothing further.

He scanned the kitchen, noting the dishes in the sink, the scraps of food on the bench, the unwashed plates on the table beside an ashtray loaded with butts. Had anyone searched the house? If so, what had they found? Where was the fight? What was it about?

A chipped green enamel cooker stood in the alcove beside an open doorway. Beyond that, a ramp led to an attached laundry, musty, smelling of kerosene soap and mould. Three cement washtubs sat on a rickety wooden bench beside a stained copper, boxes of laundry detergent propped on the wooden diagonal bracing. A wooden box under the tubs held empty bottles all the same shape. He sniffed the neck of one. Might pass for gin, but nearer to methylated spirits was his guess. A grubby rag was stuffed behind the central washtub. He poked it gingerly and extracted a ripped shirt. What looked like a stain — coppery red — ran across the sleeve and down the front. He held it over the sink and turned on the tap. The water ran red.

Carrying the dripping cloth, he walked back through the kitchen and into the lounge where Leonard sat, a large bottle raised to his lips.

'What the devil?' he said. 'Who let you in?' The man's skin was greasy, his face unwashed, his dusty bedroom slippers worn flat at the back. Hard to believe he ran a fleet of taxis, held sway over a black-marketeering empire. Even if only a small town one.

'The door was open.'

'You've got no right to be here. I made a statement already,' Leonard said.

'Perhaps it's time to make another one. What's this?' Joe dropped the shirt onto the coffee table. Small red blobs dripped onto the carpet.

'Grease rag,' Leonard said. 'Do a lot of car work.'

'Can anyone here verify your movements on the night in question? Your wife maybe?'

'You've got no call to involve her. Anyway, a wife can't give evidence, not against her husband. She's no use to you. Nor to me, if truth be told. And you can get out. Before I ring Frank.'

'By all means,' Joe said. 'I'm on my way there now.'

※

Rose sat in the library's reading room, her volume of Blake open on the desk in front of her, her letter to James half-written, the events of last night fresh in her memory. Was she playing with Joe? It didn't seem like a game.

She heard a cough behind her and felt the hairs on her neck rise.

Frank Bischof placed a hand on her shoulder and leaned close. 'Time for a little talk,' he said and the fingers moved toward the base of her neck. She smelled aftershave and tobacco, the horsey scent of a woollen suit worn for over a week. She turned back to her book.

'I don't think so,' she said. 'I'm busy.' She shrugged off the arm.

'You'll come with me,' Frank said, 'or I'll arrest you for the murder of Robert Foster. It'd be easy to pin it on you. From what I hear, you were one of the last people to see him alive. And you were in the vicinity of the cemetery where he was found. You'll come with me. Now.' He waited, arms crossed.

Carefully she folded her book, returned it to the counter, unhooked her bag from the back of the chair and followed him to the door. The sun hit with such force that for a brief moment she could see nothing.

Bischof led her to a park bench and sat. He folded one heavy thigh over the other and patted the seat beside him. 'Now, then. How do you want to proceed? Will this be done formally, at the station? Or can we settle it together in a more civilised way?'

She sat, her bag placed between them. 'You've heard from Rifkin?' Rose watched two pigeons pecking at the curling edge of a sandwich thrown at the base of the statue.

Frank nodded imperceptibly. 'Our allies have been in contact by telephone,' he said. 'It seems they find you useful.'

'So what is there to discuss?' Rose made to stand.

'I wonder how your friend Joe would like it if he discovered you were checking up on him? Or the others? Laurie or Barrie? Thea? I don't think you'd keep many friends if they knew who you reported to, and about what.'

'What do you want?' Rose said.

'I want Alma. She's not going to get away with murder.'

'Alma's no murderer.'

'Where is she?'

'Safe. And you know as well as I do that she's not a murderer. She's a victim, if anything. You just want to protect Leonard. He's valuable to you, valuable enough to cover up a murder.'

'I'll leave you to consider,' Bischof said, 'whether you want everyone to know what you're up to, not just a good-time girl, but an informer. All that bohemianism just to cover up your double dealing. It's simple to let the details filter out. No way your American pals could know who let on. Of course it might make life uncomfortable for a while. For you.'

With that Frank stood, raised himself to his full height, straightened his vest and crossed the park.

Chapter Twenty-Seven

Back at CIB headquarters, Joe wiped his forehead, sluicing sweat from his eyebrows. Even the stained-glass windows failed to moderate the glare from the noonday sun.

'What did you get from the car?' he asked Frank.

'The report's there,' Frank said, indicating a folder on his desk. 'Some blood on the back seat. According to Baty's mob, not enough to determine if it's human or not. Doubt it'd be any use in court.'

'Murder weapon?' Joe leafed through the report.

'I told you. Nothing. We've had people scouring the cemetery, all along the riverbank. It could be anywhere.'

'What about Leonard's house? There can't have been much of a search if no one found this blood-soaked rag.' He dumped the bundle of cloth on the desk. Frank looked at it.

'If that's what it is,' said Frank, leaning back in his chair, not a worry in the world. 'We'll have to wait for the tech people. And even if it is, how often have you worked on a car and grazed your knuckles? Doesn't tell us anything.'

Joe had never worked on a car in his life, wouldn't know how to. He doubted Frank did either.

'What does Jones have to say? Have you questioned him again?'

'Still swears he fled when a fight broke out. No way to tell if he's lying or not, but it fits. He's got no history of violence from what we hear. Quite the opposite, in fact. Suffering neurasthenia, according to the medicos. Combat stress reaction — a fancy name for shell shock.'

'No other injuries?'

'No, just a psych case,' Frank said.

Joe saw again the wizened hand, the bent fingers, the claw. So Frank would do nothing. Joe had guessed this from the start, known it from the eager way in which he'd zeroed in on the lipstick, prejudging the case from the beginning.

'Who does he say started the fight?' Joe said.

'Foster, of course.'

'Not Leonard?'

'Not likely. Leonard's a businessman. Too smart to be caught up in a fight. Leonard admits there was a bit of a dust-up between him and Foster but it wasn't anything serious. He went off for gin and came back to find they'd all gone. Foster, Jones and the girl. It's Alma we have to find, but she's scarpered.'

They had little enough to go on, but Frank seemed disinclined to look for more. Joe was fascinated by his proprietorial air toward the squalid little man Leonard.

'If Leonard's a businessman, perhaps the fight was over money. Most common cause of disputes around town from what I see,' Joe said.

'Young man,' Frank said, leaning forward to fix Joe with his beady black eyes. 'When you've been around as long as I have you'll know that sex is a lot more dangerous than money.

In any case,' he cracked his knuckles as he lay his arms across the forensics report, 'I'd still like to know where your girl-friend was that night. Not telling us everything, is she? Nor you. Why's that, I wonder.'

*

As he left Morecombe House Joe kept to the shady side of George Street. He looked across the river toward the ranges, hoping for the massed darkness he'd learned meant a weather change. Always from the south-west it came, bruised clouds heavy with rain. Sometimes a yellowish tinge signalled hail. One minute a mere wisp of gossamer, the next a blackened wad of steel wool rising from the southern horizon. He'd felt it before. There'd be a wind change, the pigeons suddenly began to seek shelter, roosting on the sandstone ledges of the ornate Treasury building. The trees stirred but when he looked south he saw only white streaks of cloud in a harsh blue sky. Rain was at least a day away, but the build-up would be sultry. He'd never get used to the relentless humidity.

He crossed to the middle of Queen Street to wait in the open sun, no shelter at the tram stop. He'd come to love Brisbane's trams, the snubbed noses of the gunmetal grey giving no indication which direction they might move next, the way they waddled sedately along the rails, forcing traffic to a standstill at each stop.

'Hold on!' As he swung into the open carriage a woman leaped onto the running board. It was Rose.

The conductor, imperious but faintly silly in a kepi, tugged his leather cord, *ding-ding*, and the tram edged forward between the iron semicircles of the Victoria Bridge. Give someone a bell, with the power to leave passengers stranded, and people became tyrants of their small carriage world, Joe thought, as he slid his arm around her waist. Together they reached for the hanging leather loops to steady themselves before moving to a wooden slatted seat near the doorway.

'Been to the library again?' he said. He caught the scent of her hair, the sweet smell of sweat mingled with talcum powder on a body he hoped to know more of.

Rose caught her breath, ran her hand through her hair, bunching it up and lifting it from the back of her neck. Her cheeks were flushed, her movements jerky. The conductor caught the American accent and smirked at two men in baggy woollen uniforms.

'What happened?' Joe said.

'There are so many people in the streets these days, too much rush,' Rose said. Joe saw her return the conductor's glare but chose not to react, busy tracing the curves of her face.

The tram rolled across the Victoria Bridge and rattled into Grey Street.

'Where are you going?' Joe said. 'Can I see you later?'

'We're getting together at Clem's, an editorial meeting. You know the place. I don't know how I'd survive this northern backwater if it weren't for Clem and Nina. And *Meanjin*. I want to talk to Judith. Why don't you meet me there?'

Joe watched as she talked, her mind distant, her thoughts elsewhere.

'What time? I've got someone I've gotta see,' Joe said. The tram stopped on Sydney Street and he swung down.

She leaned toward him, holding her hat. 'Come as soon as you can.'

*

He couldn't put it off any longer. Elmer deserved an explanation, even if he didn't expect justice. Cap in hand, heart in mouth, Joe pushed open the door to the Carver Club on Wednesday afternoon, barely twenty-four hours since Duke's murder. For murder it was. Cold-blooded murder, whatever Monroe might say about escape attempts. Joe knew how it worked. There'd be a reprimand, maybe. Just one MP's word against a prisoner with no witnesses worth interviewing. Not likely the brass would listen to Mrs Lakursky.

He felt reproachful eyes follow him down the hallway to the guardroom. No matter that he offered no prejudgement, no matter his open respect for Elmer. He was white, shielded from all that these men had lived with, the insults and taunts they'd had to bear. The dirty jobs no one else wanted, the orders shouted, the batons wielded for no good cause. Boy, come over here. Now.

He knocked and waited.

'Sure, come on in now.' The velvet voice from within.

Joe stood in the doorway, uncertain of his reception. 'Duke's dead,' he said.

Elmer, seated behind his desk, waved him in with a sad smile.

'You've heard,' Joe said, standing in front of the desk. 'Officially he was shot trying to escape. No one saw it happen but that's what they'll agree. I'm sorry, is all I can say. I shouldn't have let Monroe anywhere near him.'

'No point blaming yourself,' Elmer said, pointing to a seat. 'We've seen what Monroe and his boys do, what they get up to on and off duty. It'd be nigh impossible for anyone to keep them in check, least of all here in South Brisbane — where they keep all us problem people. Or that's the way the local police act, pushing the local blacks around even worse than us. The kitchen girl's got a brother in jail, her father's been in too, even her sister's been picked up more than once. I guess we're just another part of the picture.'

Joe shouldn't have worried. Elmer was a good man, practical. He knew who was to blame and didn't waste time getting angry at people trying to help.

'Still. I do blame myself. Monroe's not to be trusted, I knew that. I should have kept a better eye on him. But there's more to it. Duke had offered to help me, and maybe that's why he was killed.'

Elmer looked up, his eyes questioning.

'Duke was in a cell next to another prisoner, Private Teague. Teague's charged with murder, a knife fight that got out of hand when the naval patrol went to bust up a brawl. They were all drunk. The only thing Teague remembers is that sailors were loading barrels onto the back of a truck somewhere near the end of Wharf Street. One of the soldiers was knifed and Teague had a weapon so he's taken the can. No witnesses who weren't drunk.'

'What's that got to do with Duke? He'd be the last person to get into a fight.' Elmer's expression was stone.

'Duke heard something, something Monroe told Teague. He didn't hear it all, wasn't sure what they were up to, something about Monroe offering help, but it sounds like they're in cahoots. I wouldn't put it past Monroe to be in league with black-marketeers. I've been following them for some time, collecting evidence. It looks like someone's stealing army gasoline and it's likely Teague saw something. Maybe gasoline drums being offloaded. Duke said he'd listen in on Teague and Monroe some more. I told him I'd get a letter to his girl, speak for him at the court martial. The least I could have done.'

'We've had gasoline go missing.' Elmer leaned toward Joe, his long arms resting on the desk. 'From the Darra camp and some from here. You think Monroe's involved? Wouldn't put it past him. Although he's not exactly sharp enough to run it himself.'

'No. That'd be his pal Hayden. In Naval Shore Patrol.'

'The big blond?'

'That's him. I saw Monroe at the Royal a couple of days ago. He met a taxi driver, one of those locals with limitless supplies of gas. But now I'm wondering if the local police are involved as well, can't be sure if they were following the crooks or meeting them. It won't be easy trapping them. Too many people involved. But legally, you know, it's sabotage.'

From behind them came the sound of a truck backing into the loading ramp at the kitchen.

'Taxi driver? Maybe the deliveryman can help, reckon he knows most of the drivers around town. Seems like he's a bit of a motor enthusiast, I've even seen him driving a Buick Series 60 Coupe.' Elmer smiled appreciatively, the Detroit machinist. 'Not what you'd expect of a deliveryman. But he knows the taxi business, too. We could sound him out.'

The deliveryman bent down from the back of the truck to pass a wooden crate to the man below. Six crates in all before he jumped from the tray to help transfer them inside. Bottles clinked as he and the soldier lugged the crates into the kitchen, where they stacked them on the floor of the store-room. Gently.

Amazing how much alcohol soldiers drank, not to mention how much they were prepared to pay for it.

'Can I have a word?' Elmer asked. 'Mr . . .?'

The black private scarpered.

The man halted at the top of the ramp.

'Dawes,' he said. 'William Dawes. What do you want? I've deliveries to make.'

'Yeah,' Elmer said. 'We know about the deliveries, of which we are most grateful. But it does rather put you in an awkward position, don't it?'

Dawes made no response.

'I hear you drive a Series 60 Coupe. Well cared for from what I hear, spotless.'

'A Buick coupe,' Dawes said. 'I look after it. So what?'

'Hear you do paying jobs sometimes, drive things around. Like this.' Elmer glanced at the crates stacked against the wall. 'Not always legit, though, is it?'

'No one's complained so far,' Dawes said. 'Why now?'

'I hear you do other paying jobs, too. Drive people around.'

'So?'

Joe moved forward. 'Know most of the taxi drivers around town, do you?'

'A few. Why?'

'Ever met one called Leonard?' Joe said.

'Sure. Everyone knows Leonard. He runs a few taxis, has a couple of drivers. I'm not one of them,' Dawes said.

'How do they manage for gas?' Elmer said. 'Can't be easy getting enough for such a big enterprise.'

Dawes stared at Joe, defiant.

'Reckon he might know someone,' he said. 'Or some of his mates.'

'It's those "mates" I need to know about,' Joe said, reaching forward to grab Dawes's collar.

'Listen, pal, you'll tell us what you know,' Elmer said, standing between the men, gently pulling Joe back. He pointed once more at the stacked crates, the cartons piled against the back wall. 'If you want us to keep sweet about all of this.'

Dawes looked around, checking no one could hear.

'I can tell you where they store some of it, but I won't take you there,' he said.

'Fine,' Elmer said. 'We'll check it out.'

Joe shrugged his shoulders, arms now relaxed at his side. 'And this Leonard,' he said. 'What else can you tell me about him? Know where he was on Friday night maybe?'

Chapter Twenty-Eight

Rose stepped onto the verandah, overwhelmed by the aroma from the jasmine twined through the lattice. The smell was sickly, like the domesticity she and James had fought so hard to escape. Yet so much had happened in the last few days that she longed for the company of friends, the simple act of sharing a cup of tea, a glass of wine. She found that, to her surprise, all she wanted was companionship and light conversation.

The murmur of voices drew her through the corridor to the kitchen at the back of the house. Judith, arms plunged into soapy water, was washing dishes that she passed to Jack, who talked ceaselessly as he dried them — haphazardly — on a tea towel. As Rose watched, he placed them onto a table from which Alma lifted them, sliding them with care onto the shelf above.

'What are you doing here?' Rose said.

'Alma's helping,' Judith said, 'and I'm most grateful. Jack's good at drying but honestly he has no idea where to put things, just piles them anyhow. Alma's already worked out where everything goes.'

Alma smiled, more at ease than Rose had ever seen her.

'So you've met,' Rose said.

'Yes,' Judith said. 'Alma arrived while we were working on the proofs. We've had a lovely time, and Alma's told me a lot about Brisbane. I must say the University Commission is very relaxed. I don't know exactly what they expect. No one tells me and no one asks me to do anything. There doesn't seem much to do, in fact. Just a bit of filing and record keeping. So no one worries if I leave for the afternoon. It's easy to come and help whenever Clem needs a hand. I can't complain.'

Judith motioned toward a room adjoining the corridor from where Rose heard the sound of paper being shuffled, a chair scraping. A door slammed as Clem emerged from within, a sheaf of papers in one hand, his mouth twisted with irritation.

'Judith, see if you can retrieve anything of this when you get a chance, will you? How can so many people mangle the English language without trying? Oh hello, Rose.' He flung the papers on the kitchen table in a messy pile before retreating to his room.

Judith pulled the plug, water gurgling as it escaped down the hole. She dried her hands on a tea towel, picked up the manuscript, neatened the pages and tapped them into a stack.

'Not much of an editorial meeting, I'm afraid,' she said. 'Clem thinks there's too much basic copyediting to do first. I'll take it all home to read in the park. I love the jacarandas at this time of year.'

'I couldn't stay there,' Alma said, her back to Rose as she finished stacking the dried plates.

'Quite right too, from what I hear,' Judith said.

Rose sighed. What was she to do? 'Were you followed?' she said.

Alma shook her head and lowered her gaze.

Judith exchanged a worried look with Jack as she packed

the manuscripts into her leather handbag. 'Remember what we talked about,' she said. 'You can do whatever you choose to do but you must be firm. With yourself above all.'

'Yes,' Alma said, her eyes locked on Judith's. 'I'll try.'

'Anyone here?'

At the familiar voice Rose turned. She watched Joe peer into the corridor, his figure silhouetted against the light.

'Through here,' she said, her hand held out to him as he threaded his way past the potted palms. 'You know Judith? Jack?' He shook hands with each in turn.

'Yes, pleased to meet you again,' he said, before focusing attention past them. 'And you must be?'

Rose watched Alma claw at the neck of her shirt, the short sleeves making her arms look even thinner.

'I'm Rose's sister,' she said, eyes lowered.

Joe held her hand lightly, watched the pulse at her neck quicken. 'Pleased to meet you, Alma.'

'How?' Alma retrieved her hand. She appealed to Rose, her mouth open.

'It's alright,' Rose said, her arm circling her waist.

'We're just about to catch the tram home,' Judith said to Joe. 'Didn't you say you lived at New Farm? I've got a room there, Jack too now. Why don't you join us? We could go to the park, it's lovely under the jacarandas in the afternoon. In fact, I vote we move the editorial meeting there. What do you all think?'

Safety in numbers, Rose thought. Why not?

Judith and Jack took the lead, arms entwined. Clem waved half-heartedly from the front door as the rest of them walked to the tram stop in the middle of the road. They stood in a huddle opposite the gates to the cemetery.

'Were you here on Friday night? Did you catch the tram?' Joe said to Alma.

She folded her arms and shivered as she stared across the road to the darkness. 'No, I wasn't,' she said.

'I was,' Rose said. 'Why do you ask?'

'Did you see anything?'

'Like what?'

'A car? People?'

Alma lowered her head, gently rocking back and forth.

'There was a car,' Rose said. 'Nearly skittled Laurie and me, we left Clem's at the same time.'

A crowded tram pulled up, talk interrupted as they boarded. Judith and Jack clung to leather straps, Joe steadied himself against the frame. Rose, wedged between Joe and a wooden seat, held Alma's arm.

'Are you heading back to work?' Rose said, confused.

'I might tag along if that's okay,' Joe said. 'I need to talk to your sister.'

The tram moved into Annerley Road and passed the brick wall of Boggo Road. Rose wanted to explain, not sure if she wanted Joe to stay or go, surprised at her depth of emotion. But his focus was on Alma, her eyes clamped shut, her fists clenched. He leaned forward to speak, his voice gentle.

'I'm glad you're out,' he said.

'How dare they lock up women,' Rose said, furious. She took Alma's hand. 'It's men who cause the trouble in the first place. It's just another hypocrisy.'

Through the open side of the tram Rose glared out into the heat of a colourless afternoon. Beyond the river, the spire of the Town Hall rose above the geometric patterns of buildings, the foreground a mass of vegetation. Splashes of red and purple among the blue haze of the afternoon. A lorry rumbled by, its cargo of soldiers leaning out of the open sides, rifles propped against their knees. On their way to Roma Street.

'Do you have anywhere to go?' Jack asked Alma in a soft voice.

'Not now,' Alma said, pulling her arm free. She glared at Rose, at Joe, at the soldiers and the dusty street. 'Nowhere. I hate this town.'

'I might know somewhere,' Jack said. 'Somewhere peaceful.' He held Judith's hand. 'After we've dropped Judith at her place.'

*

Eddie wasn't happy. Honestly, these bastards had no idea of the lie of the land, blundering around like bulls in a china shop. Didn't they know that the only way to move a mob was to lie doggo, wait for the right time, move quickly but only when necessary. A single yap was all it took, plus a bit of simple cunning. But these bloody Yanks had no clue. Pissing off the locals, starting fights, rubbing everyone up the wrong way. And in business that backfired. Now he'd have to clear the warehouse. More double handling. He'd got dragged into Leonard's troubles and the tall Yank had proved nothing but a mistake, trying to make a bit on the side, causing trouble. He was done with them all.

He parked at the back of the Mountain View, entered by the back door, slapped Sam on the back. 'Tell the bloke I'll sort this,' he said. 'And tell him thanks.'

Mo, Monroe and Hayden sat at a table against the side wall, drinks in hand, loose change scattered in front of them. Mo's cigar rested on the edge of a glass ashtray.

Eddie slid into an empty seat. 'You've got to move the goods,' he said. 'The Provos know about it. I'm not involved from here on.'

Mo lifted the cigar from the ashtray, sucking on the

moistened end. A businessman. Eddie might have dealings with this one again, but not the others. He weighed the two MPs as a dunnyman might balance two buckets of shit. Incompetent fools.

'We'll need a truck,' said Mo. 'Everything moves tonight.'

Chapter Twenty-Nine

Joe steadied himself as the truck veered into Moggill Road, swerving to avoid a hole in the road. How had he let himself be talked into this? What in heaven's name had possessed him? He glanced in the rear-vision mirror. Suspects in a murder inquiry, a lady (perhaps two) of dubious occupation. Beside him, the bushman with philosophical pretensions steered the truck around another hole, riding the bumps like a rodeo rider.

They bounced onto a dirt road that wandered through the countryside, surprisingly lush despite the dry weather. Fields of Jersey cows munched through long grass. Jack clung to the steering wheel as he swerved to avoid a huge kangaroo that leaped across the road. Behind, three smaller ones stood at the edge of the road leaning backwards, like town councillors with their hands in fob pockets, shocked at this intrusion. Joe had forgotten how close the countryside was. Apart from a few road trips on jobs for work, mostly he walked the square mile of town, only rarely venturing further afield.

Judith had scavenged blankets and clothing, some tins of bully beef and a couple of packets of biscuits. Everything piled into the back of Jack McKinney's truck beside coils of rope, a dusty saddle, boxes of tools. Joe had ushered the two women into the back seat and joined Jack on the bench seat at the front.

'I keep basics at the camp,' Jack said. 'Flour and sugar, tea, of course. There's a rainwater tank filled from the tin roof. It's only rough, but it's a wonderful place to stay. Sometimes for a week or two, while I write. Now I've got a room in the boarding house I don't need it as often. Clem's going to publish my book, so things are looking up.'

'Rose has told me a little about you,' said Joe, and turned to face the dark-haired girl huddled beside Rose. 'But I need to know more if I'm to help. You know we've been looking for you? You know why?'

'Yes,' Alma said. 'Frank and Leonard want me to take the blame. But I won't. Not this time.' She curled in on herself, her hand in Rose's.

'Why did Leonard take you to the hospital?' Joe asked her.

'It wasn't him. It was Frank. He wanted me under lock and key, so I couldn't do a flit.'

'Would you?'

'Where would I go?'

'Have the police questioned you? Did Frank interview you?'

'There's no need. They've agreed what happened. It won't matter what I say. But I didn't do it. I slept with them, got drunk. But it wasn't me who fought. I won't take the blame this time.'

Jack looked ahead, concentrating on the track that wound around itself like a corkscrew. He seemed not to hear, or at least made no comment.

Joe wondered whether Alma was as innocent as Rose believed. She certainly didn't look to have the strength — physical or emotional — to kill a man. But stranger things had happened, and alcohol added fuel to what might otherwise be small fires.

'So what *did* happen that night?' he asked the girl softly.

'It was an accident,' she said. 'Just a silly accident.'

'Tell me.'

'They came with Eddie, from the dance hall. They'd been drinking but wanted more. It was getting late but Eddie knows where to get whiskey and gin, Leonard too. Eddie left the truck but he and Leonard went to get some more drink, left them with me. You know. The little one was funny, quite shy in a way. But Slim was trouble, you could tell as soon as you saw him. Prowled around the place, complained we didn't have any decent records. Said the place was like the cat house he'd grown up in. But he was the one with the money.'

'How long were Eddie and Leonard gone?'

'About an hour or so.'

'You had sex with them?'

'Yes. They paid and I don't mind. Not when I've been drinking. But I wouldn't do what he wanted, I'm not a prostitute. I don't do those things.'

'What things?'

'I don't want to say.'

'Then what happened?'

'I said I'd make them something to eat. Just eggs and toast, but something to take their minds off waiting for the drink. And me. But then Leonard came back with the gin. Eddie went off in his cab. And there was a fight.'

'What about?'

'Money. Leonard wanted money for fuel, he'd driven all the way out to Darra and it costs. But Slim said he wouldn't pay anymore, said I'd cheated him. Said if I wouldn't do what he wanted he wouldn't pay Leonard for the gin.'

'What about Jones? Snow, the other soldier?'

'He left when Slim and Leonard started fighting. He just scarpered when they started throwing punches.'

'Just fists?' Joe asked. 'No weapons?'

'I had a knife.' Alma held her hands clasped on her lap. 'Just a kitchen knife. For the bread, you know.'

'What happened to it?'

'I put it down when the fight started.'

'Where?'

'On the floor. Beside the bed.'

'Where was Leonard's wife? Was she there in bed the whole time?'

'Deidre? Yes.'

'Did she get up?'

'She can't, or not by herself. It was all an accident. They were on the ground, rolling and punching, Deidre started crying. Leonard pulled Slim up. They were both drunk, trying to hit each other but mostly missing and falling down. It was almost funny. Then Slim swung at Leonard and fell. I didn't see all of it, just heard the noise as Slim fell forward onto Deidre's bed. Like a balloon, it sounded, like when you let out the air, you know. A sigh almost, a long wheeze. I thought it was Deidre to begin with, she can't breathe sometimes, makes that spluttery . . . She's been kind to me. And she's dying.'

Joe watched Alma's shoulders sag.

'Deidre had the knife?' Joe said.

'Yes,' Alma said.

'You have to go to the police. I'll go with you.'

'No. Never. She's been kind to me and it was just a silly accident.'

Joe turned back to look through the windscreen. The truck bounced along the dirt track and he held onto the handle.

'Tell me about Frank and Leonard,' he said without looking around.

'They're mates, known each other for years. Frank knew his parents, I think, Deidre too. They're thick as thieves. Leonard runs a book and Frank's a big gambler. Now he uses Leonard to keep an eye on his other business.'

Jack changed gears, pumping the accelerator to no effect. The engine stuttered, slowed, and finally the vehicle lumbered to a stop.

'Blast and damnation,' Jack said. 'Out of fuel.' He wrenched the door open, lowered himself to the ground and walked to the back of the truck. Alma and Rose remained inside as Joe got out and joined Jack, glad to stretch his legs and relax muscles battered from the truck's vibrations. Around them birds and insects screeched and buzzed, tree branches creaked in the gentle wind. The two men unloaded a metal drum.

'Have any trouble getting gas?' Joe said.

'Not usually,' Jack said. 'I don't use the truck as often as I used to, bicycle most places around town. So I save the coupons for when I need them.'

Rose wound down the rear window as Jack lifted the jerry can, positioning the nozzle so the fuel ran smoothly. 'Why do you ask everyone about fuel?' she said. 'Sometimes it seems like that's all you're interested in.'

Joe saw Jack's smile. 'A lot of it's going missing. Army supplies are being siphoned off somewhere.'

'Where there's money to be made,' Jack said sadly, 'there'll always be crooks.' He screwed the cap back on the jerry can.

'I wonder if I might be able to help,' Rose said, coquettishness forgotten as she remembered something. Joe recalled the coupons in the suitcase at her apartment. 'I met a schoolgirl earlier, someone I see at the library. She was lugging an enormous case of contraband. Said she'd found it near the Tower Mill, stashed in some sort of underground tanks. She had lipstick and nylons but said there was stacks of other things there. Boxes and crates. And drums, I think she said. Could they be fuel?'

'Could be.' The two men hauled themselves back into the front and Jack started the motor. 'Where's this Tower Mill?' Joe asked.

'Up behind Roma Street station. Surely you've seen it, it's the highest point in the city.'

'Convict era,' Jack said. 'Very old. I don't know about any water tanks.'

'Can you show me on the way back?'

'Sure,' Jack said. 'It's on the way.'

After a hamlet Jack said was called Brookfield, the road narrowed. Soon it deteriorated into a simple one-lane dirt track that dipped to cross gullies and twisted around grassy slopes. They drove through alternating light and shade, the pale afternoon light disappearing as they swerved between hills. The valley would be cool in winter but now it was hot and airless as the truck bounced from rut to rut. In the back seat Rose clung to the door and Alma leaned forward to grab the front seat. Jack rode the truck like a horseman. In his element. They entered a tunnel, massive trees on either side touching overhead. The sinuous roots, swirling around a central trunk, were metres tall.

'Buttress roots, they're called,' Jack said. Joe felt he had entered a place more sacred than a church. Light filtered as if through stained glass, the world hushed as if in prayer. Joe had never been anywhere so wild yet so peaceful.

A large black bird raced across the track, its head bobbing as its yellow scarf swung from side to side.

'Didn't know you had turkeys,' Joe said.

'Sure, scrub turkeys,' Jack said. 'You see lots around here. Not bad eating, if you cook them long enough.'

Joe glanced in the rear-vision mirror. Alma sat huddled in a ball, her eyes wide as she stared into the dense forest, the vines and lianas writhing out from deep shadows. Spooky. All very well for a bushman like Jack, but Joe couldn't see either girl being happy to stay here.

But then the sky opened and they passed a store, a squat wooden building with a tiny verandah and a milk truck parked outside. So there were people who lived here, although none were out at this time of day.

'Not much further,' Jack said, speaking to the girls in the back seat. 'We've got to walk a bit of a way. I'll let the milkman know you're staying. He keeps to himself, won't let on to anyone outside the valley.'

Alma turned to gaze at the milk truck through the back window.

After half a mile or so Jack parked the truck beside a track leading off the road. He led them down the pathway through the trees to a small clearing where a hut of wooden slab walls and a tin roof stood alone. Beside it, a rusty tank sat on a high platform, a slow drip falling into a muddy puddle below. Jack checked inside the hut, whistling as he propped open timber windows and shook out the woollen blanket on the single bed. Joe remained outside with Rose and Alma. Neither looked happy.

Rose shook herself and bent to retrieve the suitcase. 'It'll be like bush camping,' she said, following Jack.

'A bit more than that,' Jack said, mimicking hurt pride. 'Look, there's a kerosene stove, a shower under the rainwater tank. I've planted a garden at the back but we need rain.' He pointed to a patch of bare earth where three tomato seedlings struggled to hold their heads up.

Alma slumped onto an upturned milk crate while Joe left Rose to unpack clothes from their small suitcase and stack the supplies they'd brought. They'd manage for a few nights.

'We'll come back tomorrow,' Jack said. 'Won't we, Joe? You be alright for a night?'

A shriek from the trees made Alma leap to her feet. Rose moved to give her a hug.

'It's only cockatoos,' she said.

'Boisterous bloody birds,' Jack said. 'They won't bother you.'

'I'm back on duty in an hour,' Joe said. 'We should go.'

Jack patted Rose on the shoulder and waved in Alma's direction as he headed for the truck.

'Alma, I'll think about what you told me,' Joe said. 'But you may have to say something to the police.'

'I won't hurt Deidre,' Alma said. 'Never. Even if they charge me. She's sick. I won't do it to her; it'd kill her.'

Joe nodded. He held his arm out but Rose ignored it, instead lifting hers to the side of his face. He felt the tremble of her fingers; she was so close he could hear her breath. She held his gaze as he covered her hand with his. 'We'll come tomorrow. You'll be okay.' He released her hand, made to move.

'We'll manage,' she whispered. 'It's not as if we haven't had lots of practice.'

*

Joe caught the glint of the setting sun in the driver's mirror as they neared the Grey Street Bridge. He heard the screech of flying foxes squabbling in the massive fig trees, whistling and whirring like a child's toy, black beneath the evening sky. They turned into Roma Street, only to be held fast in a cavalcade of army trucks. Jack edged forward, caught between khaki vehicles jostling the milling crowd. Men in woollen trousers with ill-fitting jackets, polished boots, hats at a rakish angle. Women and children mingled, clutching hands as they pushed forward through the throng.

'Guns,' Jack said. 'Going north.' The battles in New Guinea were taking their toll and the push through the Pacific was gathering momentum. Guadalcanal, Tulagi. More soldiers on the move, in greater numbers. 'Poor buggers.' Jack's face was set. Old enough to have seen the other one, Joe thought.

Halted in the traffic, Joe watched men swarm towards the waiting train, kit bags slung over their shoulders. Once aboard, they hauled down heavy windows so they could lean out. *Ca-clunk. Ca-clunk.* Women waved, their children held high to see above the crowd. The heat offered an easy excuse as sweat poured down the men's faces to mingle with their tears.

Finally released from the traffic, Jack steered the truck left, climbing the hill toward the Tower Mill. To their left, Albert Park offered its grassy slopes to soldiers sleeping off an afternoon's drinking or those with no money for a few hours in a cheap hotel. He turned onto Wickham Terrace and parked beside a concrete air raid shelter. He hauled on the handbrake and opened the driver's door. He grabbed a heavy flashlight from under the front seat. 'Might as well have a look around now we're here. You can't get in, though. Been closed for years.'

Chapter Thirty

'Do you want a cup of tea?' Rose asked as she lifted a kettle from the wooden stove and walked to the corrugated iron tank. She raised the brass hinge and turned the tap, waiting for water to fill the vessel. 'It might take me some time to get the fire going,' she said. 'But we'll manage, won't we? We're good at making do.'

Immovable on the upturned crate, Alma leaned forward, arms resting on her knees, head down. 'Suppose so,' she said, not looking at Rose. 'But I'm tired of it. Making do, getting by, having to watch what I say all the time or be out on the street again. I'm sick of it. I just want to get away.'

Rose kneeled on the hard ground to scrunch old newspaper into balls. She placed them in the stove's box together with overlapped twigs to form a sort of teepee. She lit a match and the paper flared, the yellow flames licking around the twigs until they glowed red. She stood to crack three larger branches over her knee, added them to the fire and fanned the flames with a magazine she'd found on the bench in the kitchen.

'Look at us. What a pair.' She closed the firebox and dragged a second crate from the side of the room to join Alma.

'So who's Joe?' Alma raised an eyebrow. 'He's an MP. Why'd he help us get away?'

Rose bit her lower lip. 'He's a good man. At least I think he is. He seems to want to do the right thing. Even if he is a policeman. I know he'll help us, he won't let Frank take you.'

'No one stops Frank,' Alma said. 'Not when he wants something. What does Joe want? They all want something.'

'Do they?' Rose thought about the men she knew. Yes, most of them did. 'What did Bob want? Fancy, we both saw him that night. What a small town Brisbane is.'

'Slim? Did you really? Where?'

'At the Trocadero. We danced a few numbers, but he was drunk and wandered off. Eddie must have collected them and driven him and the other one to Leonard's.'

'I did hit him, you know,' Alma said. 'All those dirty things he said, swearing at me, making out I was a whore. I could have killed him. I was angry enough. Maybe it was me that caused it.'

'Why do you always want to take the blame?' Rose said.

'Why don't you want to talk about Joe?' Alma said. 'Why do you always change the topic?'

Rose stood, found a tea towel draped over a hook and wrapped it around the handle of the kettle. She watched steam rise as she poured boiling water into the enamel teapot.

'Because I don't know what to think. You know what I'm like. So does James. He wouldn't want me to mooch around by myself while he's in prison — he always called me his good-time girl! And it's not as if anyone gets hurt. But somehow I don't know. Joe's got under my skin and I'm not sure what to do about it. He's different from the others.'

'Well, don't ask me,' Alma said, blowing into the cup of

tea she'd poured for herself. 'Look at my taste in men. Creeps, all of them.'

A kookaburra rattled the start of evening and above them the wooden rafters settled into their wire hitches as the tin roof creaked with the change of temperature.

'It's not as if our mother taught us anything useful. Not about men, that's for sure.' Rose looked at the ground, where a line of ants led from the cupboard to a puddle under the water tank. 'What a line of deadbeats she strung along. I wonder why she bothered. She told me once about the first man she loved,' she said, poking the fire with a stick, watching the smouldering coals. 'I didn't believe it to begin with. He was a student at university, someone with prospects. But nothing came of it, I don't know why. She loved him always, I think, it spoiled her life in ways I never understood. "Never cry over spilt milk," she'd say. But she always did. All the sweetness went sour over time.'

'She died when I was only a baby,' Alma said. 'I didn't know her.'

Rose sighed. 'Nan said she couldn't look after us both so they took you away. I cried myself to sleep for a week and said I'd find you one day. I know it took a long time. I'm sorry.'

They sat in silence, watching the ants move resolutely from cupboard to puddle. One ant staggered, a grain of sugar balanced between its front legs. Another dragged a dead ant behind it. The line barely wobbled.

'Do you really want to stay here?' Rose looked around at the rusty tin, the dirt floor, the sagging stretcher beds, the outdoor dunny.

'Where else could we go?'

'I could try to help you get away, we could go south. Doesn't have to be forever, just until things get sorted.'

Alma bit her lip. What did she have to lose?

*

At five o'clock, Corporal Jones of the 32nd Infantry Division sat on the ground together with nearly two hundred patients, his kitbag beside him, his personal effects returned, receipted and packed. He had his pay book stamped, his service record checked, his medical release signed. In fact, Jones had never had so many pieces of paper filled out, filed away, signed, rubber-stamped and pinned together. And the day wasn't over.

A line of field ambulances from the hospital ship would convey patients to the wharf and then all he had to hope for was safe passage across the Pacific. No Jap subs patrolling the coast or targeting shipping routes. Some chance. But anything was better than going back to the duty disposition he'd feared. Every day they discharged groups of patched-up men, returning them to their platoons. It had kept him awake most nights.

In January, he'd been in the push to Buna–Gona. Nothing had prepared him for the heat, the mud, the stench of rotting bodies, the sight of so many men covered with leeches like scraps of black cloth among the green. Stretcher-bearers as skeletal as the men they carried. Then Wau and Lae. Wounded and weak with malaria, he'd been evacuated to Brisbane in June. And now he was going home. How it'd been arranged he didn't know, and he didn't care. After all that had happened, he'd be glad to see the back of Brisbane.

Chapter Thirty-One

A conical structure stood on the hill, its smooth white cement render shining like ghostly skin. The structure was a landmark in town but Joe had never seen it up close before. He followed Jack along the path and circled the tower, running his hand against the smooth surface. There was a narrow wooden door, bolted shut, but no windows that he could see. It had certainly been built to last. He leaned back and saw a narrow observation deck skirted the upper level, jutting out from the tower itself. But he could see no way of getting up there.

'The Old Windmill,' Jack said in his new role as tour guide. 'Oldest building in the settlement. Built when the place was a prison.'

'A windmill?' Joe said. 'But where are the sails?'

'It was a crazy scheme. There wasn't enough wind so they used convicts on treadmills. Ended up like much of what passes for progress in this place — a white elephant.'

Below in the Roma Street rail yards lines of soldiers, like ants from this height, moved inexorably in one direction. North.

'I heard tell they hanged Aborigines here in the old days,' Jack said. 'Two poor buggers who killed a surveyor, if I remember right. Only trying to defend their land, like all those poor chaps down there are. Against the Japs.'

Below the tower Joe noticed two wooden structures, standing so low they seemed built for midgets. One gabled roof topped by a second, smaller one above a brick base. He assumed they covered the water tanks.

'Do you reckon this might be what Rose was talking about?' he said. 'They don't look well maintained.'

'What're you doing here, Washington?'

Joe spun around, confused.

'Here. Up here. I'm waiting for them.'

Joe and Jack looked up to see a dark shape separate itself from the white wall of the tower. Joe guessed Elmer McConachy's capacity to melt into the background came from years of practice. He'd noticed how the men at the Carver Club did it, lowering their faces so no white flickered in their eyes, their expressions hard as ebony. Joe knew he stuck out, his hair, his glasses, the freckles on the reddened skin of his face, whereas Elmer melded into the dark, even the pale salmon of his uniform a kind of camouflage in the evening light.

Leaning over the rail of the observation deck, Elmer's smile was broad. 'Didn't expect you so soon,' he said.

'How'd you get up there?' Jack said. 'I thought the tower was closed.'

'Never stopped a climber,' Elmer said, pointing to a coil of rope at his feet. 'The view from up here is positively copacetic.'

'Copper?' Jack said, shaking his head.

'"Bloody beaut," I think you'd say? "Grouse."' Joe was amused to find that cryptic words were not the exclusive domain of Aussies. 'What are you doing up there? Who are you waiting for?'

'Didn't I say I'd follow that delivery man Dawes?' Elmer said, doubling the rope over the rail so he could abseil down. 'He showed me one of the warehouses where they keep the goods, but they must have been warned. The place was cleaned out. Dawes told me they'd mentioned this as a backup, so I thought I'd come and sit here a while, enjoy the view, and wait and see who turns up. You can join me in the welcoming party if you want.' He slid to the ground, retrieved his rope, and Joe made the introductions.

'Jack, meet Sergeant Elmer McConachy.'

'Pleased to meet you, sir.' Elmer shook hands before bending to coil the rope. 'I heard what you said before about defending your land. Made sense to me.'

'Delighted to meet you,' Jack said. He shook hands and winked. 'In fact, it's copacetic.'

'So you've checked inside those sheds?' Joe asked.

'Yes. See the door that's hanging loose? There's stuff stowed in the tanks already but they haven't closed up properly. More will arrive, for sure. Maybe we should wait inside, now there's three of us.'

Joe shone the flashlight through the door onto what looked like a ladder. 'You alright, Jack? Sorry to have brought you into this.'

'Most fun I've had for ages,' he said. 'Wouldn't miss it for quids.'

'I'll go first to light the way, then. Elmer, you follow up after Jack.'

Joe descended into a subterranean world, the sound of his steps receding as he moved lower. At the bottom he turned and his flashlight snaked up the ladder. The others followed. Once inside, Joe shone the light above them in a circle, lighting a series of brickwork vaults that formed an intricate pattern of interweaving arches, a marvellous geometry of light and shade. He'd make sure to come back some time with his camera.

Elmer led them to the rear, where crates and drums lined the wall. Joe bent to look closer at the drums, waist height, around two feet in diameter, three ridges to strengthen the sides, two bungs on the lid. No markings but the smell of gasoline was strong. He wondered how they'd moved all this stuff; it was heavy and unwieldy. He used the flashlight to search and found a makeshift setup — a fixed pulley attached to a wooden beam with a rope coiled ready. Propped against the wall nearby was a wooden plank; set at a low enough angle, he guessed you could roll drums down it.

'So the kiddy was right, the one Rose mentioned,' Jack said. 'Must have taken a long time to amass this lot but it's a good place to store things, dry and cool, disused.'

Joe switched off the flashlight. Darkness enveloped them, the cement cold against their backs. 'Almost like when I was a kid playing hide and seek in the quarries around the Rouge,' he said.

'You know the Rouge?' Elmer said. 'Thought you came from New Jersey?'

'We moved there after '32,' Joe said.

'Your father involved in the Hunger March, was he?'

'Yeah. He was one of the people got hurt and never worked again.'

'They had it tough,' Elmer said. 'But they were real heroes. No doubt about it.'

'It's all well and good to fight for principles but there are always victims. Life was hard for us afterward.'

'Well, they were my heroes. I wouldn't have seen the Battle of the Overpass except for all those brave men in '32.'

'You were there?'

Elmer grunted. 'Yeah, and we did have a win, even though we took some beatings.'

'I saw the photos, the ones they managed to smuggle out. It was one of the things that made me want to become a photographer.'

'I have no idea what either of you are talking about,' Jack said. 'But shouldn't we be quiet?'

'Sure,' Joe said. 'I wonder how long we've got to wait.'

*

Joe heard the low scream of brakes, a truck's engine dying and a door slamming. Then a grunt as someone dragged a heavy object over metal, followed by the crunch of boots on gravel. A wooden door banged against the outside wall and a foot slapped the top metal step, the sound echoing through the cavernous space below.

'Jesus H Christ, give us a break,' said a familiar voice. 'These crates weigh a tonne and that's a teeny little ladder.' Joe wondered how Monroe would get his girth through the entrance and down the rungs. 'It'll take all night to get them down here. Fuck that fucker Eddie.'

At the back of the tank the three men huddled, Joe between Elmer's silent bulk and the old man. He felt Jack's silent chuckle and guessed he'd make it all into a good story. Joe saw Monroe in the entrance, his shape outlined against the evening sky as he balanced on the top of the ladder, a box held in his arms. He lowered the box onto the rung below and followed it down, lifting and lowering it rung by rung, descending in this awkward manner till he reached the floor.

Joe switched on his flashlight, directing the beam at Monroe now balanced on the bottom step, one foot on the floor, the other leg bent to hold up the box. Monroe raised his arm to shield his eyes from the light.

'Bates? That you? For crying out loud, don't just stand there. Get your ass over here. Hayden's lugging more damn crates but this ladder's a bitch. Give us a hand.'

Joe watched Monroe, his face puffy and breathing strained, struggling to keep his balance. He took a moment to note the stubble, the bleary eyes, the pink bulge of flesh pushing his shirt out above the trousers. Monroe at work was a rare sight and one to relish.

'Tell me why I should,' Joe said at last.

Monroe shook his head in confusion. 'That you, Sarge?'

'How would you like to explain these crates?' Joe said. 'And these drums?' He shone the flashlight around the open space, picking out rows of metal barrels along the back wall, a stack of wooden crates, cardboard boxes set down in front.

Butt Monroe didn't think fast and he didn't think quietly. Joe watched him ruminate, spit into the corner, then lower the box to the floor. He lumbered toward Joe in what would have been a menacing fashion had he been slimmer. When he saw the two men beside him he pulled up short. 'What's the coon doing here? And the grey-hair? Wrong side of the river for you, nigger,' he said, spitting at Elmer's feet.

'You don't use language like that around me,' Jack said and moved forward, hands clenched into fists.

'Just answer the question,' Joe said, putting his hand out to calm Jack. Elmer stood motionless.

'Deliveries, stuff for the quartermaster. What's it to you, Sarge?'

'Open those drums,' Joe said. 'And the crates.'

'You'll have to check with Bates,' Monroe said, sweet as a lamb. 'We're just delivery boys, no idea what the quarter-master has in storage.'

'Where did those come from?' Joe shone light back on the drums.

'No idea.' Monroe stood, arms crossed, leaning against the wall, the discarded box at his feet.

'What's going on down there?' Hayden's voice from the top of the ladder bounced around the enclosed space. 'Give us a hand, can you? Eddie . . .'

'Come on down,' Monroe said. 'We've got quite a reception here. The fancy boy, a grey-hair and a coon.'

When it came, Elmer's speed surprised Joe, the movement so swift and silent it was over before Joe realised it had even begun. Under the yellow light Monroe's face was puce, his eyes wide, Elmer's hand circling his throat.

Joe moved forward. 'Easy now. There are better ways of dealing with this. Leave it to me.'

Elmer grunted displeasure but relaxed his grip, dropping his arm as he made to turn away. At the same moment Joe saw Monroe twist, pivoting on the spot, moving faster than Joe thought possible as he reached for the gun slung low on his hip.

Later, Joe tried to remember making the move but he couldn't. All he knew was that his world blackened, his vision narrowed to a tiny circle of light, a pinprick of absolute certainty. He found himself, once again, in the ring at the youth club in New Jersey, on the day he'd broken his right hand. The day that ended his promise as a boxer and made him who he was. He was back there now, balancing on his feet, moving from side to side, listening to the boy's taunts. 'Whose father's a kike? A cripple? Come here, Jew boy.' Mr Mailer had taught him to ignore the insults, to listen only to your breathing, deliberate and slow. 'Don't get distracted, Joe,' he'd say. 'Concentrate. Keep your movements fluid and graceful. You're not a street fighter, remember. You're a boxer. Words don't matter.' He'd learned everything he knew from Mr Mailer, been trained so well it was ingrained, second nature.

But Mr Mailer was wrong. Words *do* matter, he knew that now. In their own way words can kill. Hell, isn't that how this war began? With words? He didn't need to think. He reacted viscerally but with control. His right fist met a doughy chest, not stopping until it reached the rubbery sternum one inch below. With his left arm stabbing from underneath, Joe swung into the man's chin.

Monroe slumped to the ground, his head between his knees, and vomited onto his dusty black boots.

Chapter Thirty-Two

F rank waved to the barmaid, collected his beer and idled toward the back room of the Terminus. Eddie was set up in the corner, ready for the only midweek races left in town since the Yanks had pitched tents all over Doomben and Ascot. An American sailor leaped to his feet when he saw Frank but the dealer raised his hand to reassure him, ushered him back to his seat, all the while drawing cards from the pack.

They'd find Alma and charge her, there'd be no trouble there. He'd got one of the detectives onto it, he'd track her down. If not, there was always Rose. Leonard had rung to tell him about Joe's visit but he could deal with him, too. This was his town and he called the shots. The Yanks'd be gone soon enough.

Smoke hung low over tables littered with cards, money, bottles. Frank had never got the knack of cards. Horseflesh made more sense to him; at least you could see the muscles rippling, study the pedigree, assess the odds. Cards were a mug's game, just a matter of luck, with only the bidding itself a test of strength. And he'd never let himself be the victim of luck.

'Quiet here?' he said. He placed a glass on the table near the window, checked around the room but saw no punters he recognised.

'Eddie had things to see to.' The dealer didn't look up.

Frank settled into the deep armchair. No point wasting a good beer. From where he sat he could listen to talk around the table, pick up some gossip on what was happening around the traps. You never knew when you'd hear something interesting, pick up a titbit that might be useful. He pulled the curtain aside. Outside, patrons were queueing at the entrance to the Trocadero.

*

Joe parked the army truck at the back of the Town Hall and marched Monroe and Hayden past the cells and up the stairs to the back kitchen. Prisoners sat eating a late supper, Teague and Bryson chatting happily to each other across plates of mutton, the Japanese storekeeper ignored on the other side of the table.

He pushed both men through the door. 'Sit,' he said, pointing to two chairs in front of his desk. He pulled the telephone toward him and spun the dial. 'Lieutenant Bates? We need you at the Provost Office. Now.'

From the other end of the corridor came the sound of Mrs Lakursky's mop slopping the tiled floor, the rhythmic swish as it swept from side to side. Joe heard a soft whimper followed by an uptake of breath. A cry cut short.

'Wait here,' Joe said, going to the door to investigate. Monroe smirked while Hayden used a split match to pick his teeth.

Mrs Lakursky worked along the corridor, her mop forming watery figures of eight on the parquetry. She lowered the mop into the bucket and wiped her eyes.

'Are you alright?' Joe said. He stood close, his hand stopping the mop.

'Yes,' she said, eyes on the floor.

'No you're not,' Joe said, watching as her face crumpled, the soft lines of her wrinkles etched deeper than ever. She turned away as she hauled the mop up through the wringer.

'What happened? Is it something Monroe's done?' Joe held the mop, keeping it steady, forcing her to stop and look at him, head tilted upward. 'Tell me. Can I help?'

'No one can,' she said, reaching into the pocket of her apron for a rectangle of yellow paper, crushed and sodden. A telegram.

'Is it Danny?'

'I felt sorry for the boy, to be honest,' she said, her eyes brimming but her voice strong. 'The telegram boy. He didn't know what to say. No one does. I'll be getting on with my work, then.' She retrieved her mop from Joe's clasp. The grey strings moved in circles across the floor as she retreated, her back straight. 'They said he'd got a medal, much good it'll do him.'

Joe stood helpless, open-mouthed. Among so many deaths, this was just another. Each one a knife to someone's heart.

He returned to the room, sat behind the desk and waited.

'Don't know what we're doing here,' Hayden said. 'Butt's explained it all. Bates'll confirm it.'

'We'll see,' Joe said. The two envelopes lay on the desk among the papers strewn in across the surface. He used his finger to slide open the top one, the one he knew was from his mother. But instead of pages of writing there was only a single sheet tucked into a folded newspaper clipping. He unfolded both.

'What's going on?'

Joe looked up to see the major bearing down on him like a destroyer, torpedoes ready to fire.

'I hope you can explain where you've been for the last two hours. I've had about enough of your insubordination, we've had more complaints from the CIB. You don't have any authority to enter private houses or interrogate civilians unless they work for the army. This is a police matter. What's Monroe here for? And who's this?'

'I have arrested these men on charges associated with black-market dealing in gasoline, among other things,' Joe said.

'This is the first I've heard of any such investigation,' Mitchell said. 'You brief me before you go off half-cocked on one of your private crusades, you hear me?'

'Yes, sir,' Joe said. 'But you'll see what I mean soon enough.'

At that instant Lieutenant Bates appeared. He feigned a look of surprise. 'What are both of you doing here?' he said to Monroe and Hayden. 'I told you the stores had to be all stowed away today. The new consignment of *matériel* arrives early tomorrow and we're running out of capacity at the base.' Seeing Mitchell he quickly saluted, and with a melodramatic gesture acknowledged Joe. 'What's all this about? I hope you haven't interrupted the work of these men, Sergeant. I'm sure Major Mitchell has explained it to you.'

'I was about to do just that,' the major said, 'but I'll let you have the pleasure.' He sat at his desk, crossed his legs and arms and leaned back in his chair, a smile spreading from ear to ear.

'The Lieutenant Colonel is expecting the goods to be transferred tonight,' Bates said.

'Ah,' Joe said. 'We wouldn't be talking about Lieutenant Colonel Braidwood, by any chance?'

'Indeed we are,' Bates said.

Was it only a couple of days ago he'd read the memorandum at the CIB and mentally stacked the goods in neat rows?

He remembered the major's delight at being called to meet with the new colonel, the disgust on Frank's face as he pushed the chit across the desk, his impotent fury at the colonel's formal request to return the private goods: the oily language of officialdom, the lightly veiled threat. For once Joe agreed with Frank, mentally stacking the confiscated goods into neat piles, shocked at the not-so-subtle abuse of power. Who could forget the Electrice refrigerator? That Mrs Hamilton was a fine businesswoman, for sure. He supposed the goods would end up there, in her house in West End. The water tanks were just a transit point.

'The Lieutenant Colonel made it clear,' Bates said, 'that the transfer must occur today. Why are you involved? The major will have explained that it's not a matter for the Criminal Investigation Division. You have no authority at all.'

'There's always Batchelor,' the major said.

The major's grin made Joe wonder how bad Batchelor and its famed crocodiles might be. Could they be any worse than the threats he faced here?

So that was the end of it, Joe thought, his hands resting on a folder, his fingers retaining the faint smell of gasoline. He looked past Monroe and Hayden, down the slope to the khaki river lazily winding its way to the sea. How many people had lived along its banks, he wondered. Children playing hide and seek among the mangroves, fathers teaching their sons to fish. All gone now. How many deaths had the river seen? And how many more were being prepared at the docks, warships fitted for battle, submarines readied for stealth beneath the waters of the Pacific.

The phone trilled. Joe picked up the handset and listened. 'Sure,' he said. 'I'll be there as soon as I can.'

He replaced the Bakelite handle. Fancy being saved by Frank Bischof. Wonders would never cease.

*

As Joe pulled into the kerb on Melbourne Street he checked his watch. Nine o'clock. Leaves swirled up from the pavement and the wind pushed against the jeep's side door. Frank had said to wait at the entrance to the South Brisbane railway station, but had not said why.

A long queue formed at the ticket office, soldiers for the most part, their kit bags heavy with gear for the trip south. On leave, Joe guessed. Men whistled to each other, laughing. He caught a brief glimpse of a young woman in dowdy clothing, jostled by the crowd. She lowered the brim of her hat over dark hair as she paid at the counter. The ticket collector punched a square of cardboard which she grabbed, her other hand clutching a small cardboard suitcase like the one he'd seen in Rose's lounge room days ago. Joe tried to push through the crowd toward her but stopped when he saw Frank's black V8 pull up behind his jeep. Frank stepped from the car, leaving someone Joe recognised behind the wheel — the detective with cauliflower ears, the one he'd photographed meeting Monroe and Leonard on the street outside the Royal.

'Seen her yet?' Frank said.

'Who do you mean? Why did you tell me to come here? What's this all about?'

'She's here, you know, saw her passing the Trocadero, headed this way. Which one do you think did it? If I was a betting man — and thank heavens I'm not — I reckon your young filly's as likely as Leonard's girl to have done it. She was with him at the Trocadero, and near the cemetery. She'd make a decent suspect, but Alma's easier, don't you think? And she's here. Come with me.'

Frank led Joe up the steps to the platform where men and women pushed and shoved, their luggage dragged behind or thrown in through the window. Briefly Joe saw again the small woman, in clothing he now realised was dirty, the dark skirt crumpled, her shoes scuffed, the battered case tied loosely with rope. Without looking backward she moved with purpose toward the front of the train, pausing to look up at the southern sky. Blackened clouds massed in a line above the horizon, vast rolls above a thin sliver of dark blue. The clouds were swollen and wounded, the pigeons bedded down under the eaves of the station building. Here came the cool change.

How could he warn her?

Frank pushed his way through, shoving men and women aside as he raced to the carriage near the front of the train. Joe tried to keep up, tripping over toppled luggage, skirting piles of boxes tied with twine. The temperature dropped, the skies darkened, clouds threatening to burst. Women struggled to keep their skirts from flying up and men held fast to caps.

'There she is!' Frank yelled, quickening his pace along the platform.

'What the fuck.' A soldier grabbed his kit bag just before it fell under the wheels of the train; a boy wailed as his teddy bear was knocked from his hand.

Joe climbed over suitcases, past a grey-haired man tottering on a walking stick, hauled a child up from the edge of the platform to fling him into his mother's arms. He raced on, struggling to get to her before Frank.

Over the heads of the crowd he saw Frank reach the carriage as the woman stepped onto the boarding strip. He reached for her arm, wrenched her from the steps of the train, twisting her around to face him. Puzzled, he halted before a voice from behind called out.

'Back here!'

Joe spun around. He saw the detective, the one who'd

stayed in the car, the detective he'd seen so many times before but whose name he still didn't know.

'She's on the last carriage!' the detective yelled. Frank released the woman, shook his head, confused. Joe was too, had thought it was Alma boarding the train. Freed, the woman stepped into the carriage as Frank raced off. From above the crowd she looked back, briefly her eyes found Joe's, and for a moment he thought he understood, but from this distance with his glasses foggy in the heat, he couldn't be sure. The woman at the Trocadero?

Joe followed Frank towards the rear of the train. The wheels began to turn, the crowd moving back from the steam and sparks. Women raised their arms to wave goodbye. As the train stirred, Joe and Frank reached the detective on the steps of the final carriage, his arms held fast around a woman's waist. Her battered suitcase fell as she struggled. She spat in his face as he lifted up and placed her on the platform.

'Leave her alone!' someone yelled. 'What's she done?'

'Police,' Frank said, reassuring, avuncular. 'Just go about your business, please.'

Joe looked back to the front of the train. While the two detectives manhandled Alma through the crowd, he watched as a lone woman leaned out from the doorway of a carriage. He knew those features, had run his fingers along the lines of her face. She waved to him.

The conductor dropped his red flag, the whistle screamed and the long line of carriages rolled along the platform, the sky rumbling in reply.

Rose called out but he heard nothing above the clamour of the crowd. She smiled as she waved to him, holding aloft a black wig, a raven against the darkening sky.

A crash of thunder drowned out the sound of the engine, the drumroll blotting out the piercing cry as the train picked up speed. Rain bucketed down and pounded against the ground, as if a child had slammed a paper bag full of water against a brick wall. Speech was impossible. How could anyone think in this battering? Thought was, in any case, too logical, too rational a thing against this brutal, almost supernatural, assault. The roar was of something primeval, a beast let loose. Joe felt like a fish gulping for air.

'I saw her sneak through at the last minute,' the detective said. He hauled Alma along the platform, her sodden skirt clinging to her thighs, hair plastered to her face and suitcase drenched. He handed her across to Frank to begin the formalities. Handcuffs, warnings, a statement of rights. A charge of murder.

Joe followed the two detectives, Alma wedged between them, to the street.

Rain poured from the awning at the entrance, a wall of water slowing as the storm subsided. Joe watched streams bubble up against the sandstone kerb, churning a pallid muddy brown. Scraps of paper swirled in the frothy surface. Parrots squabbled as they sought shelter in the branches above, flashes of emerald and crimson muted in the evening sky. The noise took him back to that moment at the Trocadero, the dark-haired woman fingering the rope of beads slung around her neck. Silent and mysterious, she'd been the point of focus among the noisy, colourful throng. Was it only six days ago?

SUNDAY 17 OCTOBER 1943

Chapter Thirty-Three

The river held the cemetery in the crook of its arm. At low tide, the mudbanks gave off the rich smell of brine and rotting vegetation. Mangroves rose from the water, some as tall as a man; old men, crippled and bent. The terraced earth strained against sagging redbrick walls. Clumps of headstones leaned into the hillside, tilting against the gravity of the slope. Random words emerged. Devoted mother of . . . young . . . sadly missed . . . Here was a girl of five, an old man from County Clare, a young man dead at twenty-five. Requiescat. Beloved.

The smoke from the factories and the Powerhouse, the dust kicked up by trucks on unpaved roads and the exhaust from cars, the smoke from the funnels of warships lining the northern bank of the river — all the khaki had been swept away in last week's storm and the sky was a cerulean wash. The air smelled of nothing more than clean grass.

Joe pushed open the wrought iron gate and followed the path to where an army chaplain stood beside a mound of freshly dug earth.

Robert Foster wasn't going home. Joe closed his eyes and saw him as he kissed his mama on the top of her greying hair, hugged his wife and son, slung his knapsack over his shoulder and hauled himself up onto the back of Mr Bennett's Ford truck for a lift into Atlanta. Had he expected adventure or just known that army pay was good? Foster should have known nothing ever comes out the way you expect; that life has a funny way of turning all your expectations on their heads. The safest place he'd been in the last year and a half turned out to be the deadliest. Joe stood to attention, cap in hand, as the ritual began, the formalities observed. The sole mourner at a funeral that shouldn't be taking place on this side of the world.

Two days earlier, Alma Smith had appeared before the Queensland courts charged with murder. Eyes downcast, hair unbrushed, she stood in the dock in a floral dress as Frank Bischof, resplendent in three-piece suit and freshly ironed shirt, produced a number of exhibits — a butcher's knife, a crumpled blouse, tan shoes, a black leather shopping bag, a photo of a Hudson Sedan motorcar. In precise but emotionless prose, Frank read her history to the court — abandonment as a child in Newcastle, an adolescence of uncontrollable behaviour, committal to the Parramatta Girls Training Home at the age of fourteen, five convictions for drunkenness, offensive behaviour, stealing. As he outlined the police case, paying particular attention to claims of unwarranted sexual advances, the presiding judge repeatedly warned the jury against levity. The term 'gamarouche' was new to Joe and he'd had to phone Sergeant Doyle for an explanation.

The army chaplain held the Bible lightly in his hands, open but unread as he intoned the well-worn phrases. He'd conducted this service standing in muddy jungle gardens, beside beaches glaring white against the blue, in the hard-packed red soil of ancient deserts. For soldiers. He looked weary of this duty.

In the end, the court had taken delight in giving the Americans a taste of local justice. In finding Alma Smith not guilty of murder, Joe knew the men of the jury were passing judgement on the foreign soldiers who prowled the streets of their town day and night, who took whatever they wanted or could buy, who treated their town like a brothel or a lolly shop.

So Frank Bischof had failed to get a conviction. Yet in spite of the collapse of his case, he seemed surprisingly content as the verdict was read. Joe watched him and the arresting detective exchange words. With Alma innocent of the charge, the case against Leonard as accessory to murder collapsed. He would walk free.

In a gum tree beside the pathway, a kookaburra's call turned into a raucous laugh.

Joe had finally read his mother's short letter, along with the clipping from the paper. His father was dead, his heart finally giving out after all these years. Maybe it was just as well, with the news that the United Auto Workers had agreed to a strike ban — for the war effort. Everything his father had fought for, all his principles, the injuries he'd received when the police had attacked the marchers that day in 1932, the move to New Jersey, his mother's anguish. Everything seemed like it was for nothing. But the words his mother wrote stayed with him. 'Giuseppe, you were always angry at your papa, angry he got involved, that he fought that battle. He didn't fight a big war like the one you are a part of, I proud of you. But your papa did fight a war, a small war maybe, maybe you don't think it worth the trouble it caused. But he tried to do what was right. It cost him, I know. But I'm proud of him too.'

On the day that the newspapers reported on Alma's acquittal, another small item caught Joe's attention. The San

Toy brothel on Montague Road was closing on the orders of a magistrate who noted, with some surprise, that although there had been repeated complaints about the establishment there had been none against similar establishments elsewhere in town. Joe had a feeling he'd have further dealings with Frank Bischof.

As the blessings ended, Joe looked down the slope to the thick brown arm of the river that wound around the edge of the cemetery, protecting those within its sweep. Now another soul, he thought, and lowered his eyes. He scattered a handful of dirt over the mound and replaced his cap. With a final salute he parted company with the chaplain and made his way to the wrought iron gates. He turned left, toward the afternoon sun.

In spite of the heat, he looked forward to the climb up Gladstone Road. He wiped his brow as he trudged up and over the hill. Would there ever be a camera able to replicate these vivid colours — the orange-red poinciana, the rusty red of the corrugated iron roofs? He loved black-and-white photos, the play of light and shade, the sharp outlines and certainties. He'd never expected to be so moved by colour.

He followed the road down the slope toward the winding river, the spire of the Town Hall on the horizon, the messy town sprawling into the blue haze of the hills beyond; a town that was beginning to feel almost like home. For the first time in days he thought of Nancy, now just a photo of a girl sitting on a bench in Central Park, a place on the other side of the world.

Joe thought about the war he'd signed on for, about this place where it had brought him and the battles he'd fought there. He would do his job. It was all he could do, perhaps all that anyone could ever do. A battle fought is better than a battle lost. He would make each person count, no matter their colour or education, their cowardice or bravery. He would honour their stories, however sad. Perhaps Donne was right. In some way we are all connected; what happens to one person affects us all. No man is an island. From across the river he heard the clock ring the hour. He stood still as the bell tolled. One, two, three, four. For Duke, for Danny Lakursky, for Foster. And for his father.

He wondered how his war would end.

He patted the letter in his top pocket, smiling again at the postmark — Sydney. Would she return like MacArthur? The large looping letters of blue ink traced the possibilities.

Historical Notes

On 7 December 1941, the Japanese Navy Air Service attacked the United States Naval Base at Pearl Harbor, bringing America into World War II. A few days before, a convoy of nine ships escorted by the USS *Pensacola* had left Pearl Harbor and was immediately diverted from its planned voyage to the Philippines. On 22 December 1941, the cruiser entered Moreton Bay and tied up at Newstead Wharf.

Today it is difficult to appreciate how critical the years 1941 and 1942 were for Australia. The country, with a population of only seven million, had already suffered significant losses in the European war — over three hundred men died during the Greek campaign early in 1941, and over eight hundred died later that year during the siege of Tobruk. Now Japan was poised to move south through Asia. At the Fall of Singapore in February 1942, over 15,000 Australians became prisoners of war. In March 1942, General Douglas MacArthur, Commander in Chief for the South West Pacific Area, evacuated the Philippines and escaped to Australia. Mini-submarines entered Sydney Harbour in May that year and Japanese planes bombed Darwin and Townsville.

Brisbane was at the frontline of what looked — for a time — like imminent invasion.

Although *The Brisbane Line* is a work of fiction, many of the events and characters are real and every effort has been taken to give an authentic sound and feel to wartime Brisbane.

The Office of the American Provost Marshall was indeed located in what was once the South Brisbane Town Hall. Today the building is owned by a private school called Somerville House which, during the war, was taken over by American forces as Base Station 3 Headquarters.

The Queensland Criminal Investigation Branch (CIB) operated out of a building on the corner of George and Elizabeth streets in Queens Gardens. Formerly the Synod Hall of St John's Anglican Cathedral, it became the home of the CIB and contained the offices of the detectives of the CIB, the Fingerprint, Modus Operandi and Photography Sections. The building was demolished in 1962 when the CIB moved to a new police building on North Quay.

Frank Bischof's (1904–1979) role in the development and maintenance of a network of corruption in the Queensland Police is well known but has never been fully documented. Bischof joined the police in 1925, was promoted to sergeant in 1939 and was stationed in the CIB during World War II where he was in charge of Squad 4, responsible for investigating abortions, sex offences, arson, assaults, homicides and unlawful killing. Promoted to Police Commissioner in 1958, he served until his resignation in 1969. The Fitzgerald Commission of Inquiry into Police Misconduct (1987–1989) alluded to the fact that 'certain police were said to enjoy Bischof's favour' and to the existence of 'bag men' to collect illicit payoffs. As Fitzgerald noted, 'in some respects police corruption had acquired a quaint quasi-legitimacy by the Bischof era'.

Tom Baty was a firearms specialist in the Queensland Police. In 1939, he studied science at the University of Queensland and in 1940, he was put in charge of the newly established Scientific (Technical) Section of the Queensland Police.

Cliff Stanaway was a legendary journalist and police rounds-man at *The Courier-Mail*. His most famous reporting was into the 1942 brawl between American and Australian troops, the famous Battle of Brisbane, when one Australian soldier was killed and numerous soldiers on both sides were injured.

Two literary journals began publication in Brisbane during this period. The first, *Meanjin Papers*, was founded in 1940 by Clem Christesen (1911–2003), a journalist with *The Courier-Mail* and *The Telegraph*. In 1943, *Meanjin Papers* had a national circulation of 4000. Also that year, aspiring poet Judith Wright (1915–2000) arrived in Queensland to work at the Universities Commission and soon began helping at *Meanjin*. It was in Brisbane that she met her life partner, fifty-two-year-old philosopher and writer Jack McKinney (1891–1966).

In 1943, students in the senior year at Brisbane State High School began a journal — *Senior Tabloid* — for young writers and artists. By the fifth edition, the journal editors renamed it *Barjai* and although the principal, Isaac Waddle, banned it from the school, librarian Barrie Reid sold it on the footpath. The journal was roneoed every two months and all contributors had to be under twenty-one. Many went on to have literary and artistic careers, including writer Thea Astley (then aged seventeen and a university student), and poet, playwright and painter Laurie Collinson (aged eighteen). At its peak it had a readership of close to three hundred.

Both journals deliberately assumed Aboriginal names:

'Meanjin', the name for the bend of the river where Brisbane's CBD was situated; 'Barjai', the word for 'meeting place'. Both journals also had sponsorship from the academic Professor James Duhig, progressive nephew of the conservative Catholic Archbishop James Duhig.

Literary meetings were held regularly at the Lyceum Club situated in a building — now demolished — opposite the Brisbane GPO on Queen Street.

Lock Hospitals in Australia were used to forcibly isolate people suffering from various contagious diseases. The most notorious Lock Hospitals aimed to isolate Indigenous patients with diseases such as leprosy or venereal disease. They were essentially punitive rather than medical. In Queensland, they existed from the late nineteenth century until the 1940s — in the Torres Strait, Palm Island, Barambah, and on Peel Island in Moreton Bay. During World War II, the Queensland Director General of Health, Dr Raphael Cilento, boasted that Queensland led the way in the detention of women with venereal disease. During the war, professional sex workers who worked in illegal but recognised brothels — and other 'promiscuous amateurs' and 'delinquent girls' — were subject to weekly health checks. Those with venereal disease were detained in the Lock Hospital attached to Boggo Road. In 1943, there were one hundred and five inmates of the Brisbane Lock Hospital.

The Tower Mill, or Spring Hill Reservoirs, adjacent to the Windmill on Wickham Terrace, were used for water storage until 1962. Now heritage listed, they are the venue for the Underground Opera Company, but in World War II they were filled with water.

All American servicemen who died in Australia during the war — or were executed in New Guinea — were buried in the USAF Military Cemetery at Ipswich. Their bodies were repatriated after the war. Nonetheless, the bookending of events around the South Brisbane cemetery, although inaccurate, proved irresistible to the author.

Opposite the Customs House, the Pink Elephant opened in 1946 and was Brisbane's only postwar late-night coffee shop. It was subject to frequent police raids on suspicions of sly-grogging and was the chosen meeting place for Brisbane writers, artists and 'unwholesome characters'. The Emerald Iguana, like other pink elephants, is a figment of the writer's imagination.

Acknowledgements

Brio Books and David Henley — for their support, encouragement and meticulous attention to detail. I am enormously grateful to David for his belief in this novel and his enthusiasm for getting things right. In the process we have both learned more about cooking than we expected.

Emily Maguire — who I met at a workshop run by the Queensland Writers Centre and with whom I completed a mentorship program. Emily gave me the courage to continue, the skills to find the story among the mess, and has been a friend and inspiration ever since.

Matt Condon, chronicler *par excellence* of Queensland police corruption, with whom I've discussed Bischof and his role in the development of a culture of corruption in the Queensland Police.

The Queensland Writers Centre, whose various workshops have all taught me something. In particular I want to thank Kim Wilkins - her Novelist's Boot Camp gives students the tools to tackle what can be an impossible project.

The State Library of Queensland — for a QAnzac

Fellowship that allowed me to spend time poring through their material. I am grateful to them for accepting the Ervin Task papers (originally collected by Simon Target and Rosemary Cameron) that were the initial inspiration for this novel. I am grateful for the support of my referees — Dr Yorick Smaal and Professor Alastair Blanchard.

Special thanks to Peter Dunn whose invaluable website Ozatwar.com is essential reading for those interested in World War 2. Peter graciously agreed to review the manuscript to check historical and military details. Any remaining errors in the work are mine.

Friends and family who have read portions of this novel at various times — and who have all contributed to its final form — include: Marion Diamond, Margot Duncan, Chris Dwyer, Beth Hart, Stephen Kimber, Peter Riedlinger, Michelle Riedlinger, Yorick Smaal, Mary Swayne and Catherine Quinn.

Other people with whom I have discussed the idea for this novel and who have provided background information - Judy Higgs, Jean White, Dan Hart, Don Munro, Maureen Parfitt.

It wouldn't be possible to write without these people behind me.